P9-DZM-623

*L*ove's Unfolding
Dream

Love's Unfolding Dream

JANETTE OKE

JO

LOVE'S UNFOLDING DREAM
A Literary Express, Inc. Book
(a subsidiary of Doubleday Direct, Inc.)
Reprinted by special arrangement with:
Bethany House Publishers
A Ministry of Bethany Fellowship International

PRINTING HISTORY
A Bethany House Publication / July 1987
The Janette Oke Collection / 1997

All rights reserved.
Copyright © 1987 Lavon C. Oke Representative
Cover art by Dan Thornberg, Bethany House Publishers
staff artist.

No part of this book may be produced or transmitted in any
form or by any means, electronic or mechanical, including
photocopying, recording, or by any information storage
and retrieval system, without permission in writing from
the publisher.

If you would be interested in purchasing additional copies of this
book, or have any questions concerning the Janette Oke
Collection and your membership, or if you would like to
correspond with the author, please contact us at:

The Janette Oke Collection
Literary Express, Inc.
1540 Broadway
New York, NY 10036
Telephone #973-473-4800

ISBN: 1-58165-139-2

Printed in the United States of America

Dedicated
with love and deep respect
to the memory of
three wonderful fathers—
Frederick George Steeves,
the daddy I have loved from infancy on;
John Gifford Steeves,
the uncle who was like a father to me;
Harold Edward Oke,
my kind and loving father through marriage.

JANETTE OKE was born in Champion, Alberta, during the depression years, to a Canadian prairie farmer and his wife. She is a graduate of Mountain View Bible College in Didsbury, Alberta, where she met her husband, Edward. They were married in May of 1957, and went on to pastor churches in Indiana as well as Calgary and Edmonton, Canada.

The Okes have three sons and one daughter and are enjoying the addition to the family of grandchildren. Edward and Janette have both been active in their local church, serving in various capacities as Sunday-school teachers and board members. They make their home in Didsbury, Alberta.

Table of Contents

The Davis Family

The Davis family has grown in size and maturity over the years. You may need a bit of help to keep them all straight:

Clark and Marty each lost the first partner in marriage and joined together to form a new family unit.

Nandry, their foster daughter, married Josh Coffins. Their children are Tina, Andrew, Mary, and Jane.

Clae, the Davises' second foster daughter, married a pastor, Joe Berwick. Their children are Esther Sue, Joey, and Paul.

Missie, Clark's daughter from his first marriage, married Willie LaHaye, and they moved out West. Their children are Nathan, Josiah, Melissa Joy, and Julia.

Clare, Marty's son from her first marriage, married Kate, and their children are Amy Jo, Dan, David, and Dack.

Arnie, Clark and Marty's first son from their marriage, married Anne. Their children are Silas, John, and Abe.

Ellie married Lane Howard. Their children are Brenda and twins, William and Willis.

Luke married Abbie. Their children are Thomas and Aaron.

Chapter 1

Belinda

"Mama! Look!"

At the cry from her youngest, Marty turned quickly from the biscuits she was shaping, toward the kitchen doorway. She knew by the tone of her daughter's voice that there would be some kind of trouble, for Belinda's cry trembled in the air between them. A chill gripped at Marty. *What is wrong? Is Belinda hurt?*

Her eyes quickly traveled over the slight body of young Belinda, expecting to see blood some place. Belinda's dress, clean and neatly pressed when she had gone out just a short time before, was rumpled and dirty. One of her long, carefully plaited braids had come loose from its ribbon and hung in disarray about her slim shoulders. Her face was smudged and tear-streaked. But to her mother's practiced eye, she seemed whole and unharmed. Marty, unconscious of the small sigh of relief that escaped her, lifted her gaze to meet blue, troubled and tear-filled eyes.

"Look!" Belinda cried again in a choking voice.

Then Marty's eyes fell on Belinda's outstretched hand. In it lay a small sparrow, its feathers ruffled and wet, its head dipping awkwardly to the side. Even as Marty watched, she saw the small body quiver, and Marty shivered in sympathy.

Why Belinda? mourned the mother heart. *Why did she have to find the bird?* Marty knew the tender heart of her daughter.

She would sorrow over the bird all day long.

Marty wiped floury hands on her apron and reached out to draw Belinda close. She made no comment on the dirty dress or the messy hair.

"Where did ya find 'im?" she asked instead, her voice full of sympathy.

"The mother cat had it!" Belinda wailed. "I had to chase her all over the barn and then—then—"

She could not go on. Tears fell uncontrollably, and the small girl buried her head against Marty and let the sobs shake her.

Marty just held her until the crying subsided. Then Belinda turned large blue eyes to her mother's face, the tiny bird still held carefully in her hand.

"It's gonna die, isn't it?" she quavered.

"Well I—I don't know," stammered Marty and took another look at the injured bird. Yes—it would die. Barring a miracle, it would die. But it was difficult for her to say those words to Belinda. Besides, she had seen miracles before. *Oh, God,* she inwardly prayed, *I know it's jest a sparrow, but Ya said that Ya see each sparrow thet falls. If Yer heart is as heavy as Belinda's over this one, then could Ya please make it well again?*

"We need to make it warm," Belinda was saying hopefully.

"There's an empty basket on my closet shelf. I'll get a flannel rag from the ragbag," Marty responded.

Belinda hurried off to get the little basket and Marty went to her pantry where she kept the supply of old garments and sheets for cleaning purposes. She found a soft piece of flannel and returned to the kitchen just as Belinda ran back into the room.

Together they made a warm bed, and Belinda carefully deposited the tiny bird. It was in even worse shape than Marty had feared. Its little head flopped uncontrollably as it was moved and except for a slight tremble there was little sign of life. Belinda's tears began to flow again.

"Can we take it to Luke?" she pleaded.

Oh, my, thought Marty. *A trip to town for a dying sparrow.* How many of Belinda's casualties had Luke doctored over the years? Yet he was always so patient, doing all in his power to save each tiny animal. *But this one—this one is beyond his help,* Marty was sure. But she didn't say so to Belinda. Instead, she said, "We'll ask yer pa. He'll be in soon."

Marty's attention returned to her biscuits. Clark *would* be in soon, and he'd be hungry and looking for his supper. She went to wash her hands so she could get the biscuits into the oven.

Belinda took the basket with its injured sparrow and settled into her favorite corner by the kitchen stove. Her tears had stopped but her eyes were still red and shadowed with the horror of it all. Why did cats kill birds? Actually, Belinda loved the farmyard cats. She would have fought just as hard to save the life of one of them—and had at times, along with big brother Luke's help. But why did they insist on hunting the little birds? It just wasn't fair. Belinda let a finger gently trace the curve of the small body. The little bird no longer even trembled.

The outer door opened and banged shut, and Marty knew before she heard the voice that Amy Jo, Clare and Kate's oldest child, was on her way in.

"Gramma?" Amy Jo called before she even entered the kitchen. "Gramma, do you know where Lindy is?"

Amy Jo was the only one who called Belinda "Lindy." In fact, Marty was quite sure Amy Jo was the only one who could have gotten away with it. Belinda was always very careful to pronounce her own name in full, but the laughing, teasing Amy Jo disregarded such personal taste and called Belinda after her own whim.

"She's right there by the stove," answered Marty without turning from her biscuits.

Marty could hear little gasps for breath as Amy Jo entered the room. She had been running again but Amy Jo always ran.

"Do you want—?" began Amy Jo as she approached Belinda's favorite corner. Then she hesitated. "What'cha got now?" she asked without too much interest. "Another mouse?"

"It's a bird," replied Belinda, her voice taut with sorrow.

"What happened?"

"The mother cat."

"Is it hurt bad?"

"Real bad."

"How come ya didn't take it to Uncle Luke?"

Amy Jo knew the usual procedure when Belinda found an injured creature.

"We're waitin' for Pa."

Belinda moved her hand slightly so Amy Jo could get a look at her newest casualty. For a moment Amy Jo's violet eyes widened with horror also. It was so tiny, so helpless, so—so crumpled.

"I—I think it's already dead," she whispered, now in genuine sympathy.

Belinda was about to burst into tears again when the small bird shuddered once more.

"Is not," she argued. "See!"

Marty placed the biscuits in the oven, disturbing Belinda and her precious burden for a moment to add more wood to the fire, and turned back to set the table just as the farm dog announced that Clark was on his way in. Marty's eyes traveled to the clock on the shelf. She was behind schedule but Clark was a bit earlier than she had expected.

"Grandpa," Amy Jo called to Clark from the door, but before he could even greet her she burst out, "Lindy's got a hurt thing again."

Concern showed in Clark's face as he entered the room. His gaze traveled quickly over the kitchen. He saw the young girl crouched in her corner by the stove holding the basket tightly in her hands. His eyes went on to meet Marty's. *What now?* he silently asked. *Is it serious?* And Marty answered with just a slight movement of her head back and forth. *It won't make it. It's hurt bad.*

At the sight of her father, Belinda's eyes filled with tears again. "It's a sparrow, Pa," she answered his unasked question. "The mother cat had 'im."

Clark looked at his dishevelled daughter. He could see that she'd had quite a chase to retrieve the small bird, which told him as well as anything what shape the bird must be in. He hung his jacket on the hook and crossed to the two girls crouching over the basket.

Clark was about to reach down and lift out the small bird, but when he saw it, he changed his mind. It *was* in bad shape. Touching it might just cause more pain.

"It is hurt bad, ain't it?" he said softly.

Clark reached out a hand to his youngest daughter, smoothing the roughness of her tangled hair, then gently brushing a smudge of dust from her cheek.

"I dunno," he said hesitantly. "I think anything thet we try to do fer this little bird will only bring it more pain."

Fresh tears began to course down Belinda's cheeks. "But Luke—"

"Yer brother would do all he could—I know thet."

The door banged open again. This time Dan, another of Clare's children, burst into the house. He was breathing hard from running and called out before he was even into the kitchen, "Amy! Ma wants ya home. It's suppertime."

Amy Jo stood slowly to her feet, secretly hoping that if a quick trip was to be made to Doctor Luke's office, she would be asked to go along. It was always exciting to visit there.

"Are ya goin' to town, Grandpa?" she dared ask.

Clark shook his head. "I don't rightly know. We'll need to talk 'bout it. I'm afraid—"

"What's wrong?" asked Dan, who had by now crossed to squat beside his grandfather and peer into the small basket.

"Oh! A dead bird," he said without even waiting for an answer.

"It's not dead," cried Belinda. "It's just hurt."

Dan's eyes traveled from Belinda's face to Clark's. Had he said something wrong? Was the bird—?

Clark reached out a hand and laid it on the boy's shoulder. "It's hurt pretty bad," he said, "but it's still hangin' on."

Marty checked her biscuits which were browning nicely. Supper would soon be ready, yet she could hardly get near her stove. Four people huddled there—all in sympathy over the injured sparrow. Marty felt sympathy herself. She did not like to see a small creature hurt and suffering. But it was, after all, the way of nature. Animals killed and were killed. It was a fact of life. Nature's food chain required it. *The mother cat has ba-*

bies to feed, Marty reminded herself. *She needs—* But her thoughts were interrupted.

"Are ya gonna take it to Uncle Luke?" asked Dan, his eyes round and questioning.

Clark slowly shook his head but before he could speak, Dan commented, "Bet he could fix it."

"Yer Uncle Luke is a good doctor, I'm not denyin' thet none," said Clark in a low voice, "but even good doctors have their limits. This here little bird is hurt bad. I don't think—"

"Luke says thet ya never, never give up," broke in Belinda. "He says thet as long as there's still life, then ya fight to save it."

"To be sure," agreed Clark. "To be sure."

"Then we can go?" pleaded Belinda.

Across the heads of the youngsters Clark's eyes met Marty's.

Surely yer not gonna—? Marty's expression asked, but Clark's shoulders shrugged slightly. *What else can I do?*

Marty looked at her husband—weary, she knew, after spending a full day in the fields. True, it was easier for him now, easier with the artificial limb that Luke had insisted on getting for him. But even so, planting was hard work for any man. He still had chores ahead of him, and here he was about to make a trip into town for a dying sparrow. It made no sense— no sense at all.

Marty looked back at Belinda. Surely the youngster should be able to understand reason. A girl of eleven should know by now that nature provided for its own by allowing death. But no—Belinda didn't understand. She fought death with every ounce in her tiny childish body, and her main ally was her older brother Luke—Luke the doctor, Luke the compassionate. Luke fought death, too. If anyone would understand a trip to town to save a sparrow, it would be Luke.

"I'll git the team," Clark was saying.

"But—but yer supper," put in Marty. "Yer—"

"It'll wait," answered Clark and his eyes asked Marty to understand.

She did understand. It was not for the small bird that Clark would take the trip to town. It was for the child whose heart was breaking.

"I'm sorry—sorry to make ya the extry work," Clark murmured. "Don't fuss none. I'll help myself when I git back."

It wasn't the work that concerned Marty. It was Clark. He needed supper. He needed the rest. And yet—

Again the door opened and four-year-old Dack bustled into the kitchen, his red hair bright. He was the youngest member of Clare's household and a favorite with everyone. His chubby, freckled face crinkled into a big grin as he spied his grandfather shrugging into the jacket he had removed just a short time before.

Dack's round little arms wrapped around the legs of the tall man and he grinned impishly up at him. One small fist began pounding on Clark's leg.

"Knock, knock!" he cried playfully. "Knock, knock on wood."

Clark could not resist the small boy. He reached down and lifted him up into his arms.

"Who's knockin' on my wood?" With mock seriousness he asked the question expected of him in their little game.

"It's me. It's Dack," he announced gleefully.

"Dack *who?*" his grandfather responded next, on cue.

The little boy paused a moment to get the words right. "Dack be nimble, Dack be quick, Dack—Dack jumped over the candlestick!" he finished in a triumphant shout.

They both laughed together as Dack's pudgy arms squeezed Clark's neck.

"And what is Dack doin' at my house?" inquired Clark.

Dack's eyes immediately turned serious. He squirmed to get down.

"Mama sent me," he said. "I'm 'posta git Amy an' Dan fer supper."

Clark looked at the two, still peering into Belinda's basket.

"You'd better git," he said. "Iffen yer pa has to come git the three of ya, he might not be too happy."

The three "got," Amy Jo, taking the hand of her little brother after one last glance at her grandpa in case she might be invited to go along.

Clark turned back to Belinda. "I'll be ready in a minute," he informed her. "Better grab a coat." Then he was gone.

With a sigh Marty turned to remove the biscuits from the oven. They were crispy brown and piping hot, just the way Clark loved them. But Clark wouldn't be eating them the way he liked them. By the time he returned, the biscuits would be cold.

Just as Marty finished taking the biscuits from the pan, Belinda gave a little cry. Marty whirled to see what new calamity had befallen.

"I think it's already dead," she said in a sobbing whisper. "Look! It's gittin' stiff."

Marty looked. Belinda was right. The sparrow was already past the help of even Doctor Luke.

Belinda burst into fresh tears and Marty put her arms around her to comfort her.

"I need to catch yer pa before he hooks up the team," she murmured, more to herself than to the weeping girl, but Belinda nodded her head in agreement.

Marty took the nod as consent and hurried to the barn for Clark, sighing deeply as she walked. She was glad Clark was spared the trip to town. She was glad the injured little bird was no longer in pain. But she was sorry that Belinda had to suffer so deeply every time some little creature suffered. It was good and noble for her daughter to be compassionate—but Belinda really took it too far. In many ways she was so much like her big brother Luke. So much! Yet she was even more tenderhearted than Luke. *Life is going to be so painful for Belinda,* Marty lamented. How many hurts—deep hurts—lay down the road for their youngest child? She trembled at the thought.

Clark was just leading the first horse from the stall.

"It's too late," said Marty. "The bird's already dead. Ya can have yer supper now."

Concern rather than the relief one could have expected was in Clark's face.

"She'll git over it," Marty assured him. "She'll cry for a while; then she'll have her little buryin' and put the sparrow to rest in the garden with her other little creatures. By tomorra she'll be herself agin."

Clark knew Marty was right. Belinda would feel the pain of the loss for a time but she would soon bounce back. They had seen it happen before. While Marty returned to the house, Clark took King back to his stall. The horse was relieved to be allowed to return and immediately resumed his eating.

As Clark removed the harness, hung it on the peg and started for the house, he realized just how hungry and tired he was. But his walk was even and steady with hardly the trace of a limp. Again, Clark had a moment of thankfulness for the limb that functioned almost as well as his own leg had. It was good to have his hands free. It was good to be able to throw aside his crutch. But he did get weary and sore. Right now the whole side of his body protested against the presence of the false limb. He was anxious to remove it and toss it in a corner for the night.

But he wouldn't. He still had chores to do. He wouldn't remove it even when the chores were all done. He knew Marty watched him carefully for signs of pain or weariness. To remove the leg before bedtime would tell Marty that he was in pain. Marty worried enough about his well-being without adding to her concern. He'd rest the leg a bit as he had his supper. By the time he went to chore, perhaps it would be feeling better. Clark was glad he would not need to make the long trip into town—with a sparrow. He smiled slightly as he thought of the many times he had wished he could rid the whole world of sparrows. Such pesky little nuisances they were, even when Belinda wasn't fussing over one! And yet—they were God's creatures, too, and Clark would have cheerfully aided Belinda in the fight to save a little life.

Chapter 2

Doctor Luke

Just as Clark and Marty thought, Belinda grieved over the dead sparrow, carefully made and lined a small box for it to be buried in, called on Amy Jo and the three boys to join her in the little ceremony after supper, and wept as the small bird joined a number of other small graves at the far end of the garden. Then it was over and the girl's thoughts returned to childhood play. The Saturday evening hours ended with a boisterous game of tag, which all five children joined.

Marty drew a sigh of relief as she threw the dishwater on her rosebush by the door. Belinda was usually a happy, well-adjusted child. *If only she did not grieve so when she found little creatures dead or dying,* Marty wished. She did hope that the young girl eventually would learn to face the realities of life with a bit less emotional turmoil. No one liked suffering. But some pain was inevitable.

Clark came toward the house, the pail he carried brimming with white foaming milk.

"She looks fine now," he stated, nodding his head slightly in Belinda's direction with a look of relief.

"Oh, she usually snaps back—but, my, what a storm of tears in the meantime," responded Marty.

They entered the house together.

"Guess I'd rather have her on the tender side than calloused an' uncarin'," Clark commented, but Marty shook her head.

More than once she had found Belinda's tender heart very difficult to deal with.

"She'll grow out of it as she gets older," Clark reasoned. "Jest hope she doesn't go off to the other extreme."

Marty could not imagine Belinda changing that much. "Don't think there be much danger of thet," she assured her husband.

"Jest pray thet all thet compassion gits put to proper use like," said Clark. "God must have Him a special place fer someone like our Belinda."

Marty thought about Clark's comment as she poured the milk through the strainer and set out the container for the cream. Clark began to turn the handle of the separator, and Marty stood and listened to the gentle hum. Soon Clark had reached the proper speed and turned the spigot to let the white milk pour into the whirling bowl of the machine. From the left hand spout the milk began to stream, and soon a smaller, richer cascade of cream descended from the right spout to splatter into the cream crock.

"She's so much like Luke," ventured Marty, picking up the conversation where they had left it minutes before.

Clark nodded. "Or Arnie," he said. "Arnie's 'bout as tender as a man could be."

It was Marty's turn to nod. Arnie *was* tender. He could not bear to see anyone or anything in pain. But Arnie had not openly cried as Belinda did. He had just withdrawn, his eyes mirroring his troubled soul.

"Poor Arnie," said Marty. "Maybe it be easier for Belinda. At least she can cry when she is hurtin'. The boys, 'specially Arnie, always tried not to cry."

"Funny where they got thet idea," returned Clark. "I never was a-tellin' 'em thet boys aren't to cry."

"Nor me. Guess they pick up some of those things at school. Kids can be heartless with one another."

The milk and cream continued to stream from the separator spouts.

"Funny!" mused Marty. "They are so much alike—an' yet different."

"Like how?"

"Well, Luke is carin' and compassionate all right, but he—
he don't hide from pain none. He gits in there an' fights it. He
sure enough had the right makin's fer a doctor. Arnie, now—
he coulda never been a doctor. Couldn't stand even to be around
pain. He'd pull away, I'm a-thinkin'."

Clark thought about Marty's comment. "I think yer right,"
he finally said somberly. "Arnie woulda had him a hard time
bein' a doctor all right. He's much better at jest bein' a pa."

Marty smiled. Arnie was truly a good pa. They had feared
at first that he might spoil his youngsters, but Arnie seemed
to know better than that. Even though it was hard for him, he
did discipline.

It was a good thing that Arnie took care of the disciplining.
He had three very rambunctious young sons who needed the
strong and steady influence of a father. Their little mother,
Anne, was hard pressed to keep up with them! Marty smiled
as she thought of the trio. Silas was Amy Jo's age. The two of
them had been born only four days apart and, having celebrated
their tenth birthday, were not quite a year younger than Belinda.

The next son was John. He was now seven and in second
grade already. Abe, the youngest, was still home but chafing to
be off to school like his big brothers. Anne had all she could do
to keep the young boy busy. He insisted that he learn to read
so he wouldn't be left out when his older brothers had their
noses buried in books. Anne had felt that teaching was the duty
of the schoolmarm; but with Abe continually pestering her, she
finally gave in and taught the small boy his letters. Now the
older boys were bringing home storybooks so young Abe could
read as well.

Marty's thoughts were interrupted by the sound of running
feet. David, Clare's third child, burst into the back entry, his
eyes shining, his cheeks flushed from running.

"Hide me. Hide me, Gramma!" he cried excitedly.

"Whoa," said Clark who had just finished the separating.
"Thought me the rule was no hidin' in the house."

David stopped short, his eyes lowered. He knew the rule. He
stood quietly for a moment and then looked up, an irrepressible
sparkle in his teasing eyes.

"Then hide me outside—will ya, Grandpa?"

Clark laughed. "Now, where would I be a hidin' ya?" he asked the small boy.

"I dunno. But you have lots of good ideas. 'Member?"

It had been a while since the children had talked Clark into joining them in their game.

"Please," coaxed Davey.

Clark looked at Marty and laughed again. His leg still aching, he had been hoping to head for his favorite chair with a book. Instead, he took Davey by the hand.

"Who's 'it'?" he asked.

"Dan. An' he really looks hard," warned Davey.

"Has anyone tried the rhubarb patch?" whispered Clark.

Davey shook his head, his eyes shining with glee. He knew about the large leaves of the rhubarb plants.

"Then how 'bout we try it?" asked Clark as he left the house with the small boy. Marty finished up her evening duties with putting the cream and milk to cool.

She gave one last wipe to the table and had scarcely turned around when she heard the dog barking. They had not been expecting company. It was getting on toward dark. *Who is coming at this hour?* she wondered.

Peering out through the evening gloom, she recognized the horse at the hitching rail immediately. Luke's black doctor's bag hung from the horn of the saddle. The noise in the yard quickly changed from cries of "One, two, three," or "Home free!" to shouts of "Uncle Luke!" Marty went to the door to add her welcome.

Belinda had already claimed Luke's attention, pouring out her sad story about the sparrow and its untimely death. Luke hunched down in front of her and listened attentively.

"An' if you woulda been here, it might not have died," Belinda finished, just a hint of reproach in her voice.

Luke did not say, as he could have, that he had more important things to be doing. He did not even excuse himself with the fact that he had no way of knowing about the bird. Instead, he laid a gentle hand on Belinda's shoulder. "I'm sorry," he said. "I'm sorry I didn't come sooner."

Seeing the look on her brother's face, Belinda knew he meant it. Though still a child, she knew Luke should not need to feel guilt that he wasn't there when he had been needed.

Feeling like bursting into fresh tears, instead, she choked them back and reached out for Luke's hand.

"It's okay," she comforted. "Ya didn't know. It was hurt pretty bad an' maybe—" She let the sentence go unfinished and brushed at her watery eyes.

"What brings ya out this way?" asked Clark as Marty joined them at the front gate.

"Baby Graham just arrived," announced Luke with a grin.

"Oh!" exclaimed Marty, her eyes shining. "Lou's? What is it?"

"Another girl."

"My land! That makes 'im five girls now." Marty laughed. "Ma was a hopin' fer a boy this time. Her with all those grand-daughters and us with all the grandsons! Seems it should even out like."

"Well, when I left, Ma Graham was busy fussing over that girl like it was the only thing she ever wanted," said Luke. "If she was disappointed, I sure didn't see it."

" 'Course!" responded Marty. " 'Course she would. Jest like I fuss over each new grandson. I am glad I've got Amy Jo close by, though."

Just then Kate's voice drifted over the farmyard. "Amy Jo, bring the boys in now. It's time ya be gittin' ready for bed."

Marty saw the disappointed looks on four small faces, but they moved to obey their mother.

Luke reached out a hand to rumple the hair of young Dack as he passed.

"We'll see you tomorrow. Remember. You are all coming for dinner after church."

The frown turned to a grin and young Dack skipped ahead to join his older brothers and his sister.

"Can ya stop in fer coffee?" asked Marty.

Luke grinned. "Thought you'd never ask," he quipped, flipping the reins of his horse over the hitching rail. "It's been a long day. I thought that baby was never going to make an appearance. Guess she just wanted to keep them all in suspense as long as she could."

Marty led the way back in and placed the coffeepot on the stove. When she had cut some slices of pumpkin bread and placed them on the table, Luke didn't even wait for the coffee but reached out to help himself.

"You ought to teach Abbie how to make this," he said around the mouthful.

Marty smiled, thinking of the wife Luke had brought back with him from the East where he had trained as a doctor. Abbie was a dear girl with a heart as big as Luke's, but she had not had the advantage of knowing how to make good use of garden produce. She had been raised in a city where a garden other than flowers was unknown. But she was trying. She had her own vegetable garden now; she loved to watch things grow and was learning how to use all its produce.

"She's welcome to the recipe," responded Marty with a pat on Luke's shoulder as she went for the coffee. A secret smile creased her face as she remembered her own early culinary efforts as Clark's new wife.

Luke pulled a small book from his pocket and began to pencil in an entry. "That's thirty-seven," he said.

"Thirty-seven what?" Belinda piped up from her perch on the woodbox.

"Thirty-seven babies. Thirty-seven that I have delivered since becoming a doctor."

"Thet's quite a number," remarked Marty.

"Its been almost seven years already. Seven years! Just think of it."

"It's hard to believe," said Clark. "Seems ya jest got yerself back."

"Deliverin' babies must be 'bout the nicest part of yer work," Marty commented as she poured the coffee.

"It's exciting all right—but I like the rest of it, too. I think I'd soon get weary of just waiting on little ones to decide it's the right time."

"Do you like makin' stitches?" asked Belinda. Her question

reminded Marty that the young girl should be getting ready for bed.

"Belinda, ya hurry an' wash fer bed now. It's already past yer bedtime," she chided mildly.

Belinda wished she had kept quiet—maybe her mother wouldn't have noticed her. She was about to argue that she just wanted to see Luke when she caught her father's eye. It told her plainly that she was not to question her mother. Reluctantly she rose to do as she was bidden.

"As soon as you're ready, I'll tuck you in," Luke called after her, and she rushed out to do her washing up.

True to his word, Luke went to tuck Belinda in. He felt a special closeness to his little sister. He remembered that he had waited a long time to have a family member younger than himself. Belinda was special in another way as well. Luke could already sense in her a kindred spirit. Belinda loved to nurse things back to health.

He smoothed back her hair with a hand still smelling of medicine. Belinda loved the doctor smells. She turned her face slightly toward the hand and breathed more deeply.

"Do you like makin' stitches?" she asked again.

"Sure. Sure I do. I'm sorry that folks need stitches—but I'm glad that I know how to sew them up properly."

Belinda's eyes shone. "I would too," she confided.

Luke brushed back the wispy gold hair that curled around her face.

"I wish I was a boy," sighed Belinda.

"A boy?" There had been a time when Luke had hoped that Belinda would be a boy. Now he wondered why. This dear little sister was one of the most special people in his world.

"Why?" he asked. "Why a boy?"

"Then I could be a doctor," answered Belinda. She sighed more deeply and looked into Luke's eyes. "Iffen I was a doctor," she said, "I'd never have to wait for someone else to come. I could help things myself."

"Like the little bird?" asked Luke softly.

Belinda just nodded, her blue eyes looking troubled again.

"You don't need to be a doctor to learn to help things," Luke assured her. "You could be a nurse."

"Could I?" breathed Belinda, her eyes wide and shining at the thought.

"Of course."

Belinda smiled—then a dark frown replaced the happiness on her face.

"It'd never work," she moaned. "Mama would never let me go way back East to learn how to be a nurse."

Luke could not keep the amusement from showing on his face. "Maybe not," he said evenly. "Maybe not—at least not now. Mama didn't want me to go away when I was eleven, either. I had to do some growing up first."

"But—but—" began Belinda, and Luke interrupted her.

"It's hard to wait to grow up, isn't it?"

Belinda nodded solemnly.

"That's what I used to think. That's why I tagged along with Dr. Watkins. I wanted to learn all I could—as fast as I could."

The disappointment did not leave Belinda's eyes. "But Dr. Watkins is dead now," she said, and a stab of pain went through Luke as he thought of the kind doctor. He had died only two years after Luke took over the practice. The doctor had been out fishing all alone, and Luke often wondered if he could have been saved if only someone had been with him at the time. But all of Luke's "if onlys" could not bring the dear doctor back.

He shifted his eyes to Belinda's face. "Well, *I'm* here," he stated simply.

She stared at him. "Would you teach me?" she ventured.

"Why not? I think you'd make a good nurse. If you work hard and—"

"Oh, I will. I will. I promise!" she exclaimed, sitting up to throw her arms around her brother.

Luke tweaked the soft cheek, then kissed his sister's forehead.

"Then you'd best get some sleep," he said. "Being a nurse is awfully hard work. You'll need your rest."

Belinda held him close for a minute.

"Thank you, Luke," she whispered.

"Sure," he responded and kissed her again before tucking

the blankets under her chin. Luke joined his parents again in the big farm kitchen, and his mother poured one more cup of coffee for him.

Luke stretched his legs wearily.

"So you had you quite a time with Belinda today?" he asked.

"She sure made a fuss all right," responded Marty. "Yer poor pa was 'bout to head fer town without even havin' him some supper."

Luke looked at his father and grinned. "Didn't know you felt so strongly about sparrows," he teased. "Seems to me I remember you destroying a nest or two when I was a kid."

Clark ran a hand through his thick hair, flushing slightly, then smiled a bit shamefacedly at his son. "Ya won't go mentionin' that to Belinda, now, will ya?" After Luke laughed, Clark said, "Ya think I spoil 'er?"

Luke sobered and looked at his father. "Didn't say that," he said slowly. Then he added with a flush of his own, "If you had brought her in, you know who would have been looking up medicine for 'bird shock' and fighting to save that little birdie's life."

Then they all laughed.

Marty looked at her son and said solemnly, "I worry 'bout her, Luke. She is so tenderhearted thet I fear lest she won't be able to cope with the world out there, with life and death. She grieves so when anything is in pain."

Luke thought for many moments.

"She wants to be a nurse," he finally said slowly.

Marty gasped. "Belinda? Why, it would kill 'er! She would never be able to stand seein' folks who were hurt and in pain."

"Did ya talk about it with her—discourage her somehow?" asked Clark.

"Me?" responded Luke and shuffled about uncomfortably. "Well, no—not really. Fact is, I—I—well, I promised to help her."

Both his parents looked at Luke as if he had lost his senses.

"But—but, she'll never be able to . . ."

"It'll break her heart fer sure."

"Maybe not," stated Luke. "I know she can't face the suffering of any little creature now. But maybe—just maybe—learning to do something about the suffering is just what she needs. Can't you see? If she feels she is actually helping those who suffer, then she might make a good nurse. A great nurse! She'll try—she'll really try hard . . ."

Luke let the thought drift away, watching carefully the eyes of his mother and father as he spoke.

Marty shook her head and reached for her coffeecup, toying with the handle. She really didn't need another one—she had poured it just to keep Luke company at the table.

Clark reached down and unconsciously began to rub his aching leg. *Maybe Luke is right,* he debated with himself. *Maybe—in time—Belinda should be given the opportunity to nurse if she really wants to.* But that—that was way off somewhere in the future. She was not yet twelve. There was lots of time to think about it.

"I'd like to take her with me on some of my house calls," said Luke matter-of-factly.

Two heads jerked up. Two pairs of eyes fastened on Luke's face to see if he was serious. No one spoke.

"That okay?" questioned Luke.

There was silence as Clark and Marty exchanged unspoken messages.

"Well?" Luke pressed.

Clark straightened in his chair. He cleared his throat and looked again at Marty.

"Sure," he began slowly. "Sure—when the time comes—"

"Pa," Luke cut in. "Pa, I think the time has come."

"But she's jest a child! Only eleven," Marty exclaimed.

"I knew when I was eleven. I knew." Luke's quiet voice stopped her.

Marty found her voice again. "It's just so sudden. It jest—well—we haven't had us time to think on it—to pray. How 'bout we talk it over some—"

Luke placed his cup back on the table and rose to his feet.

"Sure," he smiled. "Sure. You think about it, talk it over, pray. I think Belinda and I can wait for that."

Clark rose from the table too.

"I best be running," said Luke. "Abbie will want to know all about that new Graham baby."

He leaned over to kiss Marty on the cheek, then reached for his coat.

"Don't worry, Ma," he said. "She's still a little girl. She won't be leaving you for a long time yet. And we won't push. If it's not right for Belinda—why, we'll steer her in another direction."

Marty smiled weakly at her son. She patted his hand, then let him go. She knew she shouldn't worry. There was no one she would sooner trust her Belinda to than Luke.

Chapter 3

Sunday

In spite of her resolve to pray rather than to worry, Marty awoke still troubled the next morning. If only they could be sure that they were doing the right thing. Was Belinda really cut out to be a nurse? Could she know at age eleven? Was she ready to go with Luke on house calls? It was true that Luke had started accompanying Dr. Watkins when he had been very young—but even Luke had been older than eleven.

Belinda had no such doubts.

"Guess what?" she informed them proudly at the breakfast table. "Luke says I can go with him when he goes out to take care of sick people."

Marty looked at Clark. They had talked long into the night about Luke's suggestion. She wasn't sure if they were ready yet to allow Belinda the privilege; but they had agreed that if it was what Belinda really wanted, they would not refuse their permission.

"Are ya sure ya wanna go?" asked Clark. It was a needless question. Belinda's eyes fairly glowed.

"Can I?" pleaded Belinda.

"Yer ma and me are talkin' it over," answered Clark without committing himself.

"Why do you want to go?" asked Marty softly.

Belinda looked puzzled by the question. She seemed to feel her mother should understand without it being explained.

"Why?" repeated Marty. "Ya know thet Luke sees some pretty bad things at times. People really sick. Some hurt bad. You wanna see thet?"

Belinda grimaced.

" 'Member the little bird," Marty continued. "It was limp and suffering. Well, sometimes hurt people look thet bad, too. Do ya really think thet ya can stand to see people hurt like thet?"

It was a fair question and Belinda knew it. Her face went pale as she thought about it, but she answered honestly, "I'll hate it. I know I'll hate it. But someone has to be there to help 'em git better. That's what Luke does. But sometimes he needs help. He doesn't have a nurse to help him. I could be a nurse. I could help 'im sew up people an'—"

"All right," said Marty with a nod of her head. "Iffen ya really want to. I—I guess I thought thet ya might like to be a schoolteacher like Clae or Missie, but iffen yer really sure—"

Belinda's face still was white but she shook her head solemnly. "I'm sure," she said. Then for a moment she looked doubtful. "I *think* I'm sure." She hesitated before she spoke again. "I'll never know unless I try, will I?"

Clark nodded. "Guess not," he said. "But we don't believe us none in rushin' in, either. Yer awful young to be thinkin' on nursin'. Yer ma and me will give it some more thought."

Belinda understood that for now the matter was to be dropped.

Following the Sunday morning service, they all went to Luke and Abbie's for dinner as planned. The family members shared in providing the food. There were too many of them to be expecting one woman to do all the work.

Tables were set up under a large maple tree in the backyard, and dishes of summer foods began to pile up on them as the teams brought each family from church.

The cousins had a delightful day. There were enough of them to form several games when they all got together, and they began to sort themselves out according to ages and likes and to gather in various spots in the yard for some good, clean Sunday afternoon fun.

Nandry's children were the oldest, but not all of them were there that day. Tina was already married and living in a small town several miles from her parents. It was hard for Marty to believe that she actually had a married grandchild—even if that grandchild was the oldest one of her foster daughter.

Andrew was now eighteen and working on a neighboring farm, so he did not join the family for Sunday dinner either. Mary and Jane were both there, but they considered themselves too grown-up to join in the childish play. Instead, they busied themselves with caring for Luke's two little sons, the youngest members of the family.

Marty let her eyes travel lovingly over the family members as they gathered, a smile playing on her lips.

Clark caught the look.

"What you be grinnin' at?" he asked playfully.

"Jest thinkin'," said Marty. "Look at the size of this family— an' half of 'em ain't even here. Clae an' Joe are missin', Missie an' Willie are missin' and Ellie an' Lane are missin'. What would we ever do iffen we could *all* be together?"

Clark's eyes followed her around the circle. He too smiled at his family.

"We'd manage," he said comfortably. "Somehow we'd manage."

Then he turned back to Marty. "How many we got, anyway?" he asked her.

Marty laughed at his sudden question.

"Ya don't even know yer own offspring," she teased.

"Jest never sat me down to count," responded Clark.

"Well, best ya sit ya down and figure it out," said Marty pertly. "Me, I'm needed in the kitchen," and so saying she lifted the hem of her skirt and climbed the steps to Abbie's back door.

It was after dinner when they were all relaxing on the back porch that Clark brought up the matter of family numbers again.

"Got it figured," he said to Marty as she lifted young Aaron onto her lap.

"Got what figured?" asked Marty, a puzzled frown lightly wrinkling her brow.

"Our offspring. Counted up thirty-eight of 'em."

"You what?" asked Arnie leaning forward in his chair.

"Counted up the offspring."

"Whose offspring?" queried Luke.

"Our offspring. Yer mother's an' mine. Thirty-eight—thet's what I counted."

"Can't be," said Luke in disbelief.

"Figure it yerself. 'Course I counted the ones thet we got by adoption, by you young'uns marryin', an' by us joinin' families—the whole bunch. Anyway, we got 'em—I counted 'em."

"Thet's cheatin' a bit, ain't it?" asked Arnie with a good-natured grin.

"How so? They're all ours, ain't they?"

Dack came thundering up the steps, hooting like an Indian on the warpath. His shirttail was out, his coppery hair every which way and his trouser knees green with grass stains.

" 'Ceptin' him, now," laughed Clark, catching Dack around the waist as he ran past. "Don't know iffen I'm gonna claim me thet one."

They all joined in the hearty laughter and Clark tossed his wild grandson up into the air and swung him in wide arcs while the little boy squealed with delight. As soon as he was placed back on the ground, a small fist reached out to pound on Clark's artificial leg.

"Knock, knock," cried Dack. "Knock on wood."

"Iffen thet boy ever gits 'im the wrong leg, Pa ain't got no one to blame but hisself," said Clare. "Thet little game of his might backfire some."

Clark had to complete the game to Dack's satisfaction.

"Who's thet knockin' on my wood?" he said, pretending to be upset, and Dack squealed again and dodged out of reach of his grandfather.

The young girls were by far outnumbered when the Davis family met for Sunday dinner. Since Nandry's two older girls stayed with the women or appointed themselves babysitters for the younger members, Belinda and Amy Jo were left to find their own amusement. Most of the time they chose to play the games that the boys were playing, but on occasion the boys got too rough, and the two girls went off to find fun of their own making.

They were used to being together. They had shared the same farmyard for all of Amy Jo's days. The difference of nearly a year in age had never bothered them. Nor had the fact that they were very different in temperament. Belinda was soft-hearted and serious, while Amy Jo was carefree and teasing. She loved a dare, both to give and to take, plagued her mother with her carelessness and playfully tried to outdo her father in practical jokes. Kate longed for the day when her tomboy daughter would be more ladylike, but Clare seemed to enjoy the young girl's infectious laughter and rowdy spirit.

In spite of the personality differences, the girls got along well. It would be incorrect to say that Amy Jo was the leader and Belinda the follower, though it was Amy Jo who thought up the mischief for the two. Belinda led the way in other things—like shouldering responsibility, consideration for others, and spiritual aptitude. She often repeated spiritual or moral lessons she had learned at church or from her parents. If the little admonitions caught Amy Jo in the right frame of mind, she accepted them readily, but if she was not so inclined right then, she in turn reprimanded Belinda for "being so bossy."

But their little quarrels were always over quickly. For though Amy Jo had a shortness of patience, she also had shortness of memory, and soon she had quite forgotten what the fuss had been about. Indeed, she often seemed to forget there had been a fuss at all.

It was usually Amy Jo who suggested they desert the boys and find their own fun. Not that she didn't like the boyish games—Amy Jo had enough of the tomboy in her to enjoy most anything, but she also liked to be the leader and sometimes the boys were not too anxious to let her do the leading.

And so it was that after a few games of tag, followed by Red Rover, Amy Jo suggested to Belinda that they leave the boys to their own "silly" playing and go make some dandelion chains. Belinda was happy to comply. She had been bursting to tell her good news to somebody, and Amy Jo was the perfect candidate. Belinda wasn't ready to share it yet with the boys. They might laugh and tease.

"Guess what," said Belinda when the two had settled themselves in the shade of the maple, laps filled with dandelion stems. "Luke's gonna take me with 'im."

"Where's he goin'?" asked Amy Jo, a bit put out that she hadn't been asked to share the adventure, whatever it might be.

"No place," said Belinda, slightly miffed at Amy Jo's density.

"Then how's he gonna take ya?" countered Amy Jo with a toss of her reddish brown curls.

"Silly," said Belinda in disgust. "I mean, to make his house calls. He's gonna let me go along."

Amy Jo looked shocked rather than impressed. "Whatever for?" she questioned impatiently.

"So I can learn," declared Belinda. This conversation was not going at all as she had planned.

"Learn to what?"

"To sew up people and fix broken bones an'—"

"Yuck!" interrupted Amy Jo and stuck out her tongue.

Belinda bit her lip. She was tempted to call Amy Jo a child, get up and move away, dandelion chains and all. Instead, she quietly began to count to ten like her father had taught her.

"Ya really wanna learn that stuff?" asked Amy Jo.

" 'Course," answered Belinda, a stubborn set to her jaw.

"I wouldn't," Amy Jo shook her head confidently. "I hate blood an' messy cuts an' things. I wouldn't wanna do that at all."

"Well, someone has to do it," began Belinda, but Amy Jo cut in quickly, "Let Luke. He's the doctor. What's he makin' you do it for? He gits paid to fix people so why should—"

But Belinda could bear no more. She pulled one of her golden braids and sighed deeply. Amy Jo simply did not understand. Belinda wished she had never told her precious secret. She would say no more—at least not until she could find someone who would really understand.

Chapter 4

House Calls

Belinda was so anxious to get started that Luke had a hard time keeping her patient until he could talk with Clark and Marty and get their final decision. He finally found a little free time on a Saturday afternoon.

"Belinda's pushing for an answer. She won't wait much longer. Have you had enough time to think and pray yet?" he asked.

Clark nodded and reached for a ginger cookie.

"She can go."

"But—but not just anytime," Marty quickly added as she stood beside Luke pouring fresh lemonade.

"We been thinkin' thet ya might be able to sorta pick 'n choose the times," Clark explained. "So thet she won't be exposed to too much, too quick like."

"Exactly," agreed Luke. "Exactly my thinking. That's why I said house calls instead of working at the office. I have some idea ahead of time what I'll be finding when I make a house call. Office—well, I never know what might come in."

Marty breathed a sigh of relief.

"Truth is," Luke went on, "I'm on my way out to the Vickers' now. Their oldest son Sam cut himself with an axe on Wednesday. I stitched it up fer him at the office, but I said I'd stop by and see how it is doing today. Wasn't too bad a cut, but it will need the dressing changed. Can she come?"

Clark and Marty exchanged glances and the decision was made. Clark nodded their agreement.

"Good!" said Luke. He finished his cookie and reached for another.

"I'll call 'er," said Marty. "I set 'er to straightenin' fruit shelves in the cellar."

Belinda arrived in a flurry of excitement. She was ready to grab her coat and join Luke in his buggy.

"My, my!" said Marty with a laugh. "Jest don't get ya in such a state! Ya need to change thet dirty dress and wash those hands afore yer able to go anyplace."

Belinda ran to change, quickly swishing water over her hands and face.

Marty reached for the brush to straighten the tangled hair and Belinda wriggled impatiently.

"Hurry, Mama," she pleaded. "I don't want Luke to go without me."

Luke laughed. "I'll be here. Do as your mama says. We don't want you going in there all rumpled and scaring my patient, now do we?" He rose from the table to get the pitcher for another glass of the lemonade for Clark and himself.

It wasn't a long ride to the Vickers'. With Belinda on the buggy seat beside him, Luke talked to her about the case, using the proper terms and explaining about sutures, surgery, bacteria and antiseptics. Belinda listened wide-eyed. Her big brother knew so much—and he was willing to teach her! The excitement within her mounted.

When they reached the Vickers', young Ezra was sent to take the doctor's horse. With black bag in one hand and Belinda by the other, Luke proceeded to the house. They were met at the door by Mrs. Vickers. She looked a bit surprised to see Belinda.

"This yer baby sister?"

Luke said that it was.

"My child, yer a growin' up. Most old enough to be of some help to yer mama," said Mrs. Vickers.

"Today she's going to be of some help to me," Luke cut in

with a grin in Belinda's direction. "Wants to learn about medicine."

Mrs. Vickers frowned. "A girl?" The question was full of unspoken dubiousness.

Belinda was taken back—but just for a moment, for she heard her big brother declaring rather boldly, "Lots of girls train to nurse now. And we're going to need lots more in the future."

"Well, I guess yer mama knows what she be doin'," answered Mrs. Vickers, but her very tone indicated that she seriously doubted it. "Never let a girl of mine be a-doin' it, though." Then under her breath and with a click of her tongue she continued, "Nursin'. Never thought I'd hear me the day."

She led the way to the bedroom.

The bedroom smelled bad, and Belinda felt her stomach lurch a bit. Her palms were sticky with sweat and her heart was hammering.

On the bed lay Sam Vickers, his leg propped up on a pillow. Beside him on the bed lay several thongs of cowhide leather. Sam was braiding a rope of some sort. He looked bored and frustrated and Belinda could imagine that he wasn't too easy a patient for his mother to care for.

"How are we doing, Sam?" greeted Luke.

Sam's answer was a scowl.

"Bed getting a little uncomfortable?" continued Luke.

"Sure is," grumbled Sam. "Never be so glad to git outta a place as I will be this here bed."

"Well, if your leg is doing okay, maybe we can get you to a chair now and then."

Sam did not look impressed. A chair didn't sound all that much better.

Luke opened up his black bag and took out a few items that he placed on the table by the bed.

"It been givin' you much pain?" he asked Sam.

Sam shook his head, but as Belinda looked in his eyes she wondered if he was really telling the truth. She stole a quick glance at Luke and felt that he might be questioning the boy's truthfulness as well.

Luke proceeded to unwrap the injured leg.

"See it's been doing a bit of bleeding," he commented.

Sam didn't want any bleeding to keep him a prisoner in his bed.

"Not much," he mumbled. "Maybe bumped it in the night or somethin'."

Belinda watched the sure hands of her brother as they unwound the bandages. There had been bleeding all right. The closer he got to the wound, the redder the bandages were becoming.

Belinda shut her eyes tightly just as Luke went to remove the last strip of bandage, and then she chided herself and opened them again. One could never be a nurse with her eyes shut.

The bandage stuck. Luke lifted his eyes to Mrs. Vickers hovering at the door.

"Could you bring a pan of hot water and a clean cloth, please, ma'am?"

Mrs. Vickers went to do his bidding.

Soaking off the bloody bandages was a slow process. At least it seemed awfully slow to Belinda. She marveled at Luke's patience.

At last the final bit of gauze was lifted from the cut, and Belinda caught her breath as she saw the angry red tear in the flesh. It had been stitched carefully so there was no gaping, but it was still inflamed and fiery looking. Belinda lifted her eyes back to the face of the patient. *It must be very painful. How did Sam—?*

There was pain in Sam's eyes. Without even thinking, Belinda reached out a hand and brushed the shaggy hair back from his forehead. For just a second their eyes met. A message of sympathy passed from Belinda to Sam, and then the spell was broken. Quickly Belinda withdrew her hand and stepped back, and Sam restlessly moved his head on the pillow.

Luke saw it all—saw the compassion that prompted Belinda's action, saw the brief moment of accepted sympathy on the part of Sam, and saw the hasty retreat by both of them. *Why do we do it?* Luke wondered to himself. *Why do we feel we can't honestly, openly express our concern for another?*

At the same time, Luke was encouraged by the compassion showing in Belinda's eyes. Yes, she might make a good nurse. She could feel, she could empathize with the patients. That was promising in someone of her age. Perhaps she wasn't too young after all.

Luke continued with his treatment, watching Belinda closely for her reactions. He did not want to push her into a profession where she did not belong. Though he did see hesitation, even horror, at the injury and pain of the patient, he did not see Belinda flinch away. She faced the procedures honestly, squarely, though she certainly did not enjoy them for their own sake.

When the leg had been carefully rebandaged, Luke assisted Sam to a chair in the family living room. It was Belinda who placed the cushions as Luke lowered the young man to the seat. It was Belinda who eased another cushion under the extended leg. And it was Belinda who went back to the bedroom to retrieve the braided thongs so Sam might have something to busy his hands as soon as he felt up to using them.

Luke was impressed. He didn't say anything about it then to her, but he did give her a warm smile and her shoulder a slight squeeze to tell her that she had done a good job as his assistant. Belinda beamed. He would let her accompany him again.

Over the many months that followed, Luke carefully chose cases that he could invite Belinda to help him with. These times were limited. She could not go where communicable diseases were treated. He did not take her when he feared that the case might be too hard for a young girl to stomach. He did not take her when he feared the procedure would be a long one, demanding his undivided time and attention. But he did take her on a number of calls when he felt she could learn some of the principles of home care.

Always she was eager to learn. On the way to the case he explained what they would be treating and how they would go about it. She learned the names of his instruments and their use. It wasn't too long before Belinda was able to pass the instruments to him when he asked for them, if his hands were busy with other things.

Luke was amazed at how quickly she caught on. His voice held admiration and excitement whenever he reported to Clark and Marty. They exchanged glances of both relief and awe. Maybe they had done the right thing. They continued to pray for guidance.

Perhaps the only one to chafe about the arrangement was Amy Jo. She missed her playmate. Not only was Belinda occasionally gone, but when she was home she just was not the same. Amy Jo often found her poring over some medical book. She wasn't fun like she used to be. Amy Jo did wish Belinda would just forget the whole thing.

But Belinda wasn't about to forget it. Daily her interest seemed to increase rather than diminish.

Summer came again and with it another break from school. Amy Jo looked forward to the summer; it meant free time— more time for play. Belinda looked forward to the summer too; it meant more time to be with Luke—more time to make house calls. Now she would be able to go on more than just Saturdays. Her excitement mounted just thinking about it. She now had reached her thirteenth birthday. Luke had promised that when she reached fifteen, he would talk to her parents about letting her help in the office in town.

Chapter 5

A Surprise

"Belinda! Belinda!"

Marty's voice rose above the usual clamour of the farmyard flocks and herds, excitement in her call. Belinda and Amy Jo, who were in the loft of the barn enjoying a new batch of kittens, heard it. Belinda bounced to her feet. Perhaps Luke had come and they were going on another house call.

"I've gotta go," she informed her playmate.

Amy Jo pouted. "Yer always runnin' off," she said. "We never git to play anymore."

For a moment Belinda hesitated. She did hate it so when Amy was upset. She was about to apologize when her mother called again.

"Belinda! Amy Jo!"

At the sound of her own name, Amy Jo's spirits lifted. Maybe Luke wasn't there to drag Belinda off again after all. The two of them hurried down the ladder and to the house.

They reached the door breathless and flushed.

"There you are," said Marty to them as they followed her into the kitchen. Belinda had seen the shine in her eyes, and she knew her mother had news of some sort. For a moment Belinda had feared lest it just be some household chore.

"What is it?" she asked, puffing out each word.

"Clare jest got back from town and there was a letter from

Missie." She put a hand on the shoulder of each girl. "Ya can't guess what she has to say!"

Belinda couldn't remember seeing her mother so excited for a long time.

"Did she have another baby?" she asked.

Marty laughed. "No. No new baby. But it's something thet you'll—you'll find most interestin'. Both of ya." Marty picked up the letter that lay on the kitchen table and nodded toward two chairs. The girls obediently sat down.

"Listen to this," ordered Marty, and the girls prepared themselves to listen. Amy Jo cast a look in Belinda's direction and rolled her expressive eyes. The look said clearly, *All this fuss over a bit of news in a letter,* and Belinda nearly choked on the giggle bubbling up inside her.

" 'We'd like to ask a big favor of you,' " read Marty. " 'Ya know that Melissa is gittin' to be quite a young lady now. She has finished all of the grades in the local school. She thinks thet she would like to be a schoolteacher. We still are very short of teachers here. Melinda—you remember Melinda, her teacher—thinks that Melissa would make a good teacher, and we'd like to give her the chance.' "

Marty hesitated in her reading and glanced expectantly at the two girls. They waited for her to turn back to the letter before they dared to look at each other, and when she did continue, they both had to hide snickers behind girlish hands. *Why all the fuss about a far-off relative, a relative we haven't even met, wanting to become a schoolteacher?* was their unspoken question to each other.

" 'So, we have been thinkin',' " Marty read on, " 'would you mind if Melissa comes out to stay with you while she gets some more training?' "

Marty looked up at the two girls to see how the good news would affect them.

It took a few moments for it all to sink in, but when it finally did, it was Amy Jo who cheered loudly.

"Oh, boy!" she squealed. "Someone to play with while yer off with Luke."

Belinda was a bit hurt by the outburst.

"She'll be livin' at our house," she countered.

"Yeah, but—"

"Girls!" Marty interrupted. "Stop yer fussin'. I thought thet you'd be thinkin' on Melissa, 'stead of fightin' over who'd git her."

Belinda and Amy Jo had enough good training to feel a bit embarrassed.

They waited quietly for Marty to go on.

" 'She will need a couple more grades in yer local school, and then she will go on to take her normal school trainin'. By then she should have adjusted enough to bein' away from her family thet it won't be so difficult fer her. We thought thet if she could be with you first, it would be much better for her than sendin' her directly to the big city."

It was beginning to seem more real.

" 'She will arrive about a week before classes begin. We will send her out by train.' "

Amy Jo reached over and poked Belinda, mouthing some words that Belinda did not catch.

Marty continued, " 'If it's okay with you, we sure would appreciate it. It's goin' to be awfully hard for us to let her go. I understand much better now how you felt, Mama.' "

Marty's voice trailed off and her eyes began to mist. Belinda knew that tears were coming. But Amy Jo brought a quick halt to any sentiment.

"You an' Grandpa gonna let her come?" she asked in her usual boisterous fashion.

Marty looked with loving exasperation at her young granddaughter. Only Amy Jo would have deemed it necessary to ask such a question. But then she did not usually think before she spoke.

" 'Course," said Belinda, giving Amy Jo a gentle poke. "Ya know very well thet Ma and Pa'd never say no."

Amy Jo just shrugged.

The excitement of it all began to sink through to Belinda. *It will be so nice to have another girl in the house, almost like having a sister.* Belinda caught herself. She did have sisters— her foster sisters, Nandry and Clae, but they were much older and had children of their own older than herself. And she had Missie and Ellie—but the truth was she had never yet even seen Missie, and Ellie had left home for the West when she, Belinda, had been only a few months old. She had never had a sister around to share a room—or secrets—or anything else with. *Oh, true, there's Amy Jo,* she thought. Amy Jo was almost like having a sister—even if she really was a niece. *But Melissa will be right in the house with me,* she exulted.

Belinda's eyes traveled to the calendar on the wall. The letter had said Melissa would arrive a week or so before school. How many more weeks would that be? Quickly Belinda counted—*three or, at the most, four.* She could hardly wait. *Boy, will the weeks till then pass slowly!* She turned back to her mother, her eyes now shining like Marty's. She jumped from her chair and threw her arms around Marty's waist. *No wonder Mama was so excited!*

"Does Pa know? Does Pa know?" she implored.

"Not yet," said Marty, her enthusiasm matching her daughter's. "He's over to the Grahams' helpin' Lou. He should be home 'most anytime now."

"Oh, boy!" exclaimed Belinda and turned to Amy Jo. The two of them joined hands and danced around the kitchen. "Melissa's comin'! Melissa's comin'," they chanted.

Marty laughed at their foolishness, but truth was she sort of felt like joining in their dance. *It will be so good to have Melissa,* she rejoiced. It would be a little bit of Missie back home with them again. Marty's shining eyes began to fill with tears. She brushed at them with a corner of her apron.

What will she be like? she wondered. *She's most grown up now. Well, no, not quite. She's only 'bout nine months older than our Belinda.*

Marty turned back to Belinda. She was acting awfully childish at the moment, but there were times when Marty had to realize that Belinda too was quickly growing up. She was thirteen and a half and a mature girl for her age in many ways. Yes, Melissa, who was past her fourteenth birthday, could well seem quite grown-up. They'd need to remember that, in their dealings with the girl. Marty brushed at her tears again. It was going to be so wonderful.

It was Belinda who rushed out to greet Clark with the news. For a moment he thought she must be "funnin'," but when he looked over her head into the flushed and happy face of Marty, he knew she was not. He grinned then and flipped his worn work hat into the air.

"When?" he asked. "When's she comin'?"

"In just three or four weeks," responded Belinda.

"Jest early enough to git herself settled afore school classes begin," added Marty.

Clark grinned.

"Thet spare bedroom gonna need some fixin' up?" asked Clark.

Marty hadn't thought that far ahead. Belinda was about to protest that she had hoped Melissa would be able to share her room. But she held her tongue. Perhaps Melissa would not wish to do that.

Marty was busy thinking about Clark's comment. The room should be freshened up, all right. Perhaps she should sew new curtains and make a new spread as well. It had been a long time since the spare room had seen anything new. *Maybe Belinda would like to help in the choosin'.* Marty's mind continued to busy itself with many plans for the future, and she had the room nearly made new by the time she turned to walk the path back to her kitchen. But for the moment, getting supper on the table had to be her main concern.

Belinda had gone on down to the barn with Clark to tell him other news from the letter about Melissa's coming. Marty could not resist climbing the stairs for a quick peek into the room that would be for the girl. The door had not even been opened for several weeks. It smelled a bit musty and unused.

Her eyes traveled over the walls, the floor, the curtains, the bed. Clark was right. The room did need sprucing up. *Let's see,* Marty mused, *this was Missie's room before she was married. Melissa will be stayin' in her own mama's room!*

Suddenly three or four weeks did not seem very long after all. My, she had so much to do! Marty hurried back down the steps and to the kitchen as if getting supper quickly out of the way would be a great help in preparing for the arrival of her granddaughter. She smiled to herself. That was silly. There wasn't one thing she'd be able to do tonight in getting the room ready for Melissa.

Marty talked it over thoroughly with Clark and they agreed on her plans for the room.

"I do wish thet we knew a bit more about the girl's likes an' dislikes," stated Marty. "It would be jest like me to go an' choose a color thet she detests."

Clark smiled and patted her hand. "You'll do jest fine, Marty. Remember how well ya did with the chinks in our first log cabin home?"

Marty looked at him quickly to see if he was teasing her. She was deciding whether to be put out with him or not, but then couldn't help but laugh at the memory of her vigorous scrubbing of the log walls and the wet, muddy chinking falling out on the floor in clumps. Clark laughed too.

"Well, it sure weren't funny then," Marty reminded him, wiping her eyes. "I was a-feared the whole house was goin' to come down around our ears!" Marty and Clark looked at each other awhile remembering those long-ago days.

"Well, anyway," Marty said, back to the present, "I'm serious about fixin' up this room for Melissa." And she sounded serious. "Belinda likes soft blues and greens but doesn't care for loud, bright colors. Amy Jo loves bright reds and yellows and never picks a soft color in anything. Now, how do I know what Melissa might choose?"

Clark saw her point, but he still didn't seem to think it was much of an issue.

"Use soft colors on the walls and curtains and spread," he suggested, "with a bit of brightness in some pillows an' rugs."

Marty looked at him in amazement. Maybe he had more sense about such matters than she had given him credit for.

She nodded her head, in her mind picturing the room fresh with pale flowered wallpaper, fluffy curtains—maybe white eyelet fluttering at the window and a matching spread with lots of soft ruffles on the bed. Scattered on the bed would be bright pillows, maybe in shades of greens, yellows and even blues, depending on the wallpaper pattern. On the floor could be homemade rugs. Patterned in bright colors and—

Clark interrupted her thoughts. "I'll do whatever you want—wallpaper, paint—whenever yer ready," he was saying. "You an' Belinda will need to care fer the rest. I never could sew on a patch, much less make somethin' fancy."

Marty smiled a bit distractedly at his comment, her mind still busy with the room plans.

"Clark," Marty said reflectively, "I think I'm goin' to invite Amy Jo to come along with Belinda and me on our shoppin' trip. I sure don't want her feelin' left out, with Melissa livin' right here with Belinda an' all."

Clark nodded in agreement. "We'll want to be careful to make Amy Jo feel a part of things, seein' she and Belinda have been more like sisters than anything else all these years," he commented.

And so their plans were made. Marty checked with Kate before telling Amy Jo about the trip to town. Kate was happy to have Amy involved in the choosing of the new things for the room. She, too, was aware that with three, it was easy for one to feel left out at times. She and Marty discussed the situation and agreed that they would keep their eyes and ears open for possible problems.

Right after the morning chores had been done, Marty announced the shopping plans to two excited girls, and they ran to get ready for the trip into town.

The first duty was to select a pretty wallpaper. Just as Marty would have guessed, Belinda picked a soft cream with a mint green print on it, but Amy Jo insisted that it was "too dull." She wanted lavendar with large yellow roses. Marty, finally at her wit's end, decided to leave the wallpaper till later and took the girls to look at what was available in yard goods. Here again there was a difference of opinion. Marty loved the gauzy white for priscillas, Belinda favored the fluffy green organza, and Amy Jo insisted that a bright yellow with a bold pattern of purple flowers was the prettiest.

"And think how beautiful it will be with that wallpaper pattern, Gramma!" Amy Jo enthused while Marty inwardly cringed. "Ya know, the same colors, but opposite—the flowers yellow on the wallpaper an' . . ." she chattered on while Marty tried to figure out what to do.

She began to wish she had left both girls at home and gone with her own inclinations. She suggested that they take a break and go to the hotel dining room for a cup of tea. The girls agreed. They really weren't all that interested in tea, but they knew the hotel served some pastries they were partial to.

Marty needed that cup of tea. She sipped it slowly, trying to sort out just how she would get around the differences of opinion. At last she decided to broach the subject head-on.

"Seems—" she began, "seems thet we don't agree much on how Melissa's room should be done. Now, we don't have Melissa here to do her own decidin', and it would be rather foolish to wait an' jest move her on in and then move her out agin whilst we do up the room. Still—it would be so much nicer iffen she could make her own choices, but—"

"Why can't she, Mama?" interrupted Belinda. "She could share my room until her room is all finished; then we wouldn't need to move her in an' out."

Marty hadn't even thought of that possibility. "Why, Belinda, thet might jest work! Let me see . . ." and Marty was off in thought, busy with more plans. It did make more sense to let Melissa do her own choosing. But what if her preferences tended toward those of Amy Jo's? Well, it would be only two years and Melissa would be moving on again. Marty supposed that she could stand nearly any color scheme for her grand-daughter's sake. She could always shut the door, she decided with an inward chuckle.

"I like yer idea," Marty said to Belinda at length. "Maybe we should jest wait. Melissa could do the choosin', an' she'd feel more at home that way."

Belinda grinned.

"Ya don't mind sharin' yer room fer a piece?" Marty inquired.

"I don't mind," Belinda assured her. She not only didn't mind but she was looking forward to the opportunity.

Amy Jo scowled like only she could. Belinda knew she was displeased about something.

"Ya jest want her in yer own room so thet ya can be friends faster," she pouted.

"Friends?" responded Marty, her head coming up. "Melissa is Belinda's niece—an' yer cousin. Ya don't need to worry none 'bout bein' jest friends. Yer *family*—both of ya."

But Amy Jo still frowned at Belinda.

Marty finished her tea and gathered her belongings.

"Well," she said, "I guess thet's what we'll do. We'll jest leave it until Melissa gits here. I think I'll work me on some new rugs, though. I can put in enough colors thet they will go with most anything. Don't want to leave everything until last."

The girls still dawdled over their pastries.

"I'm gonna go git the groceries I be a-needin'," Marty informed them. "When ya git done here, ya join me at the store."

They both nodded.

"Now mind yer manners—and don't go gittin' yerselves in any trouble," admonished Marty and she smoothed out her skirts and started for the door.

Amy Jo frowned at Belinda again.

"Yer happy 'bout it, ain't ya?" she said in an accusing voice.

" 'Bout what?"

" 'Bout waitin' till Melissa gits here. 'Bout not pickin' the room colors. 'Bout Melissa stayin' in yer room with ya."

Belinda shrugged her slim shoulders. "Guess so," she said. She didn't think it would be right to deny it.

"Well, I'm not. I wanted to help choose, too. I liked the colors I picked. An' I jest bet Melissa woulda liked 'em too."

"Maybe," said Belinda.

"I wish that I could have 'em in *my* room," went on Amy Jo, determined to be negative. "I never picked my colors yet. It's been the same, *the same*, ever since I was borned, I think."

Belinda doubted that, but she didn't say so.

Amy Jo sighed. "I'll never git my own colors. Mama wouldn't even like 'em. Green an' white—thet's all she ever likes."

Belinda saw nothing wrong with those colors but she didn't say so.

They finished their cakes and Amy Jo lifted each remaining crumb to her mouth on the tip of one long, tapering finger. Belinda watched her. She had never noticed how long and slender Amy Jo's fingers were before. She compared them to her own. Her fingers were not as long, but there was a certain strength there in her slender hands. She turned them over and over. She couldn't help but picture a scalpel there—a syringe. She forced her mind back to the present.

"We'd better go," she said. "Mama said she wouldn't be long."

Reluctantly Amy Jo pushed back her empty plate and followed Belinda from the room.

Chapter 6

Planning

During the next three weeks, even the thrill of accompanying Luke on his calls took second place in Belinda's mind. All she could think about was Melissa's coming. What would she be like? Would they like one another? Would they get along? What about Amy Jo? How would things work out with three of them to get along instead of just two?

Belinda wasn't the only one holding her breath and wondering about the future. Amy Jo wondered—and at times even shed a few tears. She was sure the two girls, sharing a room up in the big house, would forget all about her. *Well, I don't care,* she told herself with a toss of her head—or, at least, that was what she tried to tell herself, over and over again. It never quite worked. She did care, and she good and well knew it.

Marty's concerns about Amy Jo led to a chat with Belinda one day when the two of them worked together over pie crusts in the big farm kitchen.

"Excited 'bout Melissa comin'?"

"Oh, yes!" admitted Belinda. "I can hardly wait."

"Been thinkin'—it might be a bit hard fer Amy Jo."

Belinda did not argue.

"We need to be extry careful not to let her feel left out," went on Marty, and Belinda nodded, knowing her mother was really meaning "you" when she said "we."

"Have ya thought ya on any way thet we might do thet?" asked Marty.

Belinda hesitated. "No," she said slowly. "Not really—but I—I've been thinkin' on somethin' I'd sure like to do fer Amy Jo."

"What's thet?" asked Marty.

"Ya know Amy Jo's room?" ventured Belinda.

Marty nodded.

"Well, it's pale green an' white."

Marty nodded again. The room had been those colors since before Amy Jo had been born.

"Amy Jo doesn't like those colors," Belinda dared to say.

"She doesn't?"

"No. She's sick, sick, sick of green an' white. She wants somethin' bright, or somethin'—somethin' darin', I think."

Marty nodded. She could well imagine Amy Jo wanting something like that.

"Ma, do ya think thet Clare an' Kate would let Amy Jo have new colors?"

Marty thought of the colors Amy Jo was likely to pick. She wasn't sure. She was sure that *she* would have a hard time living with whatever Amy Jo picked.

"I dunno," she said honestly, thinking on it as she spoke. "Does this mean a lot to Amy Jo?"

"I think so," answered Belinda slowly. "She feels kinda sad 'bout Melissa." Belinda wondered if her mother might misunderstand and was quick to add, "Oh, she's excited 'bout it— same as me. But—she's sad, too, 'cause she won't have Melissa livin' at her house an—"

"I think I understand," said Marty.

Belinda stole a glance at her mother's face to see if she did understand. After studying it, she felt sure that Marty really did understand what she was trying to say.

"I'll have a chat with Kate," said Marty. "Maybe iffen yer pa an' me offer to help with the wallpaper an' the material, they'll let Amy Jo do her own choosin'. She's got a birthday comin'. We could do it fer her birthday."

Belinda wanted to hug her mother, but her hands were all

covered with flour. She smiled happily instead.

"Thanks, Mama," she said appreciatively.

But it was really Marty who felt the best about the conversation. She was pleased to know that Belinda cared enough to be thinking about Amy Jo, having been concerned that Belinda might consider only her own excitement about Melissa's arrival. She would tell Clark all about it when they had some time alone to talk. She was sure he would be pleased with the maturity of their daughter as well. She did hope that Clare and Kate would see the offer of a new room for Amy Jo as a show of love rather than interference.

Over coffee at Kate's the next morning, Marty discussed the idea of redoing Amy Jo's room. Kate was thrilled.

"I should have thought to let her do her own choosin' before," said Kate.

"I saw, firsthand, some of Amy Jo's choices," Marty informed Kate. "Ya better be preparin' yerself is all thet I can say. I hope thet ya like yer rooms colorful an' bright."

Kate laughed. "I've seen a few of her choices. They are a bit shockin', aren't they? Well, I guess we will jest learn to live with 'em. I'm realizin' more an' more thet it's like you an' Pa have often said, they grow up awful fast, an' soon they won't be with us at all." Kate poured more coffee, then went on reflectively, "Besides feedin' an' clothin' and trainin' our children, Clare an' I need to be listenin' to 'em an' learnin' to know 'em as people on their own whilst we've still got the chance."

Marty nodded, thinking of her own scattered family.

"Ya know how Amy Jo has always liked to be drawin' an' colorin'?" Kate continued.

Marty smiled in acknowledgment, remembering Amy Jo drawing and coloring pictures even before she started off to school. They often laughed about her color choices, but Amy Jo had loved the brightness and insisted on using the most colorful watercolors she had.

"I've been talkin' to Clare," went on Kate. "I've been thinkin' on gettin' Amy Jo some things for drawin' an' paintin' fer her birthday. Let her show her love fer color in her own way. What d'ya think?"

Marty quickly agreed. "Maybe we shoulda done thet ages ago," she mused aloud. "Why didn't we think of it?"

"Guess we've been too busy thinkin' shoes an' vittles," Kate responded.

Marty nodded. It did seem to take all a mother's time just thinking of the physical needs of her family. "I think thet she'd love it," Marty went on, after giving Kate's suggestion some thought. "She's always loved bright an' colorful things."

"Maybe Clare could make a little table for her room so thet she could work with a bit of privacy," Kate went on as though to herself. "Wouldn't she love thet, though?"

"When shall we tell her?" asked Marty, anticipating her granddaughter's surprise and joy.

"Let's leave it fer her birthday surprise. It's only two months away. By then the excitement of Melissa's comin' will sorta've died down. Then she can do her own pickin' and have her room the way she likes it by Christmastime."

Marty agreed, but here was something else she'd have to wait for.

When Marty shared the secret plans with Belinda, she was almost as excited as they expected Amy Jo to be. If Marty thought, however, her own waiting was difficult, it paled compared to Belinda's eagerness to tell her beloved niece and friend.

Marty helped to fill the days before Melissa's arrival by thinking of things they could do that the girl might enjoy when she joined the family—a picnic before the weather turned cold, a visit to Ma Graham, and they could drop by the schoolhouse where she'd be attending.... Marty's thoughts were kept as busy as her hands with the rugs for the floor.

Belinda was not so fortunate. Every day seemed to drag by slower than the one before. Amy Jo accused Belinda of forgetting all about her now that Melissa was coming. She hinted that Belinda would disregard their friendship from past years and like Melissa better. On more than one occasion, Belinda nearly told her about the coming birthday surprise, but she always managed to bite her tongue.

Belinda was especially glad when Luke dropped by to pick her up on the way to make a house call. It did help to distract her from the tedium of the wait.

Then a telegram arrived. They crowded together to read it at the same time.

" 'Melissa to arrive on 25th by stage. Stop.' " Clark carefully read. " 'We love you all. Stop. Willie and Missie.' "

August 25th! That was only two days away. Belinda thought she'd never be able to bear it. She turned to run to tell Amy Jo and then checked herself. Maybe that wouldn't be so wise. Amy Jo might misunderstand her excitement. Instead she decided to do one last thorough cleaning of her room—the room Melissa would be sharing with Belinda until her own was ready.

She crowded her things together in the tiny closet so Melissa might have room to hang her clothes, then emptied half of the drawers in the tall dresser. She pulled out a wooden box her father had made years ago for her doll things and carefully folded her extra clothing into it. Then she carried the box to the empty room that had been shared by Arnie and Luke. She was glad her mother hadn't suggested Melissa use this room until the room that had been Ellie's was ready for her. *Funny,* Belinda thought. *Mother still thinks of the front bedroom as the "boys room."* She hadn't even thought of putting Melissa in there.

Well, Belinda didn't mind. Her niece! Just think! She would soon be meeting her niece for the first time! And her niece was almost nine months older than she!

Belinda's heart pounded with excitement and her stomach churned with just a bit of concern. What would it really be like? Well, she would soon learn. It wouldn't be long now.

Marty's heart was also racing. She could not count the number of times when she had ached to hold and to know her granddaughter—their Missie's "baby girl." Melissa Joy was no longer the baby in age or birth sequence—she had a younger sister, Julia, whom Marty had never seen either. But Melissa had been "on the way" when Clark and Marty had spent their difficult winter at the ranch of Willie and Missie. She had been the little one they had hoped to hold before they left again for the East. But Melissa had kept her appointed time for delivery and had not put in her appearance until after the grandparents had gone back home. So Melissa seemed special to Marty somehow. And now—now she was a young lady. A girl on the verge of womanhood—and Marty had never seen her.

Melissa's coming was an aching reminder to Marty of just how much she missed Missie and Ellie. She longed to see for herself how they were keeping, to hold their children in her arms.

Marty recalled all the fun she and Clark had shared with Melissa's brothers, Nathan and Josiah. *My, how they would have grown by now,* she marveled. They were well into their teens—almost men. Marty reminded herself that they would not be wanting to sit on Grandpa's lap for a story, or cuddle close with Grandma for a bedtime lullaby. Those days were over—never to be reclaimed. She thanked God for the time they had been able to have with the growing boys.

And Julia. Julia was now a little girl of ten. Would Marty have the same privilege of one day welcoming Julia into their home? Would Julia also wish to be a schoolteacher? Marty decided it did no harm for her to hope so.

Ellie, too, was a mother now. Their daughter Brenda was almost seven, and twin sons, William and Willis, were busy four-year-olds. Tears came unbidden as Marty yearned to see them, to get to know them as more than just names of their far-away offspring.

But Melissa—Melissa was like an earnest, a promise of things to come, a little part of those Marty loved from out West. Was she like Missie? Like Willie? Marty had not even seen a tintype of the young girl.

Oh, how she wished her "Western family" could all come for a family reunion. But at least Melissa could catch them up on all the news—that is, if Melissa was the kind of person who would talk freely to them. Would she be shy? After all, she didn't know them—not any of them. Marty felt her stomach tighten again, and, as many times over the past few days, she bowed her head. *Lord, please bring Melissa safely here, an' help us to get to know each other quick,* she prayed earnestly, *an' help her not to be fearful.* . . .

Chapter 7

Melissa Joy

The whole household was in a frenzy. Marty had checked and rechecked the supper preparations. Belinda had dusted, straightened and fussed over her bedroom that would be theirs. Amy Jo had made any number of trips to the big house to see if it was time to leave. Even Clark paced around restlessly, caught up in the excitement. Only the horses, already hitched to the buggy, waited patiently.

At last the slowly moving hands of the clock conceded that they could begin their trip into town without being ridiculously ahead of schedule, so they scrambled excitedly into the buggy and Clark clucked to the team.

"What do you think she'll be like?" asked Amy Jo of Belinda for the umpteenth time.

Belinda sighed deeply. If she only knew. It would be so much easier welcoming this niece if only she knew what kind of a person she was.

"Do ya think she's skinny or fat?" Amy Jo pursued her quest for information.

"I don't know," answered Belinda patiently.

"But ya can guess," insisted Amy Jo.

"Okay," responded Belinda just a bit testily. "I guess she's in between."

For a moment Amy Jo held her tongue but not for long.

"Does she look like her ma or pa?"

"We've never seen her—none of us."

"But didn't Aunt Missie ever write who she looks like?"

This question caused Belinda to stop and reflect. But after a few minutes she was unable to come up with any answer. She leaned forward and tapped Marty on the shoulder.

"Mama, did Missie ever say who Melissa takes after?"

Marty too thought for a few moments before responding. Without having a good reason, she had been mentally picturing the young Melissa Joy as looking like her mother.

"No-o," she said slowly now. "Don't recall she did, but I-I s'pose she'll look like her ma. No reason fer her not to."

The answer was unsatisfactory to Belinda but she didn't say so.

"Well," whispered Amy Jo relentlessly, "she might be real fat. She might even be ugly."

Belinda recalled a comment of her mother's from a few days back. Marty had said it was far more important how Melissa *acted* than how she *looked*. Could Melissa be difficult to get along with? Belinda had heard her ma and pa on more than one occasion talk about how the ranchhands doted on the girl. They enjoyed the boys but she was their favorite, and they were her self-appointed protectors. Yes, Melissa Joy could well be spoiled.

Belinda had a fleeting wish that she could escape the smartly moving buggy and return home to her own room. Maybe she shouldn't have been so quick in offering to share it. Maybe it would have been better if Melissa had stayed in the West instead of coming here to continue her schooling. Maybe—

But Amy Jo was talking again. "What if she has freckles?"

"Nothin' wrong with freckles."

Amy Jo tossed her head and scowled. "Oh, yeah," she sputtered, "*you* can say thet. You ain't got none. Iffen ya had 'em, ya'd know there's somethin' wrong with 'em, all right." Amy Jo had always hated her own scattering of freckles.

Belinda gave her an impatient look. They had discussed freckles many times in the past. Belinda always felt that the discussion led nowhere and accomplished nothing.

"You've hardly got any either," she said. "Don't know why ya fuss 'bout 'em so."

"Well, iffen ya had 'em you'd—"

"Girls!" said Marty sternly.

Belinda and Amy Jo exchanged glances, knowing better than to continue the bickering. Amy Jo gave Belinda an angry look and mouthed a few words Belinda did not understand. Belinda looked away. At least now Amy Jo might be quiet for awhile.

But not for long. "How big do you think she is?"

"She's past fourteen."

"Not 'old.' *Big*. How tall?"

Belinda shrugged. Amy Jo's guess was as good as hers. She couldn't understand why the girl persisted. Perhaps it hadn't been so wise to invite Amy Jo to meet the stage with them.

Amy Jo toyed with the ribbon on a long reddish brown braid. In spite of being peeved with her, Belinda found herself marveling at Amy Jo's unique coloring. It wasn't often that auburn hair was paired with large, violet-colored eyes.

Without thinking Belinda blurted out, "*You* don't look like yer ma."

Amy Jo's head jerked up, her lovely eyes wide with questions. Marty, too, was listening from the front seat.

Belinda hastened to explain her sudden comment. "I mean—ya don't look *only* like yer ma. Ya got her eyes, and her chin, too, I think, but not her hair color or the shape of her face."

"Ma says my hair is the same color as my Gramma Warren's," declared Amy Jo, flipping one braid back over her shoulder.

Belinda nodded.

"An' my face is shaped like Pa's," went on Amy Jo.

Like yer pa's, thought Marty, *an' like his pa's.* Every once in a while she caught a fleeting expression or a turn of Amy Jo's head that reminded Marty of Clare's father—her first husband, Clem.

"Ya see," pointed out Belinda, "Melissa could have bits—I mean, parts—of things that are like any of the family. She doesn't have to look like her ma or her pa—at least not *jest* like one of 'em."

Amy Jo scowled, not willing to part with her owlishness. But she did stop asking questions that had no answers.

The long ride to town finally ended. Now they faced a long wait for the stage to arrive. Inwardly Marty prayed that it would not be late.

"Why don't you two go git yerselves some ice cream?" Clark offered, fishing some coins from his pocket, and the girls gladly accepted the money and ran off down the street.

Marty turned to Clark with relief showing in her face. Clark read her thoughts. He knew how much quibbling children bothered Marty.

"They're jest all keyed up, thet's all. They'll calm down once thet stage gets here," he assured her.

"I do hope so," murmured Marty with a sigh. "Oh, I hope this works. I hope it don't turn out to be two girls agin one. I couldn't stand the bickerin' iffen it did."

"Now don't ya go borrowin' trouble," said Clark as he flipped the reins of the team over the hitching rail.

Marty stood still, her brow creased in thoughtfulness.

"Maybe we at least should have asked a few questions," she continued. "Clark—we really know nothin' 'bout this grand-daughter of ours."

"Know all we need to know," responded Clark comfortably, reaching out to take Marty's arm and steer her across the dusty street. "We know she's our granddaughter and we know she needs a place to stay whilst she gits her schoolin'. Now thet there is enough, to my thinkin'."

Marty sighed again and lifted her skirts to keep the dust from creeping over them with each step. Clark might be right, but she did hope that they weren't in for any unhappy surprises.

Marty did some shopping in the local store. She really didn't need many provisions, but it helped to fill the minutes until the stage was due. With time left over, she decided to look at the yard goods. Melissa might be needing some new frocks for school. Missie had written nothing about it, but it wouldn't hurt

Marty to know what was available should she need to do some sewing.

She noticed the bright bolt of colorful print that Amy Jo had picked for the curtains and spread was still on the shelf. She wasn't surprised. She couldn't imagine anyone else wanting it. Marty considered buying it on the sly and tucking it away until Amy Jo's birthday surprise, but she decided against it. Amy Jo was so changeable that she might pick something entirely different by the time her birthday rolled around.

Where are the girls, anyway? Marty checked the store clock. They were taking an unusual amount of time to get their ice cream. *They haven't gone and gotten themselves in some kind of trouble!* Marty laid aside the bolt of blue gingham she was holding and went to look for them.

She didn't need to look far. They were stationed on the sidewalk in front of the stagecoach office. The two girls had claimed a bench there. They sat sedately swinging their legs and talking excitedly.

Looks like they're friends agin. Relieved, Marty turned back to the yard goods. There were some very pretty pieces, and she decided to buy a length for a new dress for Belinda, who was quickly outgrowing her frocks. Marty could not decide between two pieces of material and ended up taking them both. She would need another one soon anyway, she reasoned, and this would save her an extra trip into town.

Purchasing the yard goods and the thread took several minutes, and Marty was glad for the distraction from waiting. She chatted with the store owner as the yard goods were measured. To her chagrin, her voice sounded almost as high-pitched and excited as did Belinda's and Amy Jo's.

At last she went to join the girls. Clark was already there, seated on the sidewalk talking with the local livery man. Marty slowed her steps. She must get her emotions under control. She was acting like a giddy schoolgirl! What kind of a grandmother would Melissa think she had?

Marty decided to take her parcels to the buggy and stow them beneath the seat. Clark offered to do it for her but she declined. Then Belinda jumped up and said she'd run them over, and Marty knew Belinda would most likely "run," all right.

"I'll go with ya," Amy Jo offered enthusiastically, jumping up.

"No—no, thet be fine," assured Marty. "There's still lots of time. I'll jest take 'em on over. Give me somethin' to do."

By the time she returned, others had gathered to meet the stage as well. Some were strangers to Marty, but she also noticed neighborfolk and some from the little town. They exchanged greetings and pleasantries.

"You expectin' someone in on the stage?" asked Mrs. Colson, the new grocer's wife.

Marty didn't suppose she'd be standing there in the heat and dust unless she was waiting for someone, but she smiled warmly and informed Mrs. Colson that their granddaughter from the West was joining them for the school year.

"How nice," said Mrs. Colson with a matching smile. "I got a sister comin' in. She jest lost her husband a couple months back an' don't know what to do with herself."

Marty murmured her sympathy and understanding.

"I do hope me thet she ain't a burden," Mrs. Colson went on quite frankly. "Some people in their grievin' feel thet the whole world should grieve with 'em. I ain't got the time nor the inclination to—"

But when the stagecoach rounded the bend, her words were covered by the cheer that went up from the waiting group. Though Marty did not join the cheer, the whole of her being suddenly seemed to strain forward. She wondered for a moment if she'd be able to stay on her feet, and then the dizziness quickly passed. She stepped forward to take Clark's arm, more for emotional support than for physical aid.

Clark sensed her emotion and reached down to gently squeeze the hand that rested on his arm.

What if Melissa missed the stage—or changed her mind at the last minute? flashed through Marty's mind. She shook the thought aside as Belinda pressed in against her, excitement making her tremble.

"Mama," she asked, tapping on Marty's arm for attention

as she'd done when a youngster. "Mama, how will we know her?"

Marty's face turned blankly to Belinda's upturned one. She had no answer. She had never seen her granddaughter and had not thought to ask for any "sign." She just thought—just thought they'd know her, *somehow*. What if they didn't? What if they had to ask? *How embarrassing!* thought Marty in panic. But Clark was speaking.

"Well, now, I don't s'pose thet there's gonna be too many fourteen-year-old girls a-travelin' all alone on thet there stage," he said confidently.

The worry left Belinda's eyes. Marty reached down and pulled her close. She wondered just which heart was beating the most wildly.

In a flurry of trail dust the stage skidded to a stop. The driver threw the reins to the waiting livery man and jumped to the ground. The door was opened and a well-dressed man stepped down. Marty's eyes quickly noted that he wasn't an acquaintance and she dismissed him.

A matronly lady was next, and Marty looked over at Mrs. Colson. But it was not she who claimed the woman. A man stepped forward, one Marty did not know, and the two embraced and walked off toward a bay team that stood at the nearest hitching rail.

Marty's heart hammered.

A younger man descended. He cast a glance in their direction at the two girls, nodded his head at the nearby men, claimed one piece of luggage which he shouldered, then walked toward the hotel.

Marty could feel Belinda quivering. The suspense was tying them all in knots.

And then a young lady—no, a child, or was she a young lady?—stepped carefully down from the stage. A mass of curly brown hair hung beneath her hat, and deep brown eyes looked curiously around at the crowd. Marty started to dismiss her. *Missie has fair hair*, she argued with herself. And then the girl smiled. Smiled right at them. And Marty recognized Missie's smile, and she knew with a quickening of her heart that she was looking at Melissa Joy.

Clark must have known it even before her, for he already had stepped forward and was even now reaching to claim the hand luggage that the young girl carried.

But she didn't offer her luggage—she offered herself. With a glad little cry she threw herself into his arms. It was enough to propel Marty forward. With tears streaming down her cheeks, she hugged the young girl to her, all doubts scattering like leaves in the wind as she held her close. In that one brief instance she felt she already knew her granddaughter. *She is lovely an' sweet—she's our Melissa!* Marty rejoiced.

Chapter 8

Getting Acquainted

The ride home was a merry one. They quickly discovered Melissa was not shy. She chattered excitedly about her experiences on the trip. She gave them all an extra hug from Missie and Willie. She told them about Nathan, Josiah and Julia. She talked about her father's new barn and her mother's huge garden down by the spring. Marty drank it all in, plying her with questions. There was so much she wanted to know, so much she longed to hear. Clark chuckled as he listened, wondering which one of the two would tire first from the exchange.

Belinda and Amy Jo hardly got a word in edgewise. It did not bother Belinda. She sat quietly, gathering all the information she could about her Western family. Amy Jo was not so complacent. As befitting her nature, she wished to be a part of the action. She had lots of questions of her own.

She finally nudged Belinda with an elbow. "Bet they don't even know we're here," she grumped, back to her sour mood during the ride into town.

It didn't matter all that much to Belinda. She knew she would have lots of time to talk to Melissa later. After all, they would be sharing the same room.

Amy Jo must have thought of the same thing.

"But why should *you* care?" she challenged. "Ya'll be a livin' with her. In the same room even. Ya can talk as much as ya like."

"She's gonna be here fer a couple a' years," Belinda reminded her.

"Two years," sighed Amy Jo. "Two years of not talkin'."

"Don't be silly," said Belinda. She was truly weary of it all.

"See," pouted Amy Jo. "Ya don't like me already."

"I do like ya," hissed Belinda in her ear.

"Ya do not. I *knew* it would be like this. I knew ya'd like her better."

"Oh, stop it," Belinda chided. "I don't even know 'er yet. Iffen ya keep on bein' so silly, nobody'll like ya."

Amy Jo turned to her corner to pout, and Belinda went back to listening to the conversation. Melissa had been tucked in securely between her grandma and grandpa so they might get acquainted on the way home.

". . . And Mother said to be sure to give it to you the minute I arrived," Melissa was saying, and then added with a laugh, "I hope she meant the minute I arrived at the farm, 'cause it's packed securely in my trunk."

They joined in her light merriment.

It was the first that Belinda had known anyone who said "mother" rather than "ma" or "mama." It sounded so grown-up somehow.

But Melissa was going on, "And Julia sent you a doily that she made all by herself."

"Tell us about Julia," coaxed Marty. "Is she like you?"

"Oh, no," and Melissa laughed again. "She's not at all like me. She does have brown eyes. Guess we all have Papa's brown eyes. But she is quite fair—more like Mother—and she is very quiet. Mama says God must have known that our house could only bear one talker—and that's me."

Melissa laughed again, a joyful little laugh that seemed to make the sun shine just a bit brighter.

"Julia is—Julia is sweet," said Melissa reflectively. "She's very unselfish, and she helps Mother, without her asking, and she loves animals, and—and—I'm really going to miss her," she finished quickly and there was a hint of tears in her voice.

"But Mother says that time will pass very quickly," Melissa continued bravely. "I sure hope so. I'm going to miss all of them.

I've never been away from the ranch before—not even for overnight. We used to coax Papa to let us go with him to the city, but he never took us—just Mother. She did all of our shopping. Papa isn't too fond of the city, I guess. But my, I did see some interesting things on the way out . . ." and she went off again with her entertaining descriptions of people, places and events as she covered nearly half a continent by train.

Marty thought back to her own trip by train and stagecoach. Yes, she was sure that Melissa had seen some interesting things.

"There was this young gentleman who offered to help me with my things," Melissa was saying, "but Mother and Papa gave me strict orders not to talk to strangers, and so I just smiled as politely as I could and said I wasn't allowed to accept help. He was nice enough about it."

"An' how are yer brothers?" asked Marty, her mind's eye picturing the sweet young Nathan and Josiah of their own stay out West.

"Fine! Nathan is taller than Papa, and Joe—he wants to be called Joe now—Joe is just a couple inches shorter. But he might be the taller of the two when he stops growing. At least, that's what Mother thinks."

Oh, my, thought Marty. *Oh, my. I never dreamed—*

"Papa is helping Nathan to buy his own spread. It's not far from ours. He wants to ranch, too. And Joe has some cattle of his own. He loves his cattle, but he says he might just wait and share the ranch with Papa. Joe is more of a 'homebody,' at least that's what Mother calls him."

"Nathan have his eye on any young lady?" Clark interrupted to ask.

"We've been teasing him about my teacher's daughter— Elisa is the same age as Joe—but he's not saying anything yet," Melissa responded.

"An' yer pa?"

"Papa's fine. He loves having Grandpa LaHaye there with him, but Grandpa is at Uncle Nathan's ranch right now— though he did come over to tell me goodbye. They all came over, Uncle Nathan, Aunt Callie and the family. And they all sent their greetings."

"Is Cookie still with you?"

"Oh, he'll never leave. He's family!"

Marty could well imagine Melissa feeling that way. She was sure Cookie had had a share in raising the family of Willie and Missie. He would have been more like a grandfather than the faraway Clark would be able to be.

"How many of the hands are still around—the ones thet we knew when we were a stayin' out there?"

Melissa had to think about that. She wasn't sure who had been there when her grandparents had visited the West. She decided just to name all the ranchhands.

"Well," she said slowly, "let's see. We have Jake and Browny and Clyde and Tom and Hooper."

"They be new," put in Marty. "This Tom an' Hooper, we didn't know 'em."

"And there is Shorty and Burt and Charlie."

"Didn't know none of them, either. Is Smith still there?"

"No, Smith left when I was still small."

"Does Wong still do the cookin'?"

"Wong? No, Wong died. About five years ago. We have a friend of Wong's from San Francisco, Yen Soo, now."

"Oh," said Marty. "I'm sorry to hear thet Wong died—we liked him."

"Mother liked him, too. She had a hard time getting used to Yen, at first."

"What happened to Wong?"

"We really don't know. He refused to go to a doctor. He said he had his own medicine, but he just got weaker and weaker. Cookie nursed him for months. But he didn't get better."

A silence hung over them for a few minutes as Marty's thoughts went back to Wong. She wondered if the kind Chinese man had ever come to know the Lord Jesus himself.

"Well, thet's our farm, jest up there," Clark was telling Melissa.

"Oh, it looks lovely—so big. I mean, the house looks so big. Ours is adobe and built low to the ground, but yours looks so tall—and so white. I love it! Mother said that I would."

"You will have yer own room of course," put in Marty, "but

it needs redoin', an' we thought thet ya might like to choose yer own colors. So we decided thet while we were workin' on it, ya could jest spend some time with Belinda in her room—iffen ya don't mind."

For the first time Melissa turned around to look at Belinda. She gave her a glowing smile.

"That will be fun," she assured them. "Julia and I share a room at home. I was afraid that I would be lonely." Then as an afterthought she added, "Do you mind, Belinda? I mean—you've had your own room—"

"I don't mind," Belinda said immediately, shaking her head. She would have said much more—more about looking forward to it, counting the days, hoping that Melissa might never move out—but she caught Amy Jo looking at her and she decided not to make further comment.

"We were goin' to have the whole family in fer supper so thet ya could meet them all," Marty said, "an' then we thought it best to take it a bit at a time. You'd never git us all straight at one time," she laughed softly. "So it will be jest the five of us to supper. Amy Jo will join us at table."

Melissa flashed Amy Jo a smile that Amy Jo tried to return. It came out a little crooked and wobbly. Melissa turned back to her grandmother.

"Mother says that Uncle Clare and Aunt Kate live right near you—right across the yard. That must be so—o fun!"

"It is," smiled Marty. "You'll git to meet 'em all in good time."

And then Clark was halting the team and helping each one safely down. All but Amy Jo—she jumped down herself, casting a peeved glance over her shoulder as Clark helped Melissa over the wheel.

"I'll care for thet luggage later," Clark informed them and began to unhitch the team. The rest of them proceeded to the house, Melissa exclaiming about everything as she went. Over and over she made comments like, "Oh, Mother told me about this," or "It's just like Mother said!" Marty knew Missie must have done a thorough job of acquainting her daughter with her new surroundings.

Belinda was asked to show Melissa their room and invited Amy Jo to join them, but she shook her head. She'd help Marty with the final supper preparations, she said. Belinda knew Amy Jo was still pouting, but she made no comment.

Belinda led the way to the room and Melissa exclaimed many times about how much she loved it. Then Belinda took Melissa to see the room that eventually would be hers, explaining that Melissa was to choose her own wallpaper and curtains and spread.

"Oh, I'll love it. I'll love it!" cried Melissa. "Mother has always done the choosing. I've never even been to the city. When do we get to go shopping?"

Belinda shook her head. She wasn't sure what to say. Would the yard goods in their little town suit Melissa?

"We don't go to the city, much," Belinda said slowly. "We shop in town here."

"They have those things here?" asked Melissa incredulously.

Belinda nodded. Of course they had those things.

"Mother always had to go to the city for shopping. They had only very crude, basic things in the local stores."

Belinda did hope Melissa wouldn't consider the storebought yard goods "crude."

"Your town will be just as much fun as a city," Melissa assured her. "I still get to pick."

The supper hour was a busy time. Melissa still chatted away—although, in her defense, much of it was in answer to the many questions that she was asked.

As soon as the meal was over and the family had read the Bible and prayed together—"We do this too," Melissa told them—she began clearing away the supper dishes.

"Do you like to wash or dry?" she asked Belinda.

Marty was pleased to see the young girl offering to help. She cast a glance at Clark to be sure he had also noticed. Clark had and nodded to her in answer.

"You'll need to tell me about my chores," went on Melissa. "Julia and I had a list. Once in a while we'd change jobs—just so we wouldn't get bored doing the same things over and over.

Mother didn't care—just as long as all of the chores were properly done."

Belinda nodded, glad to have someone to share the household duties.

"What do you like to do, Amy Jo?" asked Melissa.

"I don't live here," Amy Jo was quick to inform her. There was no way she would let herself be trapped into their "work list." She had enough chores of her own.

"Oh, I know—you live in the log house. Right? That must be so much fun! I've never lived in a log house—but my mother lived in a soddy once. Anyway, I just meant for tonight—for now. What would you like to do for now?"

Amy Jo hated to wash the dishes and she wasn't too fond of wiping them either. She liked more creative things—like sewing or needlework.

"I'll put things away," she stated.

Clare came over to help Clark with the luggage. Melissa seemed to have brought enough things for three or four girls. One trunk was especially heavy.

"Whewee!" exclaimed Clare. "What's thet little lady got in here? Gold?"

"Didn't see much gold layin' 'round when I was out there," Clark responded.

"Maybe she brought some of the cows," Clare joked and Clark just smiled.

The luggage was all carried up to Belinda's room. Melissa could now begin to unpack. Belinda showed her the empty drawers and the closet space, and she and Amy Jo both lounged on the bed to watch the unpacking.

Belinda was sure that Melissa's things would never fit in the allotted space. *She must have scores of dresses*, Belinda thought with a twinge of envy.

Melissa's clothes were of fine quality and good workmanship. Marty certainly would not need to worry about preparing Melissa's wardrobe for the school term. But it was not the clothes that took all the space. Melissa's garments were really no more plentiful than Belinda's own. Books filled the heavy trunk. Books seemed to be Melissa's prized possessions—books that seemed to capture her time and attention. Belinda and Amy Jo looked on in wide-eyed disbelief.

"Where'd ya git 'em all?" asked the candid Amy.

"As gifts," responded Melissa. "I love books. That's what I always ask for when Mother and Papa go to the city. That's what I ask for on birthdays and Christmas—and other times, too."

Belinda let one finger trace the leather cover of a book lying on the top of the stack.

"Do you like books?" Melissa was asking.

Belinda could just nod but Amy Jo spoke for herself.

"I love 'em. I *love* 'em—but I've never see'd so many—not in all my life."

"You can borrow my books if you wish," Melissa was quick to inform them.

"Oh, could we? Could we? I'd love to. What's this one?" asked Amy Jo, hopping off the bed to carefully lift one from the trunk that had caught her eye.

"It's a book on nature," replied Melissa.

"It's got lots of pictures!" exclaimed Amy Jo excitedly.

"Illustrations," Melissa corrected softly.

"How'd they git these pictures?" continued Amy Jo, disregarding Melissa's comment.

"An artist drew them."

"Drew 'em? Ya mean—with a pencil?"

"Or paints—or inks."

"Drew 'em," Amy Jo mused in a daze. "They look so real."

Melissa was called downstairs to come to meet her Aunt Kate and three boy cousins. Amy Jo did not move from her seat on the edge of the bed. Her eyes were still fixed to the pages of illustrations. *How anyone could make such true-life drawings!* she marveled. But she'd sure like to try. She'd *love* to try. Something deep within her responded to the artwork in the book. Her eyes grew bright with hope as she studied the work. *Oh, if only I had such a book.* Her eyes went back to the trunk. So many—she'd had no idea that this cousin from the West would have such treasures. And to think that she would share! It was almost too good to be true.

Clark and Marty knew Melissa must be terribly weary after her long trip. She did not protest when they suggested bed, saying that they could catch up on the rest of the news later. Clare, Kate and their family had returned to their log home across the yard, Amy Jo tightly clutching the illustrated nature book that Melissa had been so willing to lend. Amy Jo promised she would be back in the morning as soon as her chores were done.

Marty sat fingering the gifts from Missie that Melissa had promptly dug from her opened trunk as soon as she was able. The evening had been a satisfying and exciting beginning for all of them.

Melissa followed Belinda up the wide stairway and into the bedroom still strewn with books from her unpacking. As she gathered them up, she was glad she did not need to spend this first night alone in another room. She missed Julia. She missed her mother and papa. She even missed her two teasing big brothers.

Belinda shyly folded back the spread. She had never shared a room with anyone before.

"Do ya want the back or the front side?" she asked.

"You pick," encouraged Melissa. "It's your bed."

"I don't care," insisted Belinda.

"Then I'll take the back. That's where I sleep with Julia."

Without further comment the two prepared for bed, said their prayers and climbed between the fresh sheets. They said a simple goodnight to one another and did not talk any further.

Melissa's thoughts unwillingly took her back over the miles to those she had left behind—to her home, her room, her family as she had left them.

Belinda's thoughts went forward. What were the days ahead going to be like? Would they like one another? Would they become good friends as well as kin? How would Amy Jo feel? She had seemed so happy over the books that Belinda was hoping that perhaps Amy Jo now also would be pleased that Melissa had come.

It was not long until Melissa's even breathing told Belinda that she was asleep. Still, Belinda could not stop her thoughts from tumbling over one another. It was all so new and different—so strange. It was much later before she was able to quiet her busy mind and follow Melissa to dreamland.

"She's a real sweetheart, ain't she?" asked Marty after she and Clark had settled themselves in bed.

Clark chuckled. "Sweetheart—an' a real chatterbox," he responded.

"She had a lot to talk 'bout. I'm glad she's not tight-lipped. I woulda hated it iffen she had come from Missie an' not told us anything 'bout what's goin' on there."

"She does a bit of talkin'," said Clark, and he chuckled again.

"She's a pretty little thing, too," Marty commented further. "Those flashin' dark eyes an' that glossy brown hair. Her smile is like her ma's, though—but her colorin' sure isn't."

"Uh huh," agreed Clark.

"An' she has nice things, too. I didn't know iffen I'd hafta git out my sewin' machine to have her ready fer school, or what."

"Missie wouldn't a sent her to us without the things she be needin'."

"No, I guess not. I shoulda knowed better."

The pressure of Clark's hand on hers didn't mean "I told you so," but Marty realized Clark was right when he encouraged her not to worry about things.

There was silence for a few minutes as both grandparents thought about their "new" grandchild.

"She's not 'uppity' though," continued Marty.

"Ya thought she might be?"

"I wasn't sure. Ya know how Missie always talked 'bout all those ranchhands makin' such a fuss over her an' all."

"Well, I'm right glad she's not spoilt none," Clark was quick to point out.

Silence again.

"Did notice me one thing though," said Clark thoughtfully.

"What's thet?"

"Did you notice how edjacated she be?"

Marty was silent. She had noticed *something*, come to think on it, but had not put it into words. "She's had her one more year of schoolin' than Belinda," she said at last.

"It's more'n thet. She talks—well she talks careful like—not—not like you'd 'spect someone from out West to talk."

"Her ma an' pa was both edjacated."

"Yeah, but she's even more careful than either of 'em. Didn't ya notice?"

"Guess I didn't."

"You will," promised Clark.

"Maybe it's got somethin' to do with her wantin' to be a teacher."

"Missie was a teacher."

Marty thought about it. Melissa did talk more carefully than any of them. Well, it wouldn't hurt for them all to pay a bit more attention to how they spoke. It might be especially good for Belinda and Amy Jo.

"Ya know what thet there trunk was full of?" Marty asked.

"The one thet ya groaned over carryin' it up the stairs?"

"What? Felt like bricks."

"Books."

"Books?"

"More'n half full of books," announced Marty. "Saw it myself. An' she was quick to share 'em with the other girls, too. Didn't ya see Amy Jo a-huggin' one to herself like she'd never let go of it?"

"So she's a book lover, huh?" mused Clark. "Maybe *thet's* why she talks so proper."

"Could be," agreed Marty. But after thinking about it for a minute, she added another thought. "Do ya s'pose thet some of it might be Melissa's schoolteacher, Henry's wife Melinda? 'Member how careful she always spoke?"

"I'll jest bet yer right. She probl'y drills her students on proper word talk. Melissa might notice a difference 'round here," said Clark. He was quiet for a few moments. "We'll hafta troad oaroful liko," ho wont on. "She's got an awful lot of changes ahead of her."

"She has, thet," agreed Marty. "Won't be hard to be thoughtful of her. She's 'most won my heart already."

Clark reached out a hand to smooth Marty's hair back from her face.

"I'm glad she came," he said softly. "Glad we're gettin' a chance to know her a bit. Makes one glad an' sad all at one time, don't it—doesn't it?" he corrected himself.

Marty agreed. As usual, he had read her thoughts perfectly.

Chapter 9

Cousins

The other family members were all anxious to meet Melissa, so after the next Sunday's church service, they planned to gather at Clark and Marty's. They had all been introduced to her in the churchyard, but Marty was sure Melissa would never be able to keep all her cousins straight after just one meeting. And it was important to Marty for Melissa to really know her own kin.

Melissa already had posted a fat letter home to her family, telling all of her experiences on the trip east and how exciting it was to meet her grandparents. She covered a whole page about Belinda and another about Uncle Clare and his family.

Marty had carefully planned the Sunday dinner and the time the family would spend together. The grown-ups were to sit at the table in the big kitchen, but the children would be allowed to take their dinner out on the wide back veranda. Marty debated about where to put Melissa. Would she feel more comfortable with the youngsters or the adults? Marty was getting herself in a stew over it when Clark interrupted her little argument with herself.

"Be good for Melissa to git to know her cousins afore school starts. Why, with the knowin' of all of 'em, she oughta know 'bout half the school." He chuckled at his own little joke.

Marty knew he was exaggerating, but she made no reply. Clark's comment served to make up her mind. She would put

Melissa on the veranda with the rest of the youngsters. There were already enough adults at the table. Mary and Jane always wanted to sit at the table with the grown-ups. That made twelve and that was about all the big table could hold. Marty instructed Belinda about the setting of the table.

It wasn't long until teams began to arrive, filling the farm-yard with excited voices as cousins noisily greeted one another.

Melissa, who was busy helping cut apple pies, smiled as she heard the racket.

"Wouldn't Mother love to be here?" she commented.

Marty smiled back, sure that Missie would.

Arnie's family was the first to come into the house. Clark took care of introductions.

"Now, ya've met Arnie an' Anne at church. They have three rascals. They all look alike—only come in different sizes. Silas is the oldest. He's thet big fella carryin' thet lemon pie."

Silas smiled a rather shy smile and Melissa greeted him warmly.

"Then there be John. Don't call 'im Johnny. *He* might not mind—but his ma won't like it." Clark winked playfully at Anne and she smiled at the good-natured teasing.

John gave his cousin a big grin and Melissa took to him immediately.

"An' this here little fella—make thet 'this here big fella'— is Abe."

Abe grinned quickly and looked about to bolt. Melissa knew he had been ushered in to meet her when he would rather have been out with the boy cousins his own age. He did give her a quick hug and then he was gone.

Luke's family came in next, Abbie carrying a large potato salad. Melissa had them sorted out from church. Thomas and Aaron were both anxious to get out to play as well. Aaron was the baby of the bunch. Clare's Dack and Thomas were about the same age. Aaron wrapped his chubby arms around Melissa for a big bear hug but Thomas backed shyly away.

Clare and Kate joined the group. Except for Amy Jo, their children did not come in, but Melissa had already become ac-quainted with Dan, Davey and Dack.

Nandry and Josh were the last to arrive. Mary and Jane, both a bit shy, welcomed Melissa. Rather plain like their mother, they were friendly and warm after they got to know Melissa better. Mary went to work in the kitchen and Jane went in search of Aaron, her special charge. Aaron did not object. He basked in all the special attention showered on the youngest. Free to pick his activity, his first choice was Grandpa's porch swing, and Jane willingly obliged.

They were just ready to sit down to their chicken dinner when Dan brought a wailing Davey in. He had fallen from the steps and cut his forehead. Uncle Luke had him patched up and smiling in no time.

The mothers fixed plates of food for all who were to eat on the veranda. Even Aaron was allowed to join them, "all by myself," he announced proudly as he knelt on the bottom step in front of his food on the next step up. Belinda promised to keep an eye on him. Melissa didn't know what went on around the big folks' table, but she wouldn't have given up her spot on the veranda for the world.

Over the babble of excited voices, Dan and Silas tried to outdo one another in telling jokes. Most of them were corny, but their audience laughed heartily anyway.

Amy Jo spent most of her time scolding her young brothers. Dan was too silly, Davey too careless and Dack too—too *everything,* she announced in exasperation while she went to get a rag for his spilled milk.

John was sitting nearest to Melissa. He eyed her openly and then asked in awe, "Do ya got yer own horse?"

Melissa nodded. "I have three of them, in fact," she told him.

"Three! Wow! All yer own?"

"All my own."

"What're their names?"

"Sandy—he was my first horse. He's getting quite old now. Pepper is black and really pretty, and there's Star. She has a white patch on her forehead that looks like a star. She's Pepper's mother."

"Wow!" said John again.

"Do you have a horse?" asked Melissa.

"No. Not my own. We have a pony—but we all gotta share it."

"Do you like horses?"

John's face answered the question for Melissa. She wasn't surprised.

"Sure do," the boy told her. "I'd give anything to have my own. Anything!"

"I've got a book about horses," offered Melissa. "You can look at it if you want to."

John's face lit up. He'd love to look at a book about horses.

"It tells all about the different kinds and how to train them and everything," Melissa said.

"Wow!" said John again. Melissa decided that "wow" must be his favorite word.

"I'll get it for you as soon as dinner is over," promised Melissa.

From that moment on, Melissa could have asked whatever she wished and John would have done his very best to oblige her.

True to her promise, after they had finished their meal she brought the book for John to see. Several other cousins clamored to be close enough to look at the pictures too.

"I have other books," said Melissa generously. "Would you like to see them?"

Several of the cousins declared that they would, and Melissa turned to Belinda.

"Do you mind if we go up to your room?" she asked, and when Belinda assured her that would be fine, Melissa led the way up the stairs. Soon the bedroom floor was covered with young bodies poring over all the exciting books. John was given the book about horses; then the others were allowed to choose.

"Boy!" said Silas. "How'd ya git ya so many? It's even more'n we have at our school."

"They've all been given to me," explained Melissa as she gently caressed the cover of one of her treasures.

Never had the household been so quiet on a Sunday when all the Davis family members were gathered together at home. Soon this little fellow or that began to coax for a book to be read aloud, and one after the other Melissa read some of the shorter ones. All eyes were on her face, all ears attentive to the reading. Downstairs, the adults interrupted their conversation to wonder where all of the children had gone.

"With this much peace 'n quiet, they're all either asleep or in trouble!" Luke declared from his comfortable position on the davenport.

It was Kate who climbed the stairs to peek into Belinda's room. There she saw arms and legs crisscrossed across the rug-covered wooden floor as children listened in fascination to the voice of Melissa. Kate stood and stared in disbelief before she tiptoed back down the stairs.

"Yer never gonna believe what I jest saw," she informed the others. "The whole passel of 'em, all in Belinda's room, listenin' as quiet as can be whilst Melissa is readin' to 'em."

"Yer joshin'," stated Luke.

"Cross my heart," Kate insisted. "The whole bunch of 'em—jest spellbound."

"We shoulda brought thet there little gal out here years ago," Clare said loudly. "Jest think of the gray hairs it woulda saved."

The others laughed.

Marty could not resist quietly going up to see for herself. Just as Kate had said—there they all were, sprawled on the bed or on rugs and pillows across the floor of Belinda's room, all eyes fixed on Melissa. No one even stirred as Marty peeked around the door.

Well I declare, she said to herself. *Iffen thet don't beat all.*

She went back down the stairs to assure the rest that Kate had not been fooling.

"Never seed nothin' like it," she stated. "Every last one of 'em. Quiet as you please."

"Guess she'll make her a schoolteacher, all right," said Arnie. "Anyone who can keep my three rascals quiet can handle 'bout anything."

"Sure didn't take her long to get acquainted," put in Luke.

"She already shared one of her books with Amy Jo," Kate told them. "I've never seen the girl so excited. Been copyin' it, she has. Tries to draw every picture. Some of 'em are kinda hard, too, but Amy Jo does a fair job of 'em, iffen I do say so." She paused to gaze reflectively out the window. "She sure has been eager to git to 'em. Never argues 'bout her chores now, 'cause she knows thet she is free to draw jest as soon as they are done."

Marty's eyes filled with tears. "It sure is nice to have Melissa here," she said softly. "Missie's gonna miss 'er. She's the sweet-est thing ya ever saw."

Clare nodded in agreement. "She's sweet, thet's fer sure— but let's not put the burden of perfection on 'er."

Marty looked at Clare in surprise.

"Meanin'?"

"Well, she's human after all, Ma. Let's leave her some room to make some mistakes—have some flaws. She's gonna find plenty of 'em in us, her kin. Reckon we ought to allow her a few as well."

Marty's face took on a thoughtful look. Clare was right. Melissa was bound to have *some* weaknesses. They just hadn't seen them yet. Well, whatever they were, Marty would still love her, she decided. But even as Marty assured herself of that, she couldn't imagine anything that could possibly be wrong with Missie's little girl.

In spite of the rather rocky beginning during their drive home from the station, Marty was very happy at how well the three girls seemed to be adjusting to one another. There were times when two of them spent time together when the third girl was not included, but it was not a case of two shutting the other out. When the third girl arrived on the scene, she was always warmly welcomed to become a part of the little group. There was no gossiping or vying for position or attention that Marty could see, and she thanked the Lord for that.

All of the girls had their own unique personalities. Amy Jo, vibrant, alive and artistic in nature, was apt to act and react spontaneously and sometimes to regret it later. She was quick to speak her mind, but quick to initiate a restoration of the relationship if she felt she had done or said something out of line.

Belinda had always been warm and compassionate. She felt it deeply if someone hurt her or was hurt. She was slow to become upset and quick to offer her aid. She loved to share and give. At times her loving nature brought her pain, and she suffered deeply with the suffering of another. But Belinda did not find it as easy to put aside words spoken in the heat of the moment. Often, the impetuous and careless barbs of Amy Jo could cause Belinda grief for days. She forgave, but it was difficult for her to get over the memory of her pain, and it affected her appetite, her rest, and her very being.

Melissa was somewhere in between the two. She loved to be with people and to share in their experiences. She was open and caring without taking charge, as Amy Jo was wont to do. Melissa was a communicator, though she chose her words with more care and consideration of the other person's feelings than Amy Jo, and her words never seemed to be used as an implement of war. Melissa spent very little of her time alone, where as Belinda could entertain herself with her own thoughts and company for hours on end. Amy Jo liked people if she was in the right mood.

And so the three girls interacted with one another, learning and growing from their friendship. Marty felt the experience would benefit all three of them.

All three went to town with Marty on the day Melissa was to choose her room colors and fabrics. From her previous experience, Marty wondered at the wisdom of taking three girls to choose for one room; but Amy Jo and Belinda wanted to be a part of it and Melissa begged for them to be included. Clark smiled at Marty as he handed her the reins for the team. She was sure he understood her misgivings.

The girls had worked themselves up to a feverish pitch at the thought of their trip to town. Amy Jo this time was doing most of the high-spirited chattering.

"I already found the most be-autiful print," she was informing Melissa. "You'll jest love it—I know ya will."

"Oh, Amy Jo," admonished Belinda, "Remember, Melissa

gits to choose for herself. We aren't gonna tell her what she should git."

"I won't tell her," replied Amy Jo rather hotly with a toss of her red-brown pigtails, "but that doesn't mean thet I shouldn't even show her the pretty piece we found before."

"Sure you can show me," offered Melissa. "And you can show me your choice, too, Belinda."

"I haven't chosen one," said Belinda. "Ma and I decided thet you should choose."

"And I will," Melissa said excitedly. "I can hardly wait. I wrote Mother and Papa all about it."

"I jest bet you'll love the colored print. It is so-so-*vibrant!*" exclaimed Amy Jo. "Vibrant" was a new word she had found in one of Melissa's art books and she loved it. The family would hear the word over and over during the next few months.

"Maybe Melissa doesn't like 'vibrant,' " Belinda said softly.

"Oh, Lindy," Amy Jo responded impatiently. "Do you think she's a child? She'll say if she likes it or not."

Marty feared a quarrel was about to commence.

"I think thet we'll go to the hardware store first an' pick out the wallpaper," she hurried to inform the girls, snapping the reins over the horses' backs; "then we'll go look at the yard goods."

Her little plan for diverting an argument did not work. Amy Jo began to suggest a "good choice" for Melissa's walls. Belinda frowned, and Marty felt she had to move the conversation onto other ground entirely.

"Jest up ahead there is the school, Melissa," she announced, pointing to a white building set back in some trees. "Would ya like to stop an' peek in the winda? The door will likely be bolted, but we should be able to git us a bit of a look-see."

It worked, at least temporarily. The girls were soon excitedly talking about school. Marty sighed with relief and urged the team on a little faster. They would stop briefly at the schoolhouse, but then there was still a long road into town. Could she manage to keep the conversation even and controlled?

Chapter 10

School

It was a weary Marty who turned the team back over to Clark when they arrived back home. His eyes questioned her as he helped her down over the wheel, but he asked nothing aloud.

"Later," she whispered to him, and he nodded his head.

The three girls were gathering parcels and excitedly carrying them into the house.

"When will you do the wallpaperin'?" Amy Jo was asking. "I'll help."

"Grandpa will be doin' it," Marty was quick to inform the girl. "I think he'll ask Clare if he needs 'im any help."

"Aw," groaned Amy Jo. "It woulda been fun iffen we three coulda did it."

"Done it," corrected Melissa without any maliciousness.

"Grandpa will do the wallpaperin' tomorra," Marty went on. There was no way she would be talked into allowing three young girls the pleasure of messing around in the wallpaper paste. One, maybe, but not three!

"What 'bout the curtains?" continued Amy Jo, her freckled face crinkled in disappointment.

"I'll sew up the curtains an' spread," answered Marty.

"Then we don't git to do nothin'," argued Amy Jo.

"You did the choosin'," Marty reminded her.

And what a job that was! she could have added. Belinda,

though she had said very little, liked the soft pastel prints. Amy Jo had argued vociferously for the "vibrant" colors. Melissa had held her ground and picked a blue and white gingham. And her walls would have tiny blue flowers in vertical rows on a white background. For accents around the room she chose some bright blue for toss cushions, tie-backs and bows for trimmings.

It wasn't what Marty would have selected. An all blue-and-white room seemed a little boring to her. But Marty did not try to sway Melissa. They had promised her own choice, and Marty intended to keep her word.

"I'll do the kitchen work while you sew," offered Melissa, and Marty nodded her appreciation.

"I still wish thet we could do some work on the room," grumbled Amy Jo.

"Ya can," said Marty with a tired sigh. "When yer Grandpa's done his paperin', ya can scrub the floor an' move back the furniture."

At Amy Jo's look of disgust, Marty added, "Maybe Melissa will let ya help arrange the furniture a new way," but Amy Jo was not to be cheered up so easily. Her disagreeable attitude quickly changed to one of defeat when Marty held her ground with an even and determined look of her own. Amy Jo knew Marty was serious: it would be the girls' job to clean the room and move Melissa in after it had been redone. For a moment Amy Jo wished she'd held her tongue.

" 'Course we will," Belinda was saying. "That will be fun. We can put everything jest where Melissa wants it."

Amy Jo looked around and decided there was nothing for it but to cooperate. It might be a little fun at that.

The room was papered, the curtains and spread made and the little pillows stuffed with soft, old material. The girls began their housecleaning as Marty finished off the last of the sewing.

Melissa set up the ironing board and carefully ironed the new curtains, ruffle by ruffle. Belinda scrubbed the floor and Amy Jo dusted the furniture but mostly fluttered about giving orders and excitedly exclaiming over everything.

The bed and dresser were moved back into the room with

the help of Clare who had come to see how the job was pro-
gressing. He said some nice things about its appearance and
left the three girls to do the arranging. They all agreed, much
to Marty's relief, that the bed should be under the window, the
new curtains framing its head. The dresser fit nicely on the
north wall, and the desk Clark was working on would stand in
the corner near the door with the bookshelves.

By the end of the week the new room had its new occupant.
Belinda hated to have Melissa move, but they were just across
the hall from one another, and she knew it really was nicer for
them each to have their own room. She did like her times alone
and would soon have wearied of constant company, she told
herself.

When it was all done, Marty had to admit that Melissa had
chosen well. The gingham curtains and the bright splashes of
blue went nicely with the light-patterned wallpaper. The
shelves of books also added to the cheeriness and homeyness of
the room, and with the bright scatter rugs on the floor the room
looked inviting and warm, as well as light and airy.

Marty sighed wearily as she retired that night. She was glad
they had allowed Melissa the privilege of her own choosing.
She was also glad that the process did not need to be repeated
in the near future. It had been tiring having the three girls
excitedly rushing about the house, continually asking about
her sewing progress. And though they had willingly worked in
the kitchen, Marty really preferred being in charge there herself. She found herself redoing some of the tasks the girls had
hurried through. So Marty was glad it was over and she could
stretch out beneath the warm comfort of the soft quilt and let
the kinks of the week's "busyness" gradually work out of her
back and arms.

In just a few days' time all the children but young Dack
would be off to school for another year, and her days would be
more her own, Marty reminded herself. She both welcomed it
and dreaded it. The years were passing by so quickly. Before
they knew it, Belinda, too, would be grown and moving on to a
life of her own. *It will be so lonely in the old house when that
happens,* Marty mourned. She thought of the last few busy,

bustling days. She couldn't manage all that activity as well as she used to. But she wasn't ready to settle into a quiet and uneventful life, either.

When the first day of school arrived, it nearly matched the week Melissa's room had been redone for noise, commotion and activity. Melissa and Belinda both fussed with their frocks and their hair—Melissa had three different dresses on before settling on a pale yellow with blue flowers. Belinda decided on a pink print. They each tried several hair styles and finally both went back to the comfortable old. They dashed back and forth between their rooms, exclaiming over this, agonizing over that, until Marty felt that she would never survive until they were finally out the door.

Amy Jo stopped by for the two in her new bright green dress, and at last they were on the way. Each girl looked feminine and appealing and strangely at ease, while Marty still felt her head spinning. She sighed as she watched the three joined by Amy Jo's two younger brothers, and then all five of them walked down the long lane to the road that would take them to the small country schoolhouse. Even from where she stood at her kitchen window, Marty could hear their excited voices drifting back to her. It was always that way on the first day. At the end of the day too, they would come home eager to inform Marty and Clark and anyone who would listen about all the experiences of "first day." After that, Marty knew from past experience, the family was fortunate to get any information at all.

Marty turned from the window, poured herself a fresh cup of coffee and sank wearily into a kitchen chair. The back door opened and Clark's head cautiously peered around it.

"It safe to come back now?" he queried.

Marty smiled. "They all be gone, iffen thet's what ya be meanin'."

"They sure do be excited. I couldn't stand all thet flutterin' about. Guess I must be gittin' old," and so saying, Clark entered the kitchen and tossed his worn farm cap into the corner. "Any coffee left in the pot?"

Marty looked from Clark to the cap on the floor. She made no comment, but Clark responded to her look. "No use hangin' it on the peg. I'm gonna go right back out agin."

Marty made a move to get up from her chair for Clark's coffee, but he stopped her with a gentle touch on the arm, and she relaxed again.

Clark reclaimed his breakfast cup, crossed to the kitchen stove where the coffeepot still steamed, and poured himself another cup of the hot, dark liquid. He took the chair opposite Marty at the table.

"How ya holdin' up?" he asked in a teasing voice, but Marty could also sense his genuine concern.

She smiled. "Fine, I reckon—though it sure do slow a body down some."

"The first day of a new school year is always excitin', I remember, but didn't it seem to you thet they were flyin' higher 'n a kite this time?"

"Maybe so . . . maybe we jest fergit—I dunno." Marty took another sip of her coffee. "Maybe Melissa bein' here has somethin' to do with it. The other two are so anxious to show her off to all their school chums. Then, too, I s'pose thet new teacher also has 'em worked up some. They always seem to be a bit on edge until they know jest how a new teacher will be."

"Seemed nice enough to me," responded Clark.

"Good," said Marty. "It's so important for children to have a good teacher."

Marty drained her cup but she didn't leave her chair. She sat companionably while Clark finished his.

"So now do ya git to rest ya some?" Clark asked.

Marty looked around her at the table covered with dirty dishes and the kitchen still untidy from preparing the breakfast and making school lunches. She didn't bother to reply. Clark could see the answer for himself.

"Least it'll be a bit quieter," he continued.

"Oh, they'll calm down in a day or two," Marty assured him. "They always do. Afore we know it, things will be so routine agin thet we'll all feel a mite bored."

Clark nodded his head.

"Iffen I was you, though," went on Marty, "I'd be 'bout as far away as I could be, come end of the school day. They always come back in even worse than they went off. Gotta tell every little thing thet happened at the end of the first day. Who did what an' went where an' got whatever—from the whole summer long."

She stopped with a twinkle in her eye and said, "On second thought, maybe ya'd like to be here to help do some listenin'."

Clark laughed. "Thanks for the invite," he said, setting his empty cup back on the table. "But, no, I guess I'll head me fer the farthest field."

Marty reluctantly lifted herself from the comfortable kitchen chair and began to stack the dishes.

"An' what 'bout you?" Clark asked her. "How ya plannin' on protectin' yerself from the onslaught?"

"Ya ain't got any rock thet needs pickin' in thet far field, have ya?" asked Marty.

Clark laughed again and went to retrieve his cap from the corner.

"Guess we'll make it somehow," he said confidently. "We always do."

Marty knew he was right. She stirred herself to hurry more with the dishes. She had bread to bake and a stack of laundry waiting for her.

"Think I'll look 'round fer a job thet might take the help of a young'un," Clark continued. "Got me a feelin' thet it's gonna be a powerful long day fer young Dack."

It was Marty's turn to smile. True, it would be a long day for Dack. It also was a wonderful excuse for Clark to enjoy his grandson.

In spite of her warning to Clark, Marty found her excitement mounting as the clock on the wall shelf announced it was almost time for the children to be returning from school. She crossed to the window and looked out to the road several times before she heard the dog bark his welcome and knew the children would soon come bursting through the door.

Marty set out some glasses and poured cold milk. She wasn't

sure just how many of the young troop would stop at the big house. She knew Kate's family would be eager to tell about their day as well.

Marty heard the excited voice of young Dack as he enthusiastically welcomed home his brothers and the girls.

Amy Jo was first through the door of Marty's kitchen. She led Belinda and Melissa. The boys had gone on home to the log house.

"Gramma," exclaimed Amy Jo, "guess what happened at school today!"

"How 'bout ya jest tell me," responded Marty, lifting fresh sugar cookies from the cooling rack to a plate. "Never was very good at guessin' games."

"We got a new teacher!"

Marty looked up. "We already knew thet," she said. " 'Member—we talked 'bout it fer the last several days. Yer grandpa helped to move her in."

The new teacher was a recently widowed lady from a nearby town who had been most happy to get the job. She had moved into the local teacherage just as soon as she was sure the job was hers, and Clark had been one of the men who had driven a wagon over to load her furnishings.

The girls looked at one another and snickered behind their hands. Marty could not understand the joke.

"I know ya told us 'bout the teacher," explained Belinda, "but we didn't know 'bout her family."

"She has a family? I *didn't* know 'bout thet. I thought thet she was alone when yer—"

"She was," Belinda said quickly. "Her family was at their grandparents, or aunt's—or somethin'."

"I'm glad to hear she has family," said Marty as she poured one more glass of milk and set it on the table.

The girls looked at one another again, a general tittering accompanying the glances.

"So what does she have fer family?" asked Marty, innocently enough.

This brought outright giggles from all three girls.

Amy Jo was the first to recover sufficient to speak. "A boy!" she gasped out.

"A boy?" Marty looked at the giggling girls. Even Melissa was acting like a silly schoolgirl. Marty had expected her to be at least a bit more mature than the two younger girls.

"Well, does this here boy have three ears an' one eye, or what?" asked Marty.

All three girls groaned in unison. Marty wasn't sure how to interpret the answer.

"Oh, no-o," said Amy Jo. "He's—he's—well, he's *vibrant*."

"Don't be silly, Amy Jo," chided Belinda. "Boys aren't vibrant."

"Well he's—he's—" Amy Jo began again, but Melissa cut in.

"Divine," she finished with an exaggerated sigh.

All three girls went back to giggling. Marty was beginning to get the picture. Her sigh was even deeper than Melissa's. Was she ready to deal with three young girls in the middle of schoolgirl crushes on the same boy?

"You'll like 'im, Mama," said Belinda, turning in her chair to look at Marty. "He is so mannerly and so tall and so—"

"Divine," repeated Melissa.

More moans and groans, finished with giggles.

"Well, it do seem thet this boy has made hisself quite an impression," ventured Marty. "I sure hope thet his mama is equally qualified. Haven't heard one comment on what ya all think of yer new teacher."

After a pause, "She's nice," offered Belinda, "an' Jackson treats her so—so—"

"Gentle," put in Melissa.

"Yeah, gentle."

It seemed that "nice" was all Marty was to hear about the new schoolmarm.

Amy Jo reached for another sugar cookie. "An' he even treats his little brothers good."

Marty was sure that to Amy Jo, treating younger brothers "good" must be going the second mile indeed.

"He has 'im brothers?" asked Marty.

"Two. An' he doesn't even fight with 'im and they go to 'im when they need help with their work—"

"How old are they?" asked Marty.

"One in grade one an' one in grade four, an' they really like Jackson, ya can tell by the way they—"

Marty was tiring of all roads leading back to this Jackson. "Is thet all thet happened at school today? Jest this here Jackson making his impression on ya?"

Melissa stepped away from her chair and toward Marty. "Oh, Grandma," she said, "he is really nice. He is tall with broad shoulders and blondish hair and a little mark in his chin, sort of like a dimple. And he is real smart in school. He has only one more year to be taught by his mother because she has taught him everything she can, almost, and then he wants to go on to school somewhere and train in some occupation— maybe banking, or some such thing—that is, if they can afford it. His papa died, you know—with consumption—and they don't have much money, so he might have to go to work instead. He's only sixteen, but he's strong, so he could get a job easily enough, but he'd—"

"Whoa!" said Marty holding up her hand while Melissa stopped mid-sentence.

There was silence for a moment as Marty looked around the kitchen at the three girls. Marty was the one who broke it. "I'm sure he be a fine boy—but there must be other things thet took *some* of yer time at school today."

The three girls looked blank. Finally Belinda was able to come up with something. Her face brightened. "I asked the teacher an' her family fer supper," she informed Marty.

"Supper?" Marty wheeled to face her. *"Supper?"*

"Oh, not tonight," Belinda quickly amended. "Jest sometime."

Marty made no comment. She had been given quite a fright.

"Ya always invite the teacher—sometime," Belinda added, "so I thought I should tell her 'bout it."

"I see," said Marty as she turned to put another stick of wood in the stove. "I jest hope thet ya made yer new teacher an' her two younger sons feel as welcome at their new school

today as ya must have made this here Jackson fella," she remarked.

Three heads dipped slightly.

"An' I hope thet ya all three behaved yerselves like the ladies ya been taught to be," continued Marty, turning back to
look at each one squarely.

The girls stole looks at one another.

"An' I hope thet ya all are prepared to spend yer school time
learnin' what the teacher be tryin' to learn ya."

Three solemn pairs of eyes studied Marty. She decided she
had pressed it far enough.

"An' what did ya think of yer first day at this new school,
Melissa?" she asked, changing the subject.

"I like it," answered Melissa politely.

"An' did the other younguns make ya feel welcome?"

"Oh, yes," said Melissa, nodding her head vigorously.

"Good! An' ya liked the students?"

More snickering. Marty knew she shouldn't have asked that
last question.

"So—ya all like this here Jackson?"

The girls did not answer with words, but their eyes admitted
the fact.

"An' he liked us, too," ventured Amy Jo.

"All of ya?"

They all nodded.

"Well," said Marty matter-of-factly, dusting the wood chips
from her hands after feeding the fire, "thet sounds safe enough.
There ain't no boy thet I know of who can manage 'im three
girls to once. Long as this here Jackson don't go an' pick hisself
jest one, guess we needn't worry none."

The girls looked at one another. Was Marty talking to
them—or to herself? They weren't sure, but her words got
through to them. Would Jackson continue to consider all three
of them his friends? Would he "pick" one of them? If so, which
one would it be? And how would the other two feel? They turned
back to their milk glasses with more serious faces.

"Now, ya best hurry up with yer milk an' cookies," instructed Marty. "Ya need to change so thet ya can care fer yer

chores. An', Amy Jo, I'm sure thet yer mama will be wantin' to see you at home."

And so saying, Marty turned back to her kitchen counter and supper preparation. Further talk would need to wait.

Chapter 11

Passing Days

Marty watched the days on the calendar pass—busy ones with fall canning and gardening, but rather routine. For Belinda and Melissa the days were also full. They trudged the distance to school, where the teacher insisted upon close attention to what they were being taught. They walked home again to the many farm chores that awaited them. Always Amy Jo traveled with them as well as Dan and David.

Clark's days were filled with harvest work. He and Clare worked together in the fields, and when they had finished their own tasks, there was usually an ailing neighbor to help. By the time all of the crops had been cared for, the fall winds were chill and hints of winter were in the air.

Marty had been wrong about one thing: the girls did not quickly settle back to their normal emotional level. They still returned from school in an excited frenzy each day and always the talk was of Jackson. Jackson did this and Jackson said that, until Marty was truly weary of it all.

Marty still had not had the opportunity of meeting Jackson or his schoolteacher mother. She had thought they would join the community in Sunday attendance at the little church, but so far the Brown family felt strong ties to the small church in their former town. Every Sunday, according to reports, they hitched their one horse to a light buggy and drove the fifteen miles back to worship with the lifelong friends who had supported them in their bereavement.

So Marty tried not to lose patience as the three silly girls sighed at the end of the school day over young Jackson. If Marty had listened, she would have heard many things about him that she would have admired—both true and imagined. But she did not listen. She was tired of the tales. She was tired of the swooning. She wished Jackson had never arrived to upset her three girls and her world.

She even considered forbidding the girls to talk about Jackson once they were in the kitchen, but she decided not to in case the regulation would blow the situation way out of proportion. After all, it was a passing fancy. At their age, if the girls were not mooning over Jackson, they undoubtedly would have found someone else to moon over.

Marty still had not invited the teacher and her family for dinner. True, she had been unusually busy with her fall work, but Marty had always been busy and still had found time to invite guests. However, this year's teacher had not yet been given an official invitation. Even Clark noticed it.

"Not plannin' to have the teacher in this year?" he asked her one night when they were preparing for bed.

Marty's head immediately came up, her eyes showing that even the simple statement had her on the defensive.

" 'Course," she answered a bit too quickly and sharply. "Been busy."

Clark knew that for some reason he had hit a raw nerve. He wasn't sure just how to approach it from there, so he said nothing more.

Marty quickly repented. She had answered a simple question with a sting in her voice. How could Clark know she dreaded the thought of bringing the young man Jackson into her home where she would need to listen firsthand to silly girls tittering and swooning over him. Yet it seemed foolish to admit to such a ridiculous feeling.

She sighed as she slipped on her nightgown. The girls had been continually pestering her about it. She wouldn't be able to put them off much longer. Every other day, it appeared, they were informing her of which neighbor family had had the

Browns over for supper. Marty could not hold out much longer without seeming aloof and uncaring in her neighbors' eyes. Yet perhaps the neighbors did not have daughters who talked and giggled incessantly about one tall, good-looking, mannerly young fellow. Marty sighed again.

"Somethin' troublin' ya?" asked Clark patiently.

"It's jest this here Jackson fella."

"Teacher's son."

"Ya've heard of 'im?"

"How could one live in this here household an' not hear of 'im?" inquired Clark with a smile.

Marty felt some of the weight shifting from her shoulders. She was even able to laugh in return.

"Guess yer right. It's been 'most unbearable, hasn't it? I git so sick of hearin' all the tales of Jackson thet I could jest scream at times. 'Jackson said this'—an' it might be somethin' as simple as, 'It looks like it might rain,' but oh, my, it's so intelligent or so funny if *Jackson* says it."

Clark laughed at Marty's comment.

"They're jest young girls a-growin' up," he reminded her. "The others all muddled their way through the stage, too."

"Did they, Clark?" Marty asked seriously. "I've been tryin' an' tryin' to remember, but I really don't recall Nandry or Clae or Missie or Ellie actin' like this. Did they?"

Clark thought deeply as he unstrapped his artificial limb and laid it aside. *What a relief!* He tried not to let the thought show in his face.

"Don't recall 'em carryin' on like this either, come to think on it," he answered and let one hand reach down to gently massage the stub of his leg.

"I know thet they noticed the young fellas, but they didn't fill their days an' their minds with 'em like these girls do. I don't understand it—an' I guess I don't much like it, either."

"I s'pose part of it is havin' the three of 'em so close together in age. They jest sorta 'egg one another on,' so to speak."

Maybe that was it. Maybe they would be sensible too if they were each on their own instead of comparing and adding to and outdoing the stories of each other. Marty folded back the blankets and fluffed up the pillows.

"Well, as I see it," went on Clark, "we'll jest have to hold steady an' keep on prayin' for some sense to return to our girls, an' fer the strength to endure all the swoonin' an' talkin' 'til it do." He smiled slightly. "We need ta jest hang in there, knowin' thet, 'this, too, shall pass.' "

"Yer right," agreed Marty with another sigh. "An' I gotta git busy an' have thet teacher in."

The two knelt together for prayer before retiring for the night. Marty slipped her small hand into Clark's large one as they prayed together for each one of their family members, and for the needs of the community that were known to them, and especially for wisdom and understanding in all of their relationships.

Amy Jo's birthday arrived. The four from the big house joined Clare and Kate's family for the birthday supper. For Amy Jo it was a momentous event: for a few months, she was the "same age" as Belinda, and to Amy Jo that was very important.

Her young brothers were excited, too. A birthday was a celebration, and they revelled in sharing the birthday meal and cake and teased to help her open the presents. Clark and Marty's gift was a note—a note explaining to Amy Jo that by the permission of her pa and ma, Marty would take her into town and let her do her own choosing for new wallpaper for her room and yard goods for curtains and matching spread. Amy Jo bounced joyfully up and down, her auburn pigtails bobbing out behind her. Marty was sure there was no other gift they could have given her that would have made her more excited.

Her parent's gift to young Amy Jo brought equal excitement. There, in a neatly wrapped package, were art supplies and a simple book on sketching. Amy Jo was wild with her good fortune. She could hardly wait to begin her efforts. Marty wondered if the family would constantly be plagued at awkward moments with requests to pose, but she said nothing.

In spite of her granddaughter's joy, Marty really was not looking forward to the trip to town to make the purchases, but she kept her promise at the very first opportunity. Of course Amy Jo insisted that Belinda and Melissa also accompany them. Marty knew that she would be weary when the day was over—unless, of course, Amy Jo stayed with the same choice she had made previously. In that case, the task could be accomplished quite quickly.

It was not to be. Amy Jo decided to go with something completely different. She wanted something "vibrant." Marty wondered just how much more "vibrant" than the bright purple flowers a piece of yard goods could be, but she held her tongue and suffered through the long decision-making. Amy Jo took her time, vacillating between a daring yellow with scattered red flowers and leaves, and a smoky blue with green and lavendar splashes. Marty had never known that such colorful prints existed.

Amy Jo finally settled on the smokey blue and tried to match the wallpaper to the yard goods. Marty was sure the room would seem dark—though hardly dreary.

They did find a wallpaper with the same colors—the background was a bit more blue with an all-over pattern of small purple flowers and green leaves.

But Amy Jo insisted that it would look just right. Clare put up the paper while Kate sewed the curtains and Marty made the spread. Amy Jo moved into her "new" room, exclaiming over and over how *vibrant* it looked. Marty had to admit that, surprisingly, the room did look quite homey and inviting. She was glad to move on to other things. Winter was upon them and she hadn't yet had the teacher's family in for supper.

Chapter 12

Emergency

About the only events that distracted Belinda's attention from Jackson were the calls she was able to make with Luke. He still stopped by for her when he had a case in the country that he thought would be suitable for her involvement. Now that she was back in school, those times were less frequent, and Belinda undoubtedly would have chafed over the situation had not her life and her mind been so busy with Melissa, school—and Jackson. As it was, she squealed her delight whenever she saw Luke's buggy pull into their lane.

Amy Jo still turned up her nose over Belinda's medical interest, wondering how anyone could possibly enjoy seeing blood and fevers. Melissa, on the other hand, openly admired Belinda, though she had no desire to accompany her. She was considerate, however, about shouldering some of Belinda's responsibilities in the kitchen on those days when she went off with her doctor brother. Melissa always asked for a full report on the patient when Belinda returned home again, but she did look a bit pale at times when Belinda described some aspects of their service.

A brisk, cold wind blew in with Luke when he turned his team into the yard one Saturday morning. Belinda flew out the door to meet him at the hitching rail.

"Get back in there and get a coat," he scolded her. "Winter

is here, and you're out here like it was a summer day. I'll be called out to doctor you next!"

He may have been a doctor, but he was also her brother, so Belinda ignored his protest.

"Where we goin'?" she asked him.

"Out to the Simpsons'. Thought it about time you saw a broken bone. But hurry. We don't want to make the poor boy suffer any longer than we have to. A broken limb can be awfully painful."

Belinda ran back to the house to inform Marty and grab her heavy wrap. "We're gonna set a broken bone," she called over her shoulder as she rushed back out the door. "It shouldn't take long."

Luke had already swung the horses around, and the buggy left the yard at a brisk trot. While they traveled Luke told Belinda about bones—the structure of the human body and what the large bones were called. They went over the names until he was sure she had them well in her memory. Then he went on to describe different kinds of breaks and the basic treatment for each. Belinda listened with wide eyes.

"What kinda break is this one?" she asked, hardly able to wait until they got there and she could see for herself.

"I wasn't told. I was just informed that the young Simpson boy had broken a limb in a logging accident of some kind."

"Which limb?"

"I don't even know. I'm guessing it's a leg. Usually when a log rolls, it gets the leg," replied Luke and clucked again to hurry the team.

For the first time in several days, Jackson was far from Belinda's thoughts. "Are ya gonna take 'im to town?" she asked.

"Not likely. Once it's set, he should be able to rest in his own bed. I'll stop by often to see how it's coming."

"I don't think I know the Simpsons," said Belinda.

"They're new. Just moved onto the old Coffin place."

"Oh. Will they be comin' to our school?"

"I don't know a thing about the family."

"It would be nice," said Belinda. "Iffen they have young'uns, thet is."

They turned the team down the rutted, overgrown lane and pushed them hastily toward the simple log dwelling. Belinda was scrambling quickly down over the wheel when she heard the most agonized scream she had ever heard in her life. She felt, rather than saw, Luke stiffen. His head jerked up and his body seemed to become a machine of action. Without even a backward glance, he grabbed his black bag and sprang toward the house. "You tie the team," he called over his shoulder.

Belinda stood shaking. Luke had said that broken bones could be painful, but never had she dreamed they could make one scream so. Another scream pierced the air and Belinda broke from her frozen stance and began to flip the reins of the horses carefully around the post. Luke might need her help. She should get to him quickly.

But when Belinda reached the door of the log cabin, she was met by a heavyset woman in a worn and dirty apron. She placed herself solidly in the doorway, her legs slightly akimbo. Belinda could see that her eyes were red from crying and her brow covered with sweat.

"The doc says you're to stay out," she said tiredly.

Belinda could not understand the order. Luke had brought her along to learn how to set a bone. He might even need her assistance, and here was this woman trying to bar her entrance.

"But—" began Belinda, peering over the woman's shoulder toward the door at the back of the room.

"It's not a pretty sight in there," the woman continued, and her whole body trembled.

Another cry rent the stuffy air of the little cabin. For a moment Belinda went all weak and she too trembled. She had never heard such a sound in all her life. Scuffling noises came from the small room. Belinda wondered wildly just what was going on. Luke might need her. He might even be in trouble. How was she to know?

With one quick movement she ducked around the woman and ran to the room from which the awful cry had burst. Luke had already laid aside his heavy coat and even removed his jacket. His shirt sleeves were rolled up and he was bending with deep concentration over a form on the bed. A man and a boy also stood over the writhing form, pinning it to the bed sheets. Sweat beaded the brow of the man, and the boy's lip trembled.

"I thought I told you to stay out," said Luke without even turning around.

Belinda took a deep breath to help control her shaking. Her eyes were getting more accustomed to the darkness of the room. Only one small, dingy window let in any light. She looked back at Luke's strong back. The muscles rippled beneath his thin shirt as he fought to administer some kind of drug to the thrashing patient. In spite of a wave of nausea sweeping through her, Belinda swallowed hard and stepped forward.

"I thought ya might need me," she said determinedly.

"Can you?"

"I think so," she replied, swallowing hard.

"I do need you—badly—but I don't want—"

"What should I do?" asked Belinda quickly.

"Get a lamp. I need more light."

Luke had not turned to look at Belinda, his full attention having been on the injured young man.

Belinda swallowed again and hurried from the room. She must not waste time. Luke needed a light. He needed her.

The woman stood in the kitchen, her head leaning against the wall. Great sobs shook her body. Belinda wished to slip over to her and offer some kind of comfort but there wasn't time yet. "We need a lamp," she said firmly, but the woman did not seem to be able to move.

Belinda cast her eyes about the kitchen. There was a lamp on a shelf near the stove. She lifted it down and shook it to check the fuel supply. It did have oil. Hurriedly she struck a match on the stove surface and lit the lamp, then hastened with it to the bedroom.

The one on the bed was no longer screaming. He was not thrashing around as much, either. Belinda breathed a little sigh of relief. The drug Luke had given must already be working. She pushed forward with the lamp, holding it out in front of her so it would shed light on Luke's work.

It was then that she saw the patient. It was not a broken leg that Luke bent over. Neither would Belinda have called it a broken arm. Mangled and crushed beyond recognition, the appendage was only blood and bits of tangled flesh and bone. Belinda felt her stomach lurch. For a moment she was sure that the rush of blood leaving her head would put her on the floor. She reached awkwardly for the bedpost with one hand, the lamp clutched in the other, and hung on for dear life as she fought for control. The room began to come back into focus again, but Belinda feared lest she would lose her breakfast. Wave after wave of nausea swept over. Luke had no time for a second patient. Belinda fought with all her strength to bring herself under control. Luke would need her help. He would need all the help he could get.

The youth showed no sign of struggling now. Mercifully the drug had claimed him. Luke bent over the bloody mass that had been an arm and carefully examined it. Belinda held the lamp as steadily as she could, trying to avoid the scene before her, but her eyes kept returning to the sight.

Luke straightened and looked directly at the large man who still held his son, even though it was no longer necessary.

"I'm sorry, sir," Luke said as gently as he could, "I'm going to have to take the arm to save the boy."

A convulsive sob shook the man. One large hand reached up to cover his face as he wept uncontrollably. The other hand remained on the shoulder of the boy on the bed. Luke reached out a hand to the other young boy who also stood with his hands still holding his brother.

"You can go now, son," he said softly.

The boy dashed from the room. Belinda distractedly thought that he should remember a coat. It was bitterly cold out.

"I'll need lots of boiling water and some clean cloths," Luke informed the man. "You needn't worry about him throwing himself around now. He's beyond the pain."

The man wiped at his wet face with a ragged, dirty sleeve and hurried to do Luke's bidding. Belinda moved in closer with the lamp. Luke looked about at the small room and dirty bedding, but there was no way he could move the boy into his office in town.

"I'm going to need your help, Belinda. Do you think you can manage?"

Belinda nodded, her face white but determined.

"Put the lamp on that little table and pull it as close to the bed as you can. I'll need your hands to help me with this surgery."

Belinda placed the lamp and returned to do whatever else Luke needed.

The rest of the morning was only a blur in Belinda's memory. She worked alongside Luke as one in a trance. She knew that she responded to each of his orders. She handed him his instruments, reached out supporting hands, acted as she was directed, but she did it all in some kind of daze. At one point the boy stirred slightly, and Belinda had to administer more chloroform. Her hand trembled as she held the cloth with the chemical to his nose and mouth. Luke watched carefully and told her when to draw it away.

The surgery seemed to take forever. By the time the stub of the limb was bandaged and the instruments cleared away, Belinda was nearly beside herself with exhaustion. So was her brother, the doctor. He leaned his head wearily against the post of the bed and a tremor went through his body. Belinda had never seen him like this before.

He did not succumb for long. He again turned back to his patient and checked his eyes and took his pulse.

"Watch him carefully for any change," he told Belinda. "I'm going to get this mess out of here," and, so saying, Luke began to bundle the remains of the crushed limb in bloody rags so that he could dispose of it all.

Belinda allowed herself to sit on the edge of the bed. It was the first time she had taken a really good look at the patient. He was young, no more than seventeen or eighteen, she guessed. And he was deathly pale. She had never seen anyone quite so white. His breathing seemed shallow, but steady. She wondered how long it would be before the anesthesia wore off. How would he feel when he wakened? There would still be pain, Belinda knew. He would be in pain for many days—weeks, even. But he would not have an arm. Belinda thought about the anguish he would feel. What a terrible thing to happen to a young man. To lose his arm just as his life was opening up to adulthood.

Belinda thought of Clark and his missing leg. It had been hard for her pa, she knew that. Even though it had happened before her birth, her mama had told her about the pain and suffering that went with the experience. But Clark had been a grown man—a man mature enough to accept his situation. And Clark had the Lord to help him. Faith in his heavenly Father had somehow gotten him through. What about the young man before her? Did he know the Lord? For some reason, Belinda feared not. Without taking her eyes from the pale face before her, Belinda began to pray, her voice no more than a whisper.

"Oh, God," she implored, "I don't know this boy. I don't know iffen he knows You, but he's gonna need Ya, God. He's gonna need Ya to help him accept this awful thing thet has happened in his life. He's gonna need Ya to help him git better agin." Without thinking Belinda reached out a hand and brushed the hair back from the pale, sweat-dampened forehead. *His hair is a nice color—almost as shiny'n black as a raven's wing* was the thought that flashed unbidden through her mind. The face was finely formed and well proportioned, the nose straight and even. Belinda suddenly realized that in spite of the paleness and an unkempt appearance, the boy was very nice looking. Self-consciously her hand drew back. What was she doing gently stroking the face of an unknown boy? A flush began to creep up into her face.

Luke returned, bringing with him the parents. His eyes searched Belinda's face. He seemed pleased with what he saw there.

"You can leave now," he said softly. "I'll stay with him."

The woman was bending over her son, sobs shaking her body, when Belinda slipped quietly from the room. She didn't know where to go. It was really too cold to wait outside. She did long for some fresh air, though, so she grabbed her coat, wrapped it tightly around her, and left the small cabin.

There was a woodpile in a shed nearby. Belinda decided she would carry in some wood and make some coffee—if she could find the grounds and a pot. She was sure the family could do with some activity to momentarily divert them from the tragedy. Even a cup of coffee might bring some kind of relief and refreshing.

Belinda was not in a hurry. She needed to stretch her legs a bit—work the kinks out of protesting muscles. She strolled back and forth, studying the farm before her.

Kinda run-down looking, she noted. Belinda had forgotten that it had been without tenants for a number of years. The new folks certainly had their work cut out for them. The buildings were ramshackled, the fence rails down, the garden area showing unsightly weeds even through the early winter snow.

Belinda wondered just where the young boy had been working when it had happened. Luke said a logging accident. Was he busy hurrying to get in a winter supply of wood before the colder weather struck? Belinda lifted her eyes to the wooded area at the far end of the field. Was that where tragedy had struck this boy and his family?

At last Belinda turned back to the small log shack that housed the family wood supply. She went in to pick up an armload for the kitchen stove. Her eyes had not yet become accustomed to the darkness when a slight movement startled her. She jumped, a quick intake of breath escaping her lips. It was the younger boy who crouched in the corner. Belinda quickly regained her composure.

"I'm sorry," she said. "I didn't see ya there."

The boy said nothing. It was just as Belinda had feared, he had run from the house with no coat.

"Ya must be cold," said Belinda. She was glad he was at least out of the cold wind.

The boy still said nothing, only hugged his knees to his chest.

Belinda tried a smile. "Yer brother is gonna be fine, now," she told him.

The boy began to sob uncontrollably. Belinda wished to comfort him but she wasn't sure what to do. She just let him cry.

After several minutes he began to mop his tears on patched shirt sleeves.

"He's not gonna die?" he asked in disbelief.

"Oh, no!" said Belinda. "Doctor Luke is with him. He'll be okay now."

The boy succumbed to a fresh burst of tears. When they had

subsided he mopped up again, then turned large, dark eyes to Belinda.

"I was so scared he'd die," he told her shakily. "I didn't think thet anyone could live with an arm—with an arm—" He couldn't go on.

There was silence for a few minutes. The boy broke it.

"Will his arm ever git better?" he asked quietly.

Belinda did not know how to answer. Was it her place to inform the boy of his brother's amputation? Shouldn't Luke or his parents be telling him?

"Will it?" the boy insisted. Belinda decided it would be worse if she tried to evade the truth. She crossed closer to him in case he needed her, crouched down and looked him squarely in the eye. "Not—not really," she said, "but it will heal now."

His eyes grew big. "Wha'd'ya mean?" he asked her.

"The doctor—the doctor had to take off the arm—then sew it up—to save yer brother."

"Ya mean, cut it off?" His eyes were wild with fright and shock.

Belinda nodded slowly.

"But he'll *hate* thet. He'd rather die! Don't ya see? He'd rather die."

The boy leaped to his feet, his eyes challenging Belinda. By the time he finished his speech, his voice was a high-pitched scream. Belinda wondered if he was going to kick at her angrily. She was sure the temptation was in his mind. And then his whole body slumped dejectedly and he threw his arms about her and cried, the deep sobs shaking the frail body.

There was nothing Belinda could say. She just held the weeping boy and cried along with him.

Much later than they had anticipated, Luke and Belinda returned home. Marty had been frequently checking out of the kitchen window, her eyes worriedly studying the road. It was with great relief that she saw Luke's team of blacks turn into the lane.

Luke came in with Belinda, though the hour was getting late. He wanted a word with his ma and pa.

Marty met them at the door, the questions showing in her eyes. It was evident from the extreme weariness of both her offspring that something unexpected had faced them at the farm home.

"It wasn't just a break," Luke informed her quietly.

"Ya like a cup of hot tea and a sandwich?" Marty asked him.

"That would be nice," said Luke and he shrugged out of his heavy coat, then helped Belinda with hers.

"Ya be needin' me, Ma?" asked Belinda in a weary voice.

"No. No, guess not," Marty responded, then cast a glance Luke's direction.

"I think I'll go on up to bed then," said the young girl.

"Don't ya want somethin' to eat?"

"No. Thank ya, Ma. I'm not hungry. Jest tired."

Luke's eyes told Marty to let the young girl go.

Marty pulled Belinda close for a moment and then kissed her on the forehead. Belinda was glad for the comfort of her mother's arms. She was also glad that Melissa was staying overnight with Amy Jo. She just didn't feel up to answering any questions.

Luke pulled out a chair and sat down at the table. Clark joined him but shook his head "no" at Marty's offer of a cup of tea. Marty busied herself at the stove and cupboard and soon had a roast beef sandwich, made with thick slices of homemade bread and farm butter, to set before her weary son. She poured two cups of tea and sat down to join him.

"I take it this was a tough one," Clark was saying.

Luke nodded his head. " 'Bout the worse thing I've seen yet."

"Not a break, ya said."

"Crushed. Crushed beyond recognition."

"Did Belinda—?" began Marty but Luke stopped her question.

"I told her to stay out, but she came in anyway. Said I might need her help." He swallowed a sip of the hot tea and sat silent for a minute. "I did. I sure did. I don't know what I'd have done without her."

"She could—could face it?"

"At first she nearly passed out—I saw that. But she fought

against it, and she helped through the entire surgery. Did everything just like I asked her. She was a real brick about it. I was proud of her."

Marty shuddered and pushed back her cup. She did not want the tea after all. In her mind's eye she was seeing again the crushed leg of her husband.

"She's made of good stuff, that kid of yours," Luke was saying, and there was pride in his voice.

"Ya don't think it was too much fer her?" asked Clark.

"I would never have knowingly decided to let Belinda see what she did—not at her age. I would have kept her out of there if I could have—if I hadn't needed her in order to save that boy's life. There was no one else to help me. Belinda knew the names of each of my instruments as I called for them, and we were fighting against time. I hope—I hope and pray—that it wasn't too much for a girl her age. I—I don't think it was. I think—I think that she'll be fine. We've got us a nurse, to my way of thinking."

Marty felt both pride and concern at the words of her son. She would watch Belinda very carefully during the next few days—maybe try to get her to talk about her feelings and thoughts on it all.

"An' the patient?" asked Clark. "He's gonna make it?"

"He was a kid of seventeen," said Luke with deep compassion. "He'll make it—physically. He's out of danger now, barring complications. But whether he'll make it emotionally or not, only time will tell. It's going to be tough. I don't need to tell you that."

Clark nodded solemnly.

"I was wondering—would you mind making a call in a few days? Give him a bit of time to get used to—his—his misfortune, then just stop by?"

Clark nodded in agreement.

"And, Pa," said Luke quietly, "wonder if you'd mind leaving your artificial limb at home."

Clark said nothing. Just nodded again in understanding.

"Well," said Luke, getting to his feet. "I'd best be getting on home. Abbie will be concerned." Luke looked evenly at Clark and Marty and then turned toward the stairs. "First, I think I'll just go up and say good night to my little sister."

Chapter 13

The New Neighbors

Marty did watch Belinda carefully over the next few days. The girl did not seem withdrawn or troubled, but she was much more solemn than she had been. She did not even join in with the other two girls in the sighing and tittering over Jackson. Overnight, it seemed, she had become more mature—above such childish games. Marty did not know if she was thankful or regretful. Belinda was still very young. Marty did not take pleasure in life's robbing her of even a brief moment of childhood.

When Melissa returned home to the big house, she wanted to know all about Belinda's last "adventure." Belinda answered her questions very briefly. A boy's arm had been crushed in a logging accident, she informed Melissa, and Luke had needed to amputate the limb.

Melissa grimaced and looked over at Clark. She knew well the story of how her grandfather had lost his leg.

"Was it awful?" asked Melissa.

"Yes," answered Belinda and went out to get the clothes off the line.

Clark and Marty waited for a few days, and then as Luke had suggested, they hitched the team and went to call on their new neighbor. Clark felt a bit awkward returning to his crutch. He had almost forgotten how to use it.

The ride to the Coffins' old farmstead was a quiet one. A

cold wind whipped about little flurries of snow, and Marty shivered against the cold. What would happen when they got to the new neighbors? What would they say? What *could* they say? There really weren't any words in the world that would comfort them.

"Looks like winter's really settlin' in," Clark mentioned as he hurried the team with a flick of the reins. Marty shivered again. The thought of winter somehow fit with thoughts of the visit ahead.

As they turned the team down the lane to the log house, Clark and Marty both noticed the condition of the farmyard.

"Things sure do go down quickly when a farm is left vacant," Clark commented and Marty silently agreed.

Clark tied the team. They both had expected someone to come to the door, if not out to the yard, to welcome them, but there was no sign of movement anywhere. Clark led the way up to the door. A wisp of smoke was struggling from the chimney, fighting its way against the wind and snow. Marty pulled her coat more tightly about her and, too, fought her way against the wind.

Clark rapped loudly on the wooden door. They could hear some shuffling inside but the door did not open. Clark rapped again.

The door opened a crack and a pale face of a young man peeked out at them. He looked pained and hesitant.

"What ya want?" he rasped out.

"Neighbors—down the road a piece," Clark responded. "Jest thought we'd pay a call."

The door opened a bit farther. Marty could see the bandages over the stub of an arm. There were traces of blood showing on the whiteness. She shivered but not from the cold. She wasn't quite prepared for this.

"Nobody home but me," the lad said, still not inviting them in.

"Then guess we'll jest visit with you a spell," answered Clark cheerily, and he moved slightly to usher Marty in before him.

The boy moved back from the door, allowing it to open wide

enough for their entrance. Marty could tell that it was only manners, not desire, that allowed them into the cabin. She felt sorry for the young boy.

He turned to them. "Won't ya sit," he said gruffly.

Clark did not take the chair nearby, the one that had been offered. He helped Marty out of her heavy coat and seated her, then walked across the room to a chair near the window. His crutch thumped strangely on the wooden floor. There had been a time when the thumping crutch had sounded familiar to Marty. Now, after a number of years with the artificial limb, it sounded strange and eerie.

The boy had noticed. Marty saw him stiffen.

Clark seated himself and laid the crutch aside. He turned to the young man.

"Don't think I've heard yer name," he began. When the boy didn't respond, he went on, "Understand yer pa jest bought the place here."

"We're jest leasin'," answered the boy. "Got no money fer buyin'."

Clark let the comment go.

"Heard about yer accident. Powerful sorry. Terrible pain, ain't it?"

The dark eyes of the boy shadowed. Marty wondered if he was about to ask Clark what he knew about the pain, but his eyes fell again to the stump of a leg. He didn't say anything, just nodded dumbly.

"The worst should soon be over now," Clark continued. "It should soon be lettin' ya get some sleep at night."

Again the boy nodded. He still said nothing. Marty concluded that he did not want to discuss his missing arm.

"Care fer some tea?" the boy asked.

"That would be nice," exclaimed Marty a bit too enthusiastically. The young fellow moved forward to lift the teapot from a cupboard shelf and put in the tea leaves. The kettle on the stove was already boiling, and he poured the hot liquid into the pot. It slopped over some, hot water sizzling as it hit the iron of the stove surface. Clearly he was still adjusting to managing with only one hand.

"Can I give ya some help—" Marty began, rising from her chair, but as she caught the quick glance of Clark, she sat back down and busied herself with easing imaginary wrinkles from her full skirt.

The boy fumbled with cups from the cupboard. He handled them without too much problem, but when he went to slice some dry-looking bread to go with the drink, Marty turned away. She could not bear to see him struggling with the small task.

She could feel the tears stinging her eyes. *Why? Why should one so young face such pain and loss?*

Marty let her eyes travel over the small room. She needed something—anything to fill her thoughts.

The room was dingy and sparsely furnished. The little that was there needed care. The unpolished wooden floor was in need of scrubbing. Dirty dishes were stacked on the bit of cupboard space. The stove was covered with charred bits of remaining spills. The walls and windows were empty of anything that would give the place a homey look. Marty shuddered again and turned back to the young boy. It was clear that the family was not very well off. Marty felt pity for them rising within her. Determinedly she shook it off. She felt sure they would not welcome her pity.

"Jest pull up yer chairs," the boy was saying, and he placed the bread and tea on the table.

" 'Fraid we're right outta butter," he acknowledged without any real apology in his voice. He was just stating a fact.

Clark helped Marty move her chair to the table and then he pulled his own forward. Marty ached to be allowed the privilege of serving the tea but she held her tongue. The boy poured. Some of it splashed on the table but no one commented on it.

"Where you folks from?" asked Clark to get the conversation rolling.

"We jest came back from the West," said the boy. "Afore thet Pa worked in a hardware store. He was sure thet the West would make us a better livin', but we had us some hard luck."

"Sorry to hear thet," responded Clark.

"My pa got sick with some kind of lung fever, and Ma an' me jest couldn't keep things goin'. He's some better now, but by then we'd lost our claim. Pa tried to git jobs in various towns, but there weren't nothin' there neither. So we come on back. Got this far on the cash we had. We heard 'bout this here place. Fellow in town said we could live here cheap. Jest a few dollars a month, but it needs lots of fixin'. Can't rent the land though. Guess one of the boys still farms it."

That would be Josh, the Coffins' son-in-law. Clark and Marty knew that Josh farmed his father's land along with his own.

It was not intended as a hard-luck story, just a brief statement of how things were.

"Where yer folks now?" asked Clark.

"Loggin'," replied the boy. "This here fella said thet we could help ourselves to all the logs we wanted. We need firewood, an' Pa reckoned thet anything extry thet we could take out we could sell fer supplies."

Logging! Both his pa and his ma. Logging to try to get fuel supplies so that the family could survive the harshness of the prairie winter. Marty shivered again. Logging had already cost the young boy his arm.

"I got me a whole root cellar of vegetables and fruit," Marty said. "I was wonderin' what to do with all the extry. It'll jest up and spoil a-sittin' there. I hate haulin' out rotten vegetables come spring. We can jest bring some of 'em over here fer the use of you folk."

Clark caught the look on the face of the young man. The family did not ask for charity. The boy threw a glance toward Marty and she stumbled on, "In exchange for some of the logs, thet is. Thet is—iffen ya be carin' to trade?"

The boy relaxed. "I reckon we might," he said evenly. "I'll ask Pa."

Marty was wondering what they would do with the extra logs when she picked up the conversation. "I'm a member of the school board here," Clark was saying. "Ya got any sisters or brothers of school age?"

"Got me one brother. He should be in school, right enough, but I don't know as Pa can spare 'im. He's out loggin', too."

Marty's head jerked up, concern gripping her heart. *Oh,*

Clark, stop 'im, she wanted to say. *He might git hurt, too!* But she did not say it. It was really out of their control.

They drank their tea and ate their bread, Clark dipping his in his cup. Marty wanted to chide him, but the fact was, she wished she dared do the same thing. The dry bread tasted rather old.

Marty looked out at the weather. The snow had increased. She thought about the man, woman and child out in the woods chopping trees on such a day, but she made no comment.

"I was wonderin'," Clark was saying. "I have me a surplus of dry firewood—but I could sure find ways to use green logs. I'm wonderin' iffen yer pa would be willin' to make a swap. I'm in no hurry fer the green. Anytime next spring will be jest fine. I can git the firewood over to ya right away—git it outta my way."

Relief showed on the young face. "Reckon Pa would make the trade," responded the boy.

"We'll plan on thet then," Clark said and rose to go.

They thanked their host for the tea and bundled into their warm coats. Clark was about to lead Marty to the waiting buggy when the young lad stopped them.

"I didn't catch yer name," he said.

"Clark. Clark an' Marty Davis."

"My doc's name is Davis."

"Yeah, I know. He be our son." There was pride in Clark's voice in spite of his effort to disguise it. But the shadow in the eyes of the young boy quickly wrenched it away.

"Yer wonderin' iffen he coulda saved yer arm, 'stead of takin' it, aren't ya?" Clark said softly.

The boy turned slightly away. He swallowed hard. The tears that started to form were not allowed to fall. It was several minutes before he trusted his voice.

"Naw," he said. "Naw, not really. Ma an' Pa told me he didn't have no choice." He swallowed again, working hard to get his emotions under control. "He's—he's been back a number of times. He's—he's a fine doc. Nothin' he coulda done different."

Clark put out a hand and let it drop to the muscular shoulder. He said nothing except what the boy might understand from the slight pressure of his hand.

They turned to leave when the boy spoke again. "Ma said there was a girl—she helped the doc. Ma says I owe both of them my life. Ya wouldn't—ya wouldn't know who she was, would ya? I forgot to ask the doc."

"Belinda," said Clark. "Belinda. She goes with Luke some. Wants to be a nurse someday."

"Belinda," repeated the boy. "I—I guess I'm beholden to her. I'd like—I'd like to tell her thank ya someday."

Clark nodded. "I think thet could be arranged," he said, and followed Marty out into the bitter wind.

Chapter 14

Talking It Out

Marty kept thinking she would get her little girl back again, but Belinda was still thoughtful and quiet.

"Land sakes," said Marty to Clark as they prepared for bed one night, "I'm havin' me one awful time tryin' to keep up to all these sudden-like changes. Our Belinda—she's gone from one stage to the next before I can scarcely turn my head. A young gigglin' girl one day, an' the next, a serious young lady. Do ya think we'll get Belinda's childhood back fer a bit? I wasn't quite prepared to let 'er go jest yet."

Clark drew Marty close. He held her quietly for a few minutes, his hand stroking the long hair that she had allowed to fall down around her shoulders.

"I've noticed it, too," he said. "Thet there accident seems to have changed our Belinda."

"Do ya think it's eatin' away at her, Clark?"

"She doesn't seem bothered—jest more serious somehow."

"Guess what she went through would sober up anyone," Marty reasoned.

"It's hard to let her grow up so fast—I know thet—but truth is, I rather like 'er this way. She's kinda—kinda sweet, don't ya think?"

Marty smiled. "She always was yer pet. Didn't expect thet to change none jest because she adds a few years." She reached up to playfully pat Clark's cheek. "I'd expect ya to think she's sweet."

"I jest mean—well, she seems miles ahead of Amy Jo in her bearin'. She jest acts an' looks like a grown-up somehow. Even more than Melissa. Ya noticed thet?"

"I've noticed," said Marty.

There was silence for a moment.

"Clark, do ya think we should sorta help her talk it out? I mean, iffen this accident is botherin' her, we don't want it to turn up later in her life with scars we never guessed was there."

Clark thought about it. "Wouldn't hurt none, I guess."

"Speakin' of scars," went on Marty, "did ya see the young man agin when ya took over the foodstuff and the firewood?"

"Saw 'im," Clark answered simply, knowing whom she meant.

He drew back and walked to the window. He ran a hand through his still-thick hair and stood quietly looking out at the night sky. Marty knew he was troubled. She crossed over to stand beside him and look out across the dark outlines of the farm buildings by moonlight. She laid a hand gently on Clark's arm but waited for him to speak.

"He's hurtin', Marty. Really hurtin'," Clark finally said, his voice low.

"But he seemed so—so acceptin' when we saw 'im before."

"I don't think the reality of it all had hit 'im yet. He was still in so much pain with the arm—he was still in deep shock over the whole thing. But now—now he knows thet it's fer real—permanent—an' there's nothin' to be done 'bout it. He'll always be a one-armed man. Thet's tough. Thet's really tough."

"Do ya think the parson could help him any?"

"I thought so—until I talked to the parson. He'd already been there—twice. He didn't even git in the door."

Marty's eyes grew large with concern.

"Did ya—did ya say anythin' 'bout how God helped us when—?"

"Tried. Wouldn't hear it. Luke says they won't even let him make doctor calls anymore."

"Oh, my!" exclaimed Marty. "Might thet make a problem with the wound?"

"Not physically. Luke says thet the arm has healed nicely. Shouldn't be infection or anythin'. But emotionally—well, Luke worries a fair bit 'bout thet."

"Oh, dear!" Marty lamented.

Silence followed.

"Is there anythin' thet we can do, Clark?"

"I've been thinkin' and thinkin' on it. Can't think of one thing—'cept pray."

"Did he ask 'bout Belinda agin? We had promised to arrange fer 'im to see her. He wanted to thank—"

"Thet's another thing. He said to fergit the whole thing. Doesn't want to see her. Says she didn't do 'im such a favor after all."

"Ya mean—?"

"Says he'd be better off dead."

Marty's breath caught in a quick little sob. Clark put his arm around her.

"I was so taken with him," she said. "Strugglin' with thet heavy teapot an' thet dry bread, as mannerly and self-possessed as ya please. I thought he was so plucky an' brave an'—"

"Now, let's not think less of the boy," Clark was quick to say. "He is all those things. It's normal what he's feelin'. Remember, we had God and His help—or I might have done exactly what this here boy is doin'. It's a tough thing he's goin' through—an' understandable how he's feelin'. I jest hope an' pray thet he's able to sort it all out and git beyond it—thet's all. Talk 'bout scars. This young fella's got scars all right—an' the worst an' deepest ain't on thet arm."

Marty thought about the four Simpsons. So nearby, yet so shut off from the help of their neighbors. She wished there were some way—*some way* that they could reach out and break down the walls.

"They didn't refuse the food—the vegetables an' fruit?"

"No-o. But I think thet they would have iffen they hadn't been on the brink of starvation. They are proud people. It hurt them powerful to take it. Man insisted thet he'd work it off."

"So what did ya do?"

Clark shrugged. "Told 'im he could. Now I gotta come up with somethin' fer 'im to do."

"Oh, Clark. What will ya give 'im? Ya got everything done that needs doin'."

"I dunno. It's gotta be somethin' in outta the cold. His coat is so thin thet ya could sneeze clear through it."

"He could build some more fruit shelves in the cellar."

"Ya needin' more?"

"No-o. But it's warm—an' there's room there—an' it wouldn't hurt none."

"It's an idee," said Clark, reaching out to pull the window shade. Then he turned to climb into bed. Marty turned to follow him. She was surprised to find she was still holding her hairbrush.

"An' the firewood?" asked Marty as she returned the brush to her dresser.

"He's determined to pay fer thet, too. Guess we'll have us more green wood come spring."

"What ya gonna do with it?"

"Dunno. I'll check with Arnie an' Josh. See iffen either of 'em have any need. We should be able to figger out somethin'."

"Funny," murmured Marty as though to herself. "I don't care none fer a grown man with his hand out—but pride can sure enough be a hurtful thing, too."

"Makes it a bit hard to be neighborly," agreed Clark. "Still, a man needs his dignity. We've got to allow 'im thet."

Clark blew out the light and they pulled the warm blankets up around their chins. The winter nights were cold and there was no heat in the upstairs rooms except for what drifted up the stairs from the stoves below.

"Ya don't have sewin' thet ya need done, do ya?" Clark asked. "Clothes? Quilts? Rag rugs? Anythin'?"

Marty turned to him in the darkness. "Nothin' I can't git done over the winter. Why?"

"I was wonderin'—maybe the missus could help earn 'em a bit, sewin' or somethin'."

Marty was silent. There really wasn't that much the household needed. And she liked to do it. The long winter days and even longer evenings were made more bearable by the things that took shape in her hands. She looked forward to the projects and planned for them all fall as she worked hard in her garden patch. And now—?

"Might be," she answered Clark. "I'll see what I can come up with."

Marty finally had opportunity to talk with Belinda. She had been watching for an opening. She did not wish to force the issue but did want to give the girl a chance to express her feelings concerning her involvement in the amputation. But it was difficult to find time.

The occasion turned up when Melissa was sent on an errand to Kate's. She begged for some extra time because Amy Jo had sketches that she was anxious to show her. Also, now that Amy Jo had gotten some practice, she wanted to try her hand at drawing some of her kin. Melissa was picked for the first candidate.

Luke had stopped by on his way back from delivering a baby. Belinda, as yet, had not been invited to participate in a delivery. She had coaxed—more with her eyes than words—to be able to go with Luke on one of his happier duties as a doctor, but so far Luke had held back.

After Luke had drunk his coffee to warm up some from the cold and eaten some of Marty's sponge cake, he bundled up again and left for home.

Belinda, busy stirring up a batch of cookies for school lunches, opened the conversation.

"I fergot to ask 'im how the boy who lost his arm is doin'."

Marty looked at her daughter. She wasn't sure just what to say. Belinda seemed to sense her unrest. Her eyes turned to Marty questioningly.

"He's okay, isn't he? He didn't git infection or—?"

"No, no. He healed nice. Thet is, his arm healed—"

"What're ya meanin'? He wasn't hurt any place else. Luke checked him carefully fer cracked ribs or—"

"No, no," Marty said again. "Nothin' like thet."

"What is it then?" asked Belinda. "I can tell thet yer holdin' back somethin'."

"He's havin' a tough time adjustin', thet's all," said Marty slowly.

Belinda was relieved. "I would, too," she said simply. "Thet's to be expected. Luke talked 'bout it on the way home. He said thet workin' it through is one of the stages of acceptin' an amputation."

Marty nodded her head in agreement.

"So when Luke talks to 'im, does—?"

Marty didn't allow her to finish her question. "The boy don't see Luke no more."

"Ya mean Luke has quit callin' already? Why, he told me thet he'd keep goin' back jest to be sure thet—"

"They won't let Luke call. Told 'im not to come anymore."

"They did? Who did? The pa? Don't he know thet—?"

"No," said Marty. "It was the boy."

There was silence.

"I've got to git over there right away," said Belinda. "I shouldn't have waited so long. He'll think—he'll think I don't care. Do ya s'pose Pa would—?"

"He doesn't wanna see you either," Marty said softly.

Belinda's eyes turned to Marty. Marty could see the protest there.

"But ya said—"

"I know what we said."

"He wanted—"

"I know. But he changed his mind."

"But why?" Belinda cried.

"I can't answer thet. 'Cept—cept he's painin' on the inside now. He can't understand why it shoulda happened. He's sufferin' with it in a new way. He says he wishes he'd died—"

"Can't we do somethin', Ma?" Belinda cried.

"Yer pa's been tryin'. They're proud people. Hard to do things fer. They insist on payin' fer everthin', an' they can't accept the help of neighbors." Marty hesitated. She sighed deeply and turned to the troubled eyes of her youngest. "The worst is," she said slowly, "they can't seem to accept the help of God none, either."

"I wondered," said Belinda. Then to Marty's surprise her lip began to tremble and the next thing Marty knew she had thrown herself into her mother's arms and was weeping against her shoulder.

Marty let her cry. Her own tears fell in sympathy and love. The poor girl did feel this whole thing very deeply.

At last Belinda was able to talk. "Oh, Ma," she said, still clinging to Marty. "It was awful. So much blood an'—an' raw, mashed flesh and bits of broken bone—everywhere. I never knew—I never knew anything could look so—so awful!"

Belinda shuddered and Marty tightened her arms.

"An' there he laid. Quiet and still—almost like he'd already died."

Belinda stopped and blew her nose.

"But he wasn't quiet at first," she hurried on. "At first he screamed—it was awful. We heard the screamin' 'fore we even got to the house, an' Luke—he jest grabbed his bag an' ran an' left me to care fer the horses. Then when I got to the house the woman—did ya see the woman?" Marty shook her head no. "Well, she's big, an' she stood there—legs apart an' arms spread out—barrin' the door so I couldn't go in. 'The doctor told ya to stay out,' she said, and I heard the boy screamin' and throwing 'imself about. An' I knew thet Luke might need my help, so I ducked an' went past her."

Belinda stopped again, reliving the scene in the crowded bedroom of the log cabin.

"An' there he was—his pa—his pa an' a younger brother holdin' 'im down. Luke was—Luke was tryin' to give 'im somethin' to make 'im quiet. An' the blood—the blood was everywhere an' the—the mash—it was jest a *mash*, Ma, thet arm! I remember I thought, *He's dyin'. Luke will never save 'im,* an' then I remembered how Luke always says, if they still be breathin', ya *fight.* An' I looked an' he was still breathin' an' I prayed an' then I took a deep breath and started fightin' down the heaves that wanted to come. It was awful. My head went round and round an' my stomach churned and my legs went soft as jelly. But I didn't go down. For a minute I—I wished thet I could jest pass out, an' then . . ."

Belinda's face had drained white. Marty feared she might faint now.

". . . Then I made up my mind to help. Luke needed me. I could see thet. The father wouldn't be any good. 'Sides, he was too big—there wasn't room. An' he didn't know the first thing 'bout Luke's instruments. An' he looked 'most as pale as his son on the bed."

Belinda stopped again. Marty did not prompt her.

"Funny," she mused. "Once we started workin', it was all different somehow. The mass of blood and flesh no longer seemed like an arm. It was somethin' to fight against—somethin' thet was threatenin' to take a life. We had to stop it, Luke an' me. I forgot all 'bout bein' squeamish. I jest wanted to git thet job done in time to stop thet boy from dyin'. It was—it was so important, Ma. Can ya understand thet? There was death an' pain in thet room—an' only Luke an' me to fight against it."

Belinda's eyes were big with the enormity of her thoughts. They had fought against death—she and her doctor brother— and they had won. Marty wanted to cheer for the victor, but instead she began to weep softly, the tears gently rolling down the curve of her cheek.

Belinda's eyes glistened. "Ya shoulda seen 'im, Ma. Ya shoulda seen Luke. He was wonderful. He knew just what to do. An' he hurried—so careful. An' he got thet blood stopped. An' he did—he did beat death. Oh, Ma! Now I understand—I understand why Luke wanted to be a doctor. It's not the broken bones or the bad cuts or the bursted appendixes. It's not the awful things thet he sees. It's the chance to fight those things— to bring healin' an' help. Thet's what doctorin' is."

Marty took her daughter by the shoulders and looked deeply into her shining eyes. She was no longer worried about Belinda. Marty feared no emotional scars in spite of Belinda's traumatic experience. Marty saw only a reflected joy. Belinda had found a way to reach out to others who were in pain.

"An' ya want to help," Marty said softly. It was a statement, not a question.

"Oh, yes," Belinda responded breathlessly.

Marty drew the young girl into her arms. "Then help, ya shall," she said simply.

They stood for a moment and then Belinda pulled back, her eyes clouded. "But, Ma, it doesn't seem right to fight to save lives an' then—an' then they wish thet they had died."

"No," agreed Marty gently. "It doesn't seem right."

"Then we hafta do somethin' fer thet boy."

"We'll keep prayin'," said Marty. "God will show us what else to do."

"Ya shoulda seen 'im, Ma. After—after it was all over. Luke left to—to care fer the—the mess—an' he left me to watch the boy. He was so pale an' so—so—" Belinda hesitated. Marty waited. "He's good-lookin', Ma," she admitted softly, honestly.

"I noticed," said Marty with a smile.

Belinda flushed slightly. She turned back to her cookie batter on the counter. For some reason Marty knew that the sharing time had come to a close.

"We've gotta do somethin'," Belinda said again, but she was speaking more to herself now than to her mother.

Chapter 15

Sunday Dinner for the Teacher

On a cold wintry day the Brown family was due to join the Davises at the Sunday dinner table. Now that winter had arrived, the Browns no longer drove the fifteen miles to their former church but were attending the small community church close to the teacherage and schoolhouse.

Marty had already met the "divine" and "vibrant" Jackson at the Sunday services. He *was* nice looking, for a young fella, she concluded. And he was gentlemanly and proper, and he did not put on airs—in spite of the fact that all the young girls were continually fluttering around him. His two brothers seemed like nice enough youngsters, too, and Marty was quite taken with Mrs. Brown, the widowed schoolteacher.

So it was without hesitation, and a twinge of conscience for not having done so sooner, that Marty extended the dinner invitation to the Brown family. They gratefully accepted, and Marty began thinking ahead in her meal planning.

Amy Jo heard the news and coaxed, begged, pleaded and bargained unmercifully to be included. Marty could have made room at the big table for Amy Jo, but she saw no reason to encourage the silliness of the girl, so she said a loving but firm, "No, not this time." Amy Jo was quite put out. For a few days she did not even drop in to visit at the big house. Marty knew that her granddaughter—impulsive and easily peeved but essentially good-hearted—would get over her miff with time and cool off enough for them to have a sensible talk about the matter.

The Davises met the Browns after the service and offered to guide them back to the farm.

"Oh, my," said Mrs. Brown. "We have a bit of a problem. Young Jordan only wore his lighter coat. I had told him—but you know children. I should have checked before we left the house. Anyway, we must drop by the teacherage to get his warmer coat before coming out. If you just give us the directions, I'm sure we can find you with no trouble."

Marty agreed. It was not difficult to find their farm. The directions would be straightforward enough. She was about to say so when she felt a tug at her sleeve. Melissa stood there.

"Someone could ride with them," she said demurely, "and show them the way."

It sounded sensible enough to Marty.

"I'm sure there's no need," Mrs. Brown said. "We hate to make trouble—"

"Oh, it wouldn't be any trouble at all. Would it, Grandma?"

"No," responded Marty. "No trouble at all."

Without even thinking about it, Marty turned to Belinda. She was used to giving Belinda orders, and Belinda was totally familiar with the country roads, so it was the most natural thing for her to send the young girl when there was an errand to be run.

"Jest grab yer coat an' go along with the Browns," she said. "They need to drop by the teacherage fer a moment."

To Marty's surprise, Belinda hesitated. It was not like Belinda to resist an order.

Marty looked at her quizzically. "Yer coat?" she prompted.

Then Marty's eyes followed Belinda's to the downcast face of Melissa, and she knew that Belinda's hesitation had something to do with the other girl.

"I jest thought thet—thet maybe I should go with you an' Pa," Belinda said carefully, "to help git dinner on an' all. Melissa will go with the Browns. Won't you, Melissa?"

Melissa's face brightened. Marty nodded in agreement. She was still puzzling the strange behavior of the two girls when she saw Melissa reach out and give Belinda a quick hug, then wrap her coat tightly about her in preparation for the trip with the Browns.

Strange creatures—girls, thought Marty and reached for her own heavy coat on the peg.

"So what was thet all 'bout?" she whispered to her daughter after the others were out of hearing.

"Oh, nothin'," said Belinda with a shrug of her slim shoulders. "Melissa likes Jackson, thet's all."

"Oh," said Marty, the truth finally dawning. Then she added, "Thought thet you like Jackson, too."

"Not the way thet Melissa does," said Belinda.

"I see," said Marty.

They left the church just as the Brown's sleigh was leaving the yard. Marty could not help but smile to herself. *Melissa must feel a mite disappointed,* she noted. The young Jackson sat in the front driving the gray. His mother shared the seat with him, and tucked in the back along with the two younger boys was Melissa. Marty was quite sure that it hadn't all worked out according to Melissa's desires.

They had been home only long enough to get the food ready to serve when their dog announced the arrival of the guests. Clark went out to lead the team to the barn and Marty went to the door to welcome the Browns. Belinda stayed where she was, busy in the kitchen.

Melissa showed them in, careful not to precede Mrs. Brown but not too concerned about the two young boys. She was busy casting sidelong glances at Jackson. He seemed to take it all in stride.

Jordan spotted Clare's David and was momentarily sidetracked. The two had become friends at school and could not understand why they should be denied the opportunity of spending some time playing together right away. Mrs. Brown had to intervene and urge Jordan on to the house.

Mrs. Brown was a delightful guest. She complimented Marty on her home, exclaimed over the delicious odors from the kitchen, said nice things to Belinda, who fussed to make the table look special, and thanked Melissa again for her kind escort. It all seemed sincere and natural and Marty found herself liking the new woman even more.

Marty, with Belinda's help, soon had the food on the table and began to seat her guests. Without giving too much thought to the arrangements, she put Mrs. Brown between the two younger boys to her right and Jackson down beside Clark so they could share some man-talk. She motioned for Belinda to sit next to him and Melissa beside her. Without hesitation Belinda suggested, "I think thet Melissa should sit in the middle. It's easier fer me to wait on the table iffen I sit on the end."

Melissa quickly took the middle chair before someone changed the arrangement. Jackson held the chair for her to be seated while Melissa flashed him the most brilliant smile. Marty only nodded dumbly.

They all took their places and Clark led in the table grace. The meal was a success in every way. The food was good and the Brown family was easy to talk to. Even the children had manners and a sense of decorum rarely seen in ones so young. Even young Jordan only whispered twice to his mother to be allowed to return to David.

Marty found herself wondering about the deceased Mr. Brown. How had he died? And when had the death taken place? She felt a deep sympathy for the young widow. *It must be hard to raise a family—especially boys—alone.* Marty felt cold at the very thought. She didn't know what she'd ever do without Clark.

"Is the teacherage meetin' yer needs?" Clark was asking the woman. As chairman of the school board, it was up to him to find out.

"It's fine," said Mrs. Brown. "A bit crowded for the four of us, but fine. I guess we had a few more things than we really needed, but I just couldn't part with them—just yet."

She did not explain, but Marty felt she really understood.

"Ya lived right in town before?" Marty asked.

"Yes. My husband worked in the bank in Chester."

Marty pictured a big frame or brick house with delicate curtains covering the windows and flowers blooming along a neat boardwalk up to a white front door . . .

"It must be quite an adjustment fer ya," she said, compassion in her voice.

"Yes," admitted Mrs. Brown, "Yes, it is."

"Had you taught before?" asked Clark.

"I was a schoolteacher when I came to Chester. That's where I met Carl—Mr. Brown. I taught for two years before we married—and a bit when the other teacher was down with pneumonia one winter. But Carl—Mr. Brown—wanted me to be at home. And then Jackson arrived, and I was happy to forget about school teaching. I likely would never have taken it up again if—"

But Mrs. Brown stopped and changed direction.

"I was so glad when I heard of the opening here. It was truly an answer to prayer—for all of us. We are so thankful for the opportunity." She turned to Clark, the chairman of the board who had hired her. "I do hope that I will live up to your expectations, Mr. Davis. If ever you question my—"

"We are pleased with your work," Clark was quick to inform her. "Very pleased."

Mrs. Brown still did not seem to relax.

Clark went on, "Now, no more talk of school," he said kindly. "Today you are not the schoolteacher—an' I am not the chairman of the board. We are neighbors—neighbors an' fellow members of the church. Let's fergit school an' jest have us a good neighborly visit."

Mrs. Brown smiled warmly. "I'd like that," she said simply.

So the visiting turned to other matters. The three Brown youngsters were included. Clark knew how to make each one feel welcome at his table.

After dinner Belinda and Melissa volunteered to do the dishes. Jordan—anticipation brightening his face—and Payne were allowed to run out to join Dan and David, who were towing their sleds toward the banks of the nearby creek. Marty led Mrs. Brown into the family living room to look at some new quilt patterns. That left Clark and Jackson. Clark suggested checkers and was answered by an enthusiastic grin.

Belinda could tell that Melissa was hurrying her through the dishes. She didn't have to ask why. Though Melissa had stopped giggling and tittering over Jackson, Belinda knew she still had a special interest in the boy. She gave him coy little smiles and watched for opportunities to be around him. Marty, who now had also noticed this new approach, wasn't sure she enjoyed this stage of interest one bit more than the earlier one.

"I think Jackson likes me," Melissa whispered confidentially to Belinda as the girls worked at the dishes.

Belinda did not respond.

"Have you seen the way he looks at me?" asked Melissa.

"How?" asked Belinda. She had noticed no difference in the way Jackson looked at Melissa or anyone else, but she didn't dare say so. Melissa seemed just a tad annoyed by the question. She had been hoping Belinda would simply say, "Yes."

"Well—well—like he likes me," she finished lamely.

"Maybe so," said Belinda without mercy. "Can't say I'd noticed anything particular."

Melissa changed her tack. "And we had such a good ride over here together," she continued. Belinda wanted to smile. She had seen with her own eyes how they had ridden over.

Suddenly Belinda felt sorry for Melissa. Melissa really did like Jackson. Belinda liked Jackson, too, but she understood there was some difference in the way the two of them felt about the boy. Well, she wouldn't stand in Melissa's way. She loved Melissa. She had no desire to hurt her. After all, Melissa was a very generous person. She shared her books, she shared her wardrobe, she shared her friendship. It was asking too much to expect her to share her first love as well. So Belinda held her tongue and smiled at Melissa in hopes that it would give her encouragement.

When the last of the dishes had been returned to the cupboards, Melissa removed her apron, rubbed a bit of sweet cream into her hands and went to join the others in the living room. The checker game had just ended in a draw. Clark had won one match and Jackson another, but the third had been a stalemate. Clark was surprised at the young man's ability.

"Yer good, boy," Clark congratulated him as they pushed back the board and rose to their feet.

"Pa an' I used to play a lot," Jackson explained.

"Bet ya miss 'im."

The boy's eyes shadowed. "Yeah," he said, looking down at the toes of his shiny boots. "Yeah, I sure do."

Melissa's voice cut in. She wanted to be sure to have her say before they started another game. "Care to see where the boys are sledding?" she asked Jackson.

"Sure," he replied.

"I'll get your coat," said Melissa.

She was soon back, wearing her own coat and carrying Jackson's over her arm. Then she led the way back through the kitchen.

Belinda was still there. She had not yet removed her apron but was busy polishing the big black stove with a scrap of newspaper. Jackson stopped beside her.

"We're goin' out to see where the boys are sleddin'. Want to come?"

Belinda looked from Jackson to Melissa.

"I'm not quite done," she said simply. "You go on—"

"We'll wait," said Jackson. "Got lots of time. What you gotta do yet? Let me help." And so saying Jackson took the paper from Belinda and began to vigorously rub the iron surface. Belinda cast Melissa a helpless look over his bent shoulders.

"Really, I—I was goin' to—" began Belinda but she couldn't think of one honest excuse that she could offer.

Belinda lifted a lid and tossed the paper into the firebox. She reached for a few sticks of wood to replenish the fire. They would want coffee or tea later, but already the cake was sitting in the pantry. There was really nothing else that needed doing. She had no more excuses.

She smiled at Jackson. "Nothin'—I guess," she answered honestly.

"Then get out of that apron and grab your coat," instructed Jackson and he reached to give the bow a playful tug.

Belinda moved away toward the hook on the wall, apparently to hang up her apron, but it was really to get out of the reach of the boy.

It was Jackson who lifted her heavy coat from the coat hook on the back porch and held it for her. She shrugged it quickly onto her shoulders, avoiding any further help from him, and the three of them went out into the brightness of the winter's sunshine, squinting against the sun on snow.

From the creek came the shouts of young boys and the barking of the two farm dogs. The snow crunched and crackled under foot and even though frost hung thick in the air, the wind was not blowing and the day felt almost mild.

Belinda breathed deeply. She loved the crisp feel of winter. As long as one had a warm meal and a warm coat . . . For some reason, the face of the young boy who had lost his arm suddenly appeared before Belinda. She knew instinctively that he would not be dressed for the sharpness of the winter weather. Her eyes clouded. He had so many needs, that boy. She didn't even know his name. But Belinda ached to help him. She had been praying, just as her ma had suggested, but so far God hadn't seemed to give her any answers. She sighed deeply without meaning to. Jackson immediately turned to her.

"Something wrong?" he asked, concern warming his voice.

Belinda jerked her thoughts back to the present. She felt her cheeks coloring. Surely he couldn't read her thoughts?

"No—no-o. Nothin'. I like the winter, thet's all. I mean, it's so—"

"Me, too," Melissa the chatterbox broke in. She had no intentions of being left out. "It's so clean and fresh and bright. So bright! I think that it's even brighter than the West," she rattled on. "The sun seems so—so—intense here—or something. Oh, it's intense out West, too. Intense and bright and it shines most all the time, but here, there seems to be something different somehow."

Jackson glanced back at Melissa.

"Do you like the winter, Jackson?" Melissa pressed.

"Guess so," he said laughing slightly. "Never thought much about it. Guess I just like summer a bit more."

"Oh, me too," gushed Melissa. "I love the summer and the flowers and the birds! Out West we have wild flowers that grow all over on the hills. I used to go out and pick handfuls and handfuls of them in the spring," she said.

" 'Fraid I don't pick too many flowers," Jackson laughed again.

Melissa gave him a teasing smile. "Wouldn't be expecting you to be out picking flowers," she said. "It's not the kind of thing that a man does."

Jackson flushed a bit. He hadn't missed the term "man." But Belinda found herself wondering why Melissa had said that. Why, Clark, her pa, picked flowers all the time. He was always bringing in a handful of one kind or another. *And Ma always looks at him kinda special like,* she noted, *when he gives 'em to her.* Her brothers brought flowers to Ma too. She had seen them herself. Whatever was wrong with a man picking flowers if he wanted to?

Belinda was still sorting it out when Jackson unexpectedly asked her, "Warm enough?"

"Fine. Jest fine," she was quick to respond.

They reached the creek and stood watching the shrieking, sliding, tumbling boys as they frolicked on their favorite sliding bank. Jackson stood grinning. "It looks like fun," he commented.

Belinda smiled in reply. "It is," she said. "I've spent jest hours out there."

"You have?"

She nodded.

"Never had a sled," said Jackson. "There wasn't any place to use one in town."

"Oh, you've missed a lot of fun," responded Belinda. "There's nothin' quite like thet fast 'whis-sh' as you come down the hill. 'Course our hill isn't very big, but—it—it's fun."

"Shall we try it?" asked Jackson enthusiastically.

Belinda looked down at her skirts. She knew that tumbling in a snowbank was often a part of sledding.

"I'm hardly dressed for it," she replied, laughing, but Jackson persisted.

"We'd be careful. I'd sit in the front. All you'd need to do would be to hang on."

"I'll go," said Melissa.

Both Jackson and Belinda turned to look at her. Her cheeks were flushed and her eyes bright with challenge.

"I'll go with you. I'm not afraid," she insisted.

Without comment Jackson turned his attention back to Belinda. His eyes seemed to ask her if she had changed her mind.

"That's a great idea," Belinda was quick to agree. "Take Melissa. This is her first winter here. She's never slid the hill before, either." Belinda did not add that she thought that Melissa was foolish to be considering it now in her Sunday skirt.

Dan shared his sleigh and Jackson settled in the front, holding fast onto the rope that worked the steering bar. Melissa climbed on behind him and without hesitation quickly wrapped her arms around him to hang on for dear life. Belinda, watching, wondered if she hung on a bit tighter than was really needed, but of course she made no comment. The sled did go "whis-sh." Jackson, laughing and shouting, was thrilled with the ride. He asked for another. They went down again, Melissa hanging on just as firmly. Jackson "whooped" as the sled sped down the short hill.

He called up to Belinda, "It's great! How about trying it with me? See, we didn't spill. It's a snap!"

Belinda just laughed and shook her head.

"One more, just one more. Please?" Melissa asked Dan with exaggerated enthusiasm.

The next ride was not the "snap" that Jackson had expected. Midway down the hill the sled seemed to develop a mind of its own. It veered off the well-traveled path and hit a bank of snow. From there, matters only got worse. The sled bounced farther afield and struck a rock. Before Jackson could correct its course, the sleigh plunged into a snowdrift and skidded to a stop on its side, spilling its two passengers in a cloud of snowy dust.

The young boys at the top of the hill howled with glee, thoroughly enjoying the entertaining sight. Belinda stared openmouthed, fearful that one of the two might be hurt in the spill, but when they both climbed, a trifle unsteadily, to their feet, she relaxed. Melissa did look a bit the worse for wear. Her skirt, hanging crazily because of a huge tear at the waist, was covered with snow and her coat, also snow-covered, was hanging open as though it was missing all its buttons. Jackson brushed the snow from his coat, grinning sheepishly.

"Whoops!" he called up the hill to Belinda. "Guess it's not without calamity after all."

Belinda laughed, glad that no one had been hurt.

Jackson helped Melissa brush the snow off her coat, and asked her if she was all right. She assured him rather stiffly that she was fine, in the meantime embarrassed at the state of her clothes. He righted the sled and started up the bank.

"Now will you ride with me?" he called laughingly to Belinda as he slowly made his way back up the hill, dragging the wayward sled with him.

"No, sir. I still will not," answered Belinda cheerfully.

Melissa, after rummaging around in the snow to locate her missing buttons, left quickly for the house to change her clothes and get herself back in order.

Jackson handed the sled back to Dan and thanked him warmly for the ride. "I'd like to try it again some time," he informed the boy and Dan grinned, happy to have made an impression on an older fellow.

Belinda's eyes followed Melissa. "I'd better git in," she said to Jackson. "Mama might need me. She'll want to serve coffee soon."

He moved to fall into step beside her but she waved him away.

"Why don't ya stay out an' have another ride or two? Dan won't mind. We'll call ya as soon as lunch is ready."

"You sure?" asked Jackson, eyeing the hill again.

"I'm sure. You might not git another chance. Spring can come pretty early in these parts."

"Before Christmas?"

"Ya never know."

He grinned. "Think I will," he said. "Thanks."

Belinda nodded and hurried off toward the house. She needed to check on Melissa. She prayed that there had been damage only to Melissa's clothes and not to her pride.

Belinda found Melissa in her room. She had removed the torn dress but she had not put on another. Instead she lay on her bed, her face buried in her hands, her shoulders shaking with sobs.

"Melissa," cried Belinda in alarm. "Were you hurt?"

Melissa looked up with disgust, her eyes swollen from crying.

"As though you care," she challenged.

Belinda was taken aback. She crossed to the bed, sat down and laid a hand on the girl's arm.

"Ya know I care," she insisted. "Are you sure you're all right?"

Melissa drew herself up and slipped off the bed. "Don't get your hopes up," she threw at Belinda, "I don't need a nurse."

Belinda was completely baffled by the whole exchange. She decided to change the subject.

"We're gonna have coffee soon. I'm jest goin' to git it on now."

"Well, I won't be there," spat out Melissa.

"You *are* hurt. Where?"

"I'm not hurt," Melissa insisted impatiently. "I'm just not coming down, that's all."

"But what—what will I tell folks? They'll all wonder—"

"Tell them anything you want to. I don't care," and Melissa tossed her hair back with an angry move and reached for her bathrobe.

Belinda stood to go. She wasn't sure what to do. She didn't know what was wrong. She still wondered if Melissa really had been hurt and was refusing to say so. She wished Luke would miraculously arrive.

"Is there anythin' thet I can do?" she asked, genuinely sympathetic.

Melissa gave her an angry look. "It would seem that you have already done enough, don't you think?" she flung at her.

Belinda frowned. What in the world had she done to make the girl so angry?

"What do ya mean?" she asked.

" 'What do ya mean'?" Melissa mimicked. "You know exactly what I mean. You've been butting in on me and Jackson all day. You know he likes me—and you know I like him—yet you just keep on butting in—spoiling everything!"

The long speech ended in uncontrollable tears. Belinda stood staring at her overwrought and unreasonable niece. *Where did Melissa get such an idea?* was her frantic thought.

She had purposely tried to stay out of the way. And she had bent over backwards to—But Melissa was not going to listen to reason.

Belinda heard her mother calling her. She slipped from the room without further comment, but her heart was heavy as she went back down the stairs to help in the kitchen.

Not much had been said while their guests were still there, but as soon as the Browns had left, Marty wanted an explanation concerning Melissa. There was little Belinda could tell her. She hated to "tell on" Melissa, but there was no way that she would lie to her mother. So she finally just told the truth as simply as she knew how.

Marty's eyes widened as they sought Clark's above Belinda's head.

"Yer sure?" she asked. "Yer sure she thinks thet ya were cuttin' in?"

Belinda nodded.

"An' she's jealous?"

Again Belinda nodded.

"I find thet hard to believe," stated Marty. "Surely she'll see things different in the mornin'."

But Melissa did not see things differently in the morning. She did her chores and prepared for school, but she was not her usually cheery, chattering self. And she carefully avoided any conversation with Belinda.

"Oh, dear Lord," prayed Marty lifting her eyes heavenward. "We've got us one of them triangles. What do we do now?"

Chapter 16

Pride

At Christmastime, neighbors tried to share food baskets with the Simpson family, but each one was turned away at the door. They all wanted to help, but they did not know what to try next. The minister also was turned away again when he tried to visit—it seemed that the family wanted no comfort or aid from God, either. Marty's heart ached over their destitute and pride-filled condition, while Clark muttered under his breath. It was sheer foolishness, that's what it was.

The debt for the firewood and groceries still had not been paid. Clark would have gladly considered it a gift, but he knew that the family would not. Until they felt they had paid the debt, Clark knew that he would not be able to help them further.

He decided to drop in on them. At first he planned to take Marty with him. Then he reasoned that it might look too much like a neighborly call, so they talked it over and Clark decided to go alone. He wanted it to be as businesslike as possible.

All the way over Clark tried to think of jobs that needed doing. He really could think of none. Clark reflected on the plans he and Marty had made previously. It wouldn't be easy for Marty. In fact, it wouldn't be easy for either of them, and he feared they both might feel a bit guilty of dishonesty in the whole affair. It was hard to tell the Simpsons that they needed help when in truth they did not.

Marty had been able to come up with a short list of things she could have Mrs. Simpson sew for her. Then there was a quilt that was promised to Nandry's Mary for her birthday. Marty supposed she could use some help in the quilting, though she enjoyed it and usually did her quilting alone.

Still, those jobs wouldn't take much time.

So they had tried to figure out something else for the woman to do, but each time they came back again to the sewing.

"How much in yard goods do ya have on hand?" Clark had asked Marty.

"Four or five pieces, I reckon," she had replied.

"Well, can't ya find some way to make use of 'em?"

"I had purposes in mind fer all of 'em," Marty had told him, "but I just don't need 'em yet. One was to be a dress fer Belinda, but it's too old a print fer her yet—well, at the rate she's maturin', maybe not that long—" she quipped. "And one is fer aprons fer Kate, and one is fer the backin' fer Amy Jo's quilt when she finishes school an' another fer—"

"I'll go to town," Clark had said. "I'll go to town an' buy some material with no purpose at all."

"Then what'll I have 'er do with it?" Marty had protested.

"I dunno. We'll think of somethin'—how 'bout a new dress fer you?" Clark said with a smile and a hug.

"Oh, Clark, I don't need somethin' new," Marty protested.

"Maybe not, but maybe Mrs. Simpson does," was his gentle rejoinder, and she nodded her head in agreement.

And so he had gone to town and had come home with six lengths of yard goods. He had chosen some pretty pieces—or the clerk had, Marty wasn't sure which—but she still hadn't figured out what to do with all of them. And who knew if the woman could even sew? She might just spoil the pieces.

When Marty had mentioned that fact to Clark, he just shrugged his shoulders. "Throw 'em in the rag bag then," he had stated.

What a terrible waste! thought Marty. It would have been so much more simple, so much less costly, if the family had just allowed the neighbors to outright help them.

Clark reviewed all of this in his mind as he coaxed the team forward. He was busy trying to properly choose his words. What could he say that would be totally truthful and would not offend them?

Clark tied the team and walked toward the door. His artificial limb was making his leg ache again. Or maybe it was just the cold—Clark didn't know for sure. All he knew was that shivers of pain were shooting from the stump clear up to his hip.

He rapped loudly on the door and Mr. Simpson answered. He looked about to launch into his usual "we-don't-take-charity" speech, so Clark began quickly, "Came to see 'bout clearin' thet debt fer the wood and food stuff."

The door opened a bit wider and the man stepped back.

The woman was busy at the stove. By the smell that filled the room, Clark decided she was making stew for supper. It smelled good. Clark sniffed appreciatively and gave her a smile and a nod.

Clark looked around for the boys but only the smaller one was present, listlessly playing cat's cradle with a piece of twine in a corner of the room.

The man motioned toward a chair, though he did not ask Clark to be seated nor did he invite him to remove his coat.

Clark sat down and unbuttoned the coat to hang loosely.

"I'm listenin'," said the man in a growl.

"Well, I figured as how ya might be anxious to git the weight of this here debt offa yer shoulders," Clark began. "I have a few jobs 'round the place thet I could put ya to doin' as soon as ya can spare the time."

"Time, I got lots of," the man replied without a smile.

Clark nodded.

"How many days?" the man asked.

"Not sure. Two—maybe three."

"Thet won't pay off our debt," the man stated sullenly.

"It'll pay off the vegetables," responded Clark. "Yer gittin' out green logs next spring in exchange fer the firewood."

Mr. Simpson nodded. Maybe it would cover the vegetables. He seemed to feel that the matter was closed.

"My wife has some sewin' that—that—she could use some

help on. Wondered iffen yer wife might be interested."

"Thought ya said the work I did would pay it off," the man answered irritably.

"So it will," Clark said without ruffling. "The sewin'—thet would be fer a wage."

Clark saw the woman at the stove jerk her head upward. He pretended not to notice.

"Yer wife can't sew?" asked the big man with a hint of sarcasm.

"She can sew first rate," Clark was quick to defend Marty. "No harm in a woman gittin' a bit of help with her chores now an' then."

The man mumbled something under his breath.

"So what ya offerin' to swap?" asked Simpson.

"Thought we might pay in cash," said Clark. "We could swap but we don't know iffen there's anythin' thet we got thet ya might be needin'. But good help, now—thet's hard to come by."

His eyes brightened some. He turned slightly to the woman.

"Ya wanna do thet, Ma?" he asked her.

Clark was thankful that he had asked, not ordered. He did have good qualities in him under all that gruffness.

The woman responded with a nod of agreement.

"What ya payin'?" asked Simpson.

"What'd'ya think is fair wage?" Clark countered.

"Ten cents an hour," said the man.

Clark appeared to be thinking deeply.

"Was thinkin' on fifteen," he informed the man. "Don't wanna git the reputation of not bein' willin' to pay a fair wage."

"Fifteen," agreed Mr. Simpson and the two men shook on it.

"I'd best be gittin' on home then," said Clark, rising to his feet. "It gits dark powerful early these days, an' I got me chores to do."

"We'll be over first thing in the mornin'," the man told him.

"Then I guess I'd best tell ya where to find us," Clark said with a hint of a smile. It did not bring a responding smile to the face of the man. Clark pulled a stub of pencil and a piece of paper from his pocket and busied himself drawing a simple map. He was bending over the table when he heard the door creak open and close again. Out of the corner of his eye, he saw movement, but he purposely did not look up from drawing.

The older boy had come home. Clark finished his crude map and his bit of explanation before he lifted his head.

The boy still had not moved from the door nor removed his skimpy coat. The one sleeve had been tied into a clumsy knot to keep out the cold. A gun was tucked under his good arm, and in his hand he carried a couple of rabbits and a grouse. Clark nodded a greeting and eyed him evenly.

"Ya must be a good shot," he acknowledged with warmth.

The boy nodded in return, tossed the game into the corner and hung the gun on the wall pegs.

"Do ya always have thet kind of luck?" Clark asked with a grin.

"Mostly," said the boy simply and slipped the coat off his shoulders.

Clark moved toward the door. He buttoned his coat against the cold and reached to reclaim his hat from where he had dropped it by the chair. He could feel the boy's eyes on him.

Clark looked at him, wondering what was going on in his mind.

He had almost reached the door when the boy spoke.

"Thought ya claimed to have ya only one good leg," he said with a bit of venom.

Clark looked down at his legs. They both looked good all-right. His trouser legs fell full and nearly to his boot tops. Only if one looked closely would he have seen that the boots did not match.

"No," said Clark with a smile. "Me, I got two good legs. Now, one I borrowed, I needta admit, but I got me two."

He reached down and hiked the pantleg quickly upward, exposing the wooden leg with its straps and braces.

He saw the woman wince before she turned quickly away and the younger son, who had sat quietly in the corner of the room, suddenly leaned forward, his eyes big with wonder.

"It works 'most as good as my old one did," Clark went on. "Oh, not quite. But Luke, my doctor son, he insisted thet I git me one. I fought it at first, but now I don't know what I'd do without it. Frees my hands up"—Clark extended his hat in both his hands—"an' makes things a heap easier fer me."

The one-armed boy said nothing.

Clark turned back to the man as he slipped his hat back on. "Well, we'll see ya in the mornin' then," he said and nodded his goodbye.

He let himself out the door, closed it firmly behind him and limped his way to his restless team. He wasn't sure if he had made any headway or not.

Chapter 17

Hired Help

Clark and Marty were still at the table the next morning, enjoying a second cup of coffee after the hurry-scurry of getting the youngsters off to school, when Marty heard the dog bark. She leaned forward and lifted back the curtain. To her surprise two people were walking up their lane.

"Now, who you s'pose be out walkin' at this hour?"

Clark joined her at the window.

"Must be our hired help," he exclaimed. "Never thought 'bout 'em not havin' 'em a team or wagon."

Marty frowned. "Ya mean the Simpsons?"

"Thet's them."

"Oh, dear, Clark," Marty cried as she jumped up from the table, one hand slipping up to smooth her hair. "I sure don't know how I'm gonna use me hired help! Never had such help in my whole life. Why, I don't even know how to go about givin' orders."

Clark laughed. "Jest pretend it's one of your young'uns," he told her. "Ya never had ya problems tellin' 'em what to do."

"Well, she'll hardly seem like a young'un. An' she might resent the tellin', too. Who knows jest what we got ourselves into?"

"Do ya have ya a paper all set out?" asked Clark.

"A paper?"

"Yer gonna have to keep track of the hours. She gits paid by the hour, ya know."

"No," said Marty, shaking her head, "I don't have me a paper."

Clark was the one to go to the door. "Come on in," he invited, and held the door wide for them.

They came slowly in, looking carefully about them. Marty had never been so conscious of her own well-being and cozy, comfortable surroundings as she was at that moment. Why had God blessed her with so much when some had so little?

"Jest hang yer coats there by the door," Clark was saying.

Marty went to get two cups from the cupboard. She wondered if they had even had breakfast but she didn't dare ask.

"We was jest having us another cup of coffee before settin' to work," Clark informed them. "Won't ya sit yerselves down an' join us?"

Marty moved the plates left behind by Melissa and Belinda and wiped the table for the guests, er, hired help. Clark lifted the family Bible from the table back to its shelf in the corner.

"Yer nice an' early," Clark commented. "I like a man to be early. We'll git us a good start."

Marty poured the coffee and Clark passed the cream and sugar. The two helped themselves liberally.

"Ya got any more of those cinnamon rolls?" Clark asked Marty. "Thinkin' thet I might like one with my coffee here."

Clark had just finished a hearty breakfast, but Marty understood and hastened to the pantry to bring out half a dozen of the rolls. She placed them on the table and had hardly let go of the plate when Clark reached for one. Marty was surprised when he helped himself even before offering one to the Simpsons.

"Jest help yerself iffen ya care to," Clark said around a bite of roll.

Then it dawned on Marty why he had done that. The rolls were for the benefit of the Simpsons, both Clark and Marty knew that. But Clark did not want them to catch on to that fact and was afraid they would not help themselves if they were the only ones at the table eating. So when Marty sat back down, she too helped herself to a roll, though she didn't know how in the world she would be able to get it down.

They really didn't visit over their rolls and coffee. The new neighbors had very little to say. They seemed restless and anxious to get started, and Marty guessed that at fifteen cents an hour they wanted to waste no time.

"Best we git ourselves goin'," she finally said. "Do ya mind givin' me a hand with the dishes so thet we have the table to work on fer the cuttin'?"

Then Marty got out a piece of paper and wrote Thursday across the top. Then she looked at the time, sure to read it to the minute, for the lady's eyes were on the clock, too.

"It's seven forty-six," said Marty. "We'll start countin' the time right now." Marty cast a glance toward the big stove. "My lands," she said. "We still didn't drain thet coffeepot, an' I do hate bein' wasteful. Could ya drink another cup?"

And without waiting for an answer she rose to get the coffee and refilled the cups.

"It won't be wasted time," she informed the woman. "I'll use it to explain to ya what we'll be doin'. "

They drank their coffee slowly. Now and then Clark or Marty gave some explanation about what the two would be expected to do. They seemed to be satisfied with this procedure.

At length Marty felt she could stall no longer. Clark sensed it and rose from the table and led the way out of the kitchen. The man reached for his coat but Clark stopped him.

"Won't be needin' thet jest now," he said. "First job is more fruit shelves down in the cellar. It stays shirt-sleeve warm down there."

The man left his coat, cast a glance at his wife and followed Clark.

Marty scurried about her kitchen, her thoughts running ahead of her. They would need to get the dishes out of the way. The kitchen floor should be swept. She planned to mix up a batch of fresh bread. Could the woman be trusted to do the cutting on her own? Oh, well. If worst came to worst, she could do as Clark had said and throw the whole mess into the ragbag.

The woman spied the dishpan on the peg beside the stove and went to get it.

"The water's there in the reservoir," and Marty nodded toward the end of the stove.

The woman could not help but show her pleasure at the convenience. She lifted out dipper after dipper of the hot water until she had all she needed in the dishpan.

Marty let her begin washing up the dishes. *Pretend she's one of the young'uns,* she kept saying to herself as she dried them and put them away. She hoped that the pretending would work.

They finished the dishes with hardly a comment. *Well, she sure won't be hard to listen to,* Marty said to herself with a hint of a smile playing about her lips. *Never seen such a quiet one.*

Then Marty realized she hadn't been doing much talking either. Well, she'd change that.

"Hear you've lived in the West," Marty commented warmly.

The woman nodded her head.

"How long were ya out there?" asked Marty.

" 'Bout twelve years," said Mrs. Simpson.

"Did ya like it?"

She looked at Marty. Now the questions were getting personal. She shut her lips tightly and shrugged her shoulders. Marty got the message. She must be careful not to pry.

Marty left her to wipe the table and went for the broom. When she had her pile of kitchen woodchips and breakfast crumbs gathered, she swept them into the dustpan and pulled back the lid of the stove to dump them in. The stove needed more wood and Marty reached for a few more sticks.

"You let it burn between meals?" Mrs. Simpson asked in disbelief.

Marty nodded. "Wood be one thing we've plenty of," she said, "an' this kitchen stove be the main source of heat fer the house."

The woman said nothing.

"I be needin' to mix up my batch of bread," Marty went on. "I'll jest git it outta the way before we start our sewin'."

Mrs. Simpson nodded.

There was silence in the kitchen for many minutes as both women attended to their respective chores. Down in the cellar the sound of a hammer began to beat out a rhythmic pattern. The man was at work.

The stove was wiped up, the dishwater was discarded and the pan hung back on its peg.

"What do you want me to do next, Missus Davis?" the woman asked.

"Jest call me Marty," Marty responded. "I'm more used to thet." Then she hurried on, "We'll start on some sewin' jest as soon as I finish this kneadin'. 'Most done now."

"And what do I do while I'm waitin'?" asked Mrs. Simpson.

Marty wanted to say, "Just sit ya down," but she didn't dare. She cast her eyes about her kitchen, looking for some job—any job. It was tough having hired help.

"The back porch could be swept," she said at last.

The woman took the broom and dustpan and moved to the back porch. Marty hoped it was not too cold. The back porch, though enclosed, did not get the heat of the rest of the house.

Marty finished her bread mixing just as the woman returned with the broom.

"I'll git the material," Marty announced and went for the yard goods. She decided to bring only two pieces at a time. She didn't want it to look like she was flaunting their wealth. She had noticed the tattered and mended garment that the woman was wearing. It had recently been washed, but there was nothing to disguise the fact that it was almost worn through in the spots where it had not already been mended.

"This is the one thet I want to start on," said Marty, "an' here is the pattern. Now, the machine is right in the family livin' room there. An' the scissors and thread are in thet basket beside it."

Marty didn't know what to do next. She didn't want to appear like she was hanging around to see if the woman knew what she was doing. Yet she really had nothing else to take her immediate attention. She could churn some butter, but there was such a tiny dab of cream to be churned—she had just done the churning the day before. She could do some baking—but she didn't need anything baked at present. She wanted to take up the braided rug she had been working on and had intended to fill her day with, but it seemed foolish and awkward for her to be doing hand sewing while her hired help used the machine. She could—

Marty stopped.

"I'll be upstairs," she told the woman. "Iffen ya need anything, jest call," and she turned to the steps that led her up to her bedroom.

Marty had already made her bed and tidied her room for the day. She wandered aimlessly around for a few minutes, fluffing pillows and arranging curtains; then she sat down on the side of her bed. It was cool upstairs.

This is silly, she told herself. *Completely silly. Here I am, a grown woman, 'most a prisoner in my own home.* Her thoughts fluttered back and forth. *How am I ever gonna make it through the next few days? How many days is Clark hirin' 'em, anyway? An' what am I gonna do with my time?*

Marty shivered. It was too cold to stay upstairs for long. She grabbed a warm shawl from the chair beside her dresser and wrapped it tightly about her shoulders.

You could pray, a little voice from somewhere within her said. *Remember how you are always saying that you wish that you had more praying time?*

Marty flushed, even though there was no one in the room with her—no one visible, that is.

She knelt beside her bed. She began slowly, willing herself to concentrate on the needs of family and friends. Before long she found herself truly communicating with God—talking to Him from her heart and hearing His responses the same way. It was a time of refreshment and uplift for Marty.

Every one of her family members was remembered in a special way. She remembered her far-off daughters, her sons-in-law, and each of their children. She included Nandry and Josh and each of their children, she prayed for Clare and Kate and for Amy Jo that her life and her artistic talents would be used for God's glory. She remembered each of the three boys. She asked God to be with Arnie and Anne and their boys. She prayed for Luke in his doctoring and for Abbie and the children as they were so often alone.

Marty prayed especially for Belinda, that God would direct her in her future plans and make her useful in His kingdom. She asked God for wisdom in dealing with Melissa, Missie's little girl who was so far away from home, and she asked for special wisdom and help in dealing with the little rift and misunderstanding that was straining the relationship between Belinda and Melissa. She prayed for the neighbors, she prayed for the church. She prayed for the new schoolteacher that God would comfort her in her widowhood and help her in her adjustments and in raising her three sons.

And Marty, with tears, prayed for the Simpson family. She prayed that their somewhat awkward attempts to help would turn out for good. "An' help me to think of things fer her to do," she requested. She pleaded for special help for the young boy's adjustment to the loss of his arm.

Marty earnestly prayed on. There was no need to jump up and run to care for this task or that task. And then Marty thought of her batch of bread. *Why, it must be almost covering the cupboard by now,* she thought ruefully as she sprang to her feet and flung the shawl aside to hurry down to the kitchen.

She needn't have worried. Mrs. Simpson had cared for the punching down of the dough. She was now sitting at Marty's machine, the treadle humming along smoothly as neat seams took shape beneath her skilled fingers. Marty felt like rubbing her eyes. *The woman must be a professional seamstress!* she marveled.

"My!" said Marty, "yer good at thet!"

The woman never lifted her eyes from the cloth.

"Used to work in a dress shop back East before I was married," she said simply.

"My!" said Marty again.

She watched for a few minutes more, then roused herself.

"Well, I guess I'd better start thinkin' on dinner. My, how the time has flown."

Marty saw the woman's eyes also travel to the clock on the mantle, and she could almost hear the calculations that were taking place. *Three and a half hours at fifteen cents an hour makes fifty two and a half cents.*

Marty decided to make some milk pudding. It would be ready in plenty of time to cool. She would also fry up some pork chops and potatoes. She had carrots to warm, too. Her bread would soon be ready to make into loaves. She moved about her kitchen less self-consciously and even began to hum softly to herself. It had been a long, long time since she'd had so much of her morning to spend in prayer. *Maybe hired help isn't so bad after all,* she concluded.

Chapter 18

Adjusting

Gradually Marty adjusted to having another woman sharing the work in her home. Each morning after the dishes and early morning chores were finished, Marty slipped up to her room for prayer. Though she did not always take as much time as she had that first morning, she did appreciate the extra time she was able to spend on her knees.

Gradually the new garments took shape under the skilled hands of the hired seamstress. Marty was excited and pleased. Surely there was need for sewing skills in their little town. Marty had often overheard the local women talk about how difficult it was to find someone to sew up yard goods in proper fashion. *Well, there'd be no complaints about this woman's sewing*, Marty felt sure of that.

Marty even brought out the pieces of material she had tucked away for future use and had Mrs. Simpson sew them up as well. *No point in harborin' them*, she decided. Each of the girls could do with a new dress for Sundays.

Mr. Simpson had long since finished his assigned tasks and returned to felling trees in the woods near their home, so his wife walked the distance to the Davises alone. But still the two women did not really visit, though they shared the same house for a time each day.

Marty shivered each time she saw her neighbor trudging up their lane in the chill of the early morning, or begin the trek back home at the end of the day. But she really could think of nothing to do about it. *Iffen she jest wasn't so proud*, Marty kept saying to herself. *Iffen she jest wasn't so proud we could help her more.*

But the woman *was* proud—just like her husband, and Marty did not dare to suggest anything that might smack of charity.

Marty gathered up all of the sewing she could find and let the woman do it for her. Then she went to Kate's and carried back all the mending and stitching that Kate could gather together—quite a bundle because of their three active boys. They then finished off the rugs that Marty had prepared for her winter's sewing projects and went on to the quilting. Even in that close proximity, they mostly worked in silence—Marty had quickly run out of one-sided conversation topics. But, surprisingly, the quiet had not felt awkward. When the quilting too was done and Marty could think of no other sewing projects, she suggested they have one last cup of tea together while she figured the amount still owed.

It seemed strange to both of them, knowing this was their last time together. Marty had come to enjoy the silent presence in her home. She poured the tea, sliced the cake, and picked up her piece of paper with its calculations.

"The way I figger it," she said, "I still owe ya a dollar and ten cents."

"Thet's right," said the woman, surprising Marty. Marty had not been aware that the woman was also keeping a tally on the account. She was glad their figures had agreed.

Marty got out her purse and counted out the money, which the woman promptly put in a little cloth bag and tucked in the front of her dress.

"Ya know, I've been thinkin'," said Marty, treading carefully. "Ya really do lovely work, an' I know thet there are a number of women in town who've been lookin' fer a seamstress. Would ya be interested—?"

The woman did not even let Marty finish. "I have me no machine now," she said abruptly.

Marty did not let that stop her. "Ya could use my machine."

At the look on the woman's face she was quick to add, "I'd rent it to ya at a set rate per hour."

The woman relaxed some, but then said, "It's a long way to town. How'd I ever git my orders?"

"We go in every week," said Marty as offhandedly as she could. "Ain't no problem to pick ya up an' drop ya off."

"We live beyond ya," the woman reminded Marty.

"Well—not much beyond us. Wouldn't be—"

"I could walk on over to catch the ride, I reckon," the woman said.

"Fine," said Marty, trying to keep her voice matter-of-fact. "Thet would be fine."

"We're goin' in to town tomorra," continued Marty after a pause. "Why don't I jest take in a sample or two of yer work an' ask around a bit?"

"How much ya be chargin' fer the machine?" asked the woman.

"Ah—let's see. Ah, ten cents should do nicely."

"Ten cents an hour. I wouldn't be making much—but it might help some. Do you think that folks will be willin' to pay fifteen cents an hour for the sewin'?"

Marty didn't remind her that she had just finished paying her fifteen cents per hour and her own machine had been used.

"I didn't mean an hour," Marty said. "I meant ten cents a day. An', yes, I think thet yer work is well worth fifteen cents an hour. Yer good—an' yer fast. Folks should expect to pay thet much fer the work thet ya do."

The woman said nothing but her eyes shone with appreciation.

"I'll do it then," concluded Marty. "I'll see what I kin find out."

"I'd be obliged," mumbled the woman, the closest she had come to admitting that she was accepting something from another.

She rose to go.

Marty smiled warmly. "Then I guess thet this needn't be goodbye then. I mean, ya'll still be comin' over to use the machine an' all."

"If the plan works," said the woman shortly.

"Iffen it works," repeated Marty.

The woman nodded.

"I've enjoyed havin' ya here," Marty said a bit self-consciously. "It's been nice workin' with ya."

Mrs. Simpson nodded again.

"An' we'd be so happy iffen ya'd join us in worship at our church. It's not fancy like, but you an' yer family would be most welcome—"

She was cut short. Mrs. Simpson's eyes sparked as she flung a hand toward her tattered dress. "Like this?" she hissed. "Like this to your church? No, I'm not thinkin' that much of a welcome mat would be extended to the likes of people lookin' like this."

Before Marty could even respond, the woman grabbed her coat from the coat peg, and without waiting to put it on, she pushed her way out the door and was gone.

Marty stood looking after her in stunned silence. Though her eyes remained dry, her heart cried out in silent prayer. *Oh, God,* she prayed, *forgive us iffen we have unmeaningly given thet impression. Why would she think thet we wouldn't welcome her the way thet she be? I so much wanted her to know thet she was welcome into my house an' she'd be welcome into Yer house, too, but somehow I have failed Ya agin, Lord. I've failed Ya agin."*

And the tears came then.

But from somewhere within Marty came a reply. *Be patient,* the gentle voice said. *Just be patient. I have never failed you, and I am with the Simpsons, too, even when they are not aware of it.*

Marty did check for sewing work when she went into town. The first place she went was to the dry goods store. She showed the clerk behind the counter some of the work that Mrs. Simpson had done for her, explaining that the woman would be happy to do sewing for the ladies of the town. The shopkeeper was impressed and said she was sure she could find customers. Marty knew this would increase sales in yard goods, so this would be a help to both Mrs. Simpson and the shop owner.

The woman promised to put up a notice where interested

women could sign their names and indicate what kind of sewing they wished to have done. Marty was to check the list the next time she was in town.

The next Saturday, Marty was thrilled to see the list of names. It looked like her machine would be kept busy for several weeks. She picked up the yard goods and the patterns that the ladies had selected and took them home for Mrs. Simpson. Somehow she would get word to her neighbor that the arrangements had been made and that there was much sewing to be done.

Chapter 19

The Triangle

Things had not improved greatly between Belinda and Melissa. Marty kept hoping and praying that the situation would work itself out. Clark had been so sure that the simple solution to the problem was just to ignore it. It was a part of growing up, he said, and if allowed to take its course it would eventually go away. Well, this time Clark had misread the state of affairs. The problem did not go away.

Marty longed to sit the two girls down and talk some sense into them, but she really could not see that Belinda had been at fault in the matter. And Melissa might feel she was being "picked on" if Marty talked to her alone.

Marty found it hard to believe that their generous, sweet, sensitive Melissa could have such a stubborn streak. Well, Clare had said she would not be perfect.

Because of the strained relations, Melissa was spending more and more time at Kate's. But also she did love to be with Amy Jo and she enjoyed the small boys. She spent hours reading to them and coloring pictures or making cutouts. Melissa was a born teacher. She was the happiest when she was in charge.

Belinda did not seem to suffer greatly from Melissa's absence. She carried on her duties cheerfully and went out with Luke at each opportunity. Always, when she returned home, she had a full report for Clark and Marty. Marty herself was finding that she was learning a lot about medicine. *It's no wonder both Luke and Belinda find it so intriguin'*, she noted to herself.

Marty wondered if Kate might be feeling that Melissa was spending far too much time at the log house. She decided to walk over for coffee and have a chat with Kate.

She was met at the door by Dack. "Do ya want to read to me, Gramma?" he asked hopefully before Marty even had her coat off. He was restless with being shut in doors and glad to see her.

"Dack," scolded Kate, "let yer Gramma catch her breath." She turned to Marty, "He thinks thet's all people have to do since Melissa spoils 'im so."

Marty laid aside her coat and sat down at the kitchen table. Her fingers traced the pattern on the oilcloth as Kate busied herself fixing a cup of tea for each of them.

Kate handed Dack some raisins. "Here ya are," she said to the small boy. "Why don't ya go have yerself a party with the dolls?"

Dack left, excited about getting "official permission" to set Amy Jo's dolls all in a row and share his raisins with them. Later he would go down the row, eating the raisins on behalf of each doll baby.

"Is yer seamstress all done now?" asked Kate as she sat down with two cups of tea.

Marty nodded, then smiled. "An' guess what," she admitted a bit sheepishly, "After all my fussin' 'bout it, I'm actually missin' her."

Kate laughed with her.

"Yet it sure weren't her talkin' thet I miss. Never saw me such a quiet woman in all my born days."

"Thet's what ya told me before," responded Kate. "Well, there're plenty of days thet I'd sure settle me fer a bit of peace and quiet. I'll be right glad when thet boy can be off to school with the rest of 'em, I'm thinkin'."

Then she smiled knowingly. "Least, thet's what I tell myself now," she added. "I know when the time actually comes an' the house gits quiet, I might be changin' my words some."

Marty agreed. She knew what it was like to see the last one go off to school.

"How's Amy Jo doin' with her art?" Marty asked.

"Ya know, Ma, I think she really has talent. Clare an' me jest can't believe some of the work she does. An' it helps so much fer her to have all those books of Melissa's to learn from, too. Bless Melissa, she's been so good 'bout sharin'! I do hope thet we aren't hoggin' her too much. I know she's here a lot an' we love to have her, but I sometimes think thet ya must think we are pretty selfish."

"No," said Marty. "Iffen ya are enjoyin' her, I won't be begrudgin' ya." She paused. "I am a bit worried though," she said slowly.

"About Melissa?"

"Yeah."

"Somethin' wrong?"

"I dunno," said Marty. "Thet is, I don't know iffen it's worth stewin' 'bout or not. Clark says to jest leave it an' it'll go away, but it's been a fair while now an' it ain't gone away yet."

"What's thet?" asked Kate soberly.

"Well, ya know this here Jackson thing?"

"Ya mean all the girls moonin' over 'im?"

"Yeah. You'd think he was the one an' only boy on the face of the earth."

"I agree with Pa," said Kate comfortably. "They'll grow out of it in time. All girls seem to go through a silly stage—some worse'n others."

"Oh, it ain't the moonin' I worry 'bout. Least not directly. It's more'n thet. Melissa hasn't said anything?"

"Not to me, she hasn't. Maybe to Amy Jo. They seem to have 'em lots of little secrets that they share in her room and giggle or groan over. Me, I pay 'em no mind. I remember goin' through thet myself."

Marty smiled. She might have gone through it too, but it was a long time ago. "Well, it's more than that," she tried to explain. "Melissa seems to have a real crush on Jackson. An' she was sure thet he liked her too. Special like. Well, when we had the Brown family over a while back, Jackson seemed to pay more mind to Belinda than he did to Melissa."

"So-o," said Kate, beginning to understand. "How did Melissa take that?"

"Not well, I'm afraid. She accused Belinda of cuttin' in an' she's been miffed with Belinda ever since."

"I see," said Kate as she got up to pour more tea.

From the bedroom they could hear Dack scolding a doll for not waiting her turn.

"Have ya talked to Melissa?" asked Kate, setting the teapot on the back of the stove.

"No. I've been followin' Clark's advice—waitin' fer it to go away."

"An' it hasn't?"

"Well, not yet it hasn't, an' last night when they got home from school Melissa seemed angrier than ever. Didn't even say nothin'. Jest changed her clothes and headed down here. How did she seem to you when she got here?"

"I didn't notice anything different. But she an' Amy Jo went right to her room," said Kate, then asked, "Did ya learn what happened?"

"I asked Belinda. She tried to shrug it off. Said Melissa had seen Jackson give 'er a wink, in teasin'."

"How does Belinda feel about Jackson?" asked Kate.

"Well, iffen she cares for him, she sure doesn't let on," responded Marty. "But then, right now, 'bout all Belinda seems to care fer is her trips with Luke."

"She is excited 'bout thet, isn't she?" said Kate. "Me, I could never stomach the sight of blood. Amy Jo is jest like me thet way. We can't even wrap up a cut finger or pick out a sliver 'thout going all queasy. Clare has to do it."

"I don't care none for blood neither," admitted Marty, "but I'm beginnin' to understand what Belinda finds so excitin' 'bout it."

"How is the boy doin' who lost his arm?"

"We haven't seen or heard much 'bout him fer quite a while. I know his ma worked fer me day after day, but she never said one word 'bout 'im an' I didn't dare ask. She was touchy 'bout things she considered personal."

"I do hope thet he doesn't let it bitter 'im none," said Kate.

Marty told Kate that she and Clark had been praying for him along that very line.

Kate returned to the former issue.

"I really don't know what to say 'bout Melissa."

"I thought she might have said somethin' while she was here," said Marty. "Somethin' thet would give me a hint as to what to say or do."

"No, nothin'. She doesn't spend all that much time talkin' to me. She is either whisperin' with Amy Jo or readin' an' playin' with the boys."

"Well," said Marty, setting her empty teacup back on the table, "I don't wanna be borrowin' trouble. Maybe it will jest pass over like Clark says."

"I'll keep my eyes and ears open now thet I know," promised Kate.

Marty stopped in Amy Jo's room to see Dack before leaving for home. He had almost finished the raisins. The last doll still claimed a little pile. Dack pointed at her reproachfully. "She won't share," he stated. "It's not nice not to share."

Marty agreed that the dollie should share and Dack scooped up the few remaining raisins and popped them all into his mouth.

"There!" he exclaimed triumphantly. "Now she'll learn ta share."

Marty laughed and gathered the chubby little boy into her arms for a hug. "I'm glad yer learnin' 'bout sharin', Skeezix," she said, calling him her special name. "How 'bout sharin' dinner with Grandpa and me tomorra?" Marty invited, and Dack gave a whoop and ran off to the kitchen to get his mother's agreement.

Marty felt better as she walked back to her house. If Kate knew nothing about the little miff, then maybe it wasn't too serious. Surely Amy Jo would talk to her mother about it even if Melissa didn't. Perhaps Marty had blown it all out of proportion in her thinking. Clark was likely right. Eventually it would just go away.

But it wasn't to be that easy. Before the girls even reached the house that afternoon, Marty could tell that something had happened to make matters worse. The two girls were not even walking together. Melissa stormed on ahead, her very stride announcing the fact that she was very angry. She burst into the house and, without even acknowledging Marty's greeting, stomped up the stairs and slammed the door to her room. Marty could hear her crying all the way from the kitchen.

"Well!" said Marty, even though there was no one there to respond. "Well!"

Belinda walked in later, her cheeks streaked like she also had been crying, and Belinda did not cry easily. Unless it was to mourn over hurt pets or birds. Marty wondered what had happened now.

Belinda did greet her mother, but she too passed and would have gone straight up to her room had not Marty stopped her.

"Wait," she said. "Wait a minute. Don't ya think thet I should know what's goin' on?"

Belinda hesitated. Then the tears began to flow again.

"It's thet dumb Jackson," she wailed.

"Dumb Jackson? Why, I thought thet ya like Jackson."

"Well, I don't," insisted Belinda. Then she quickly amended, "Well, I do. I do. He's—he's—but I don't like him as much as Melissa does. She—she—an' he—he—he jest makes trouble."

"Trouble? How?" asked Marty.

"He—he—keeps doin' things—sayin' things—an then Melissa gits mad at me."

"What did he do now?"

"Yesterday he wanted—wanted to help me with my geometry. I told him, 'No thanks,' 'cause I was nearly done. The day before he asked to sit with me at lunch hour, but I made an excuse, an'—today, Ma—today he asked iffen I'd go with 'im to the church picnic!" she ended in a rush.

"The church picnic? The church picnic is months away yet."

"I know—but he said thet he wanted to ask early so thet no one else would ask me first," Belinda acknowledged with downcast eyes.

"I see," said Marty. "An Melissa found out about it, huh?"

"Found out?" cried Belinda. "She was standin' right there when he asked me!"

"Oh, my!" said Marty. "Oh, my!"

It was clear that someone was going to have to talk to Melissa. And she, Marty, seemed to be the one.

She wiped her hands on her apron and reluctantly climbed the stairs.

She rapped on Melissa's door, but there was no answer so she waited a moment and then opened the door gently. Melissa was lying on her bed, her head buried in her pillow. Marty crossed to her, praying for wisdom as she went. She lowered herself to the bed and reached out to smooth back the girl's long curls. Melissa's reply was a fresh burst of tears. Marty let her cry.

When she felt she had waited long enough, she began carefully, slowly, "Ya really do like Jackson a lot, don't ya?"

Melissa nodded and gave a shuddering sigh.

"I remember," said Marty reflectively, "I remember when I was yer age, I liked a boy a lot, too."

No answer.

"I thought thet he was the smartest, the handsomest, the nicest boy thet I had ever seen—an' he was too."

"Was it Grandpa?" asked Melissa in a muffled voice from her pillow.

"Grandpa? Oh my, no. I didn't meet yer grandpa till many years later. Then I finally learned the truth. Yer *grandpa* is the smartest and the handsomest and the nicest man I've ever seen."

Melissa was quiet. Marty let her be.

"What happened to the other one?" she asked at length, just like Marty had hoped she would.

"Clifton? Thet was his name, Clifton. Well, Clifton—it seemed like he cared more fer another girl then he did me. It nearly broke my heart. Her name was Cherry and she had long blonde hair and big green eyes. She was older'n me—maybe two years. Fact, she and Clifton were 'bout the same age. She loved to tease. Was worse than a boy 'bout it. At first I thought thet she really didn't care fer Clifton at all, jest wanted to flirt with 'im to make me mad. An' it did make me mad, too, ya can bet it did. But—I guess maybe she really did care for Clifton after all. Still—I never liked her. In fact, it was a long, long time until I could bring myself to forgive 'er."

Marty waited again.

"So-o," said Melissa.

"Well, she married Clifton, Cherry did. I could hardly stand it at first. Jest thinkin' 'bout it made me angry inside. An' then one day I did some thinkin' on it. Me moanin' around wasn't gonna git me Clifton. An' there I was spoilin' all my growin' up years a-weepin' over 'im. *Now is he really worth it?* I asked myself. *Is he really worth spoilin' my life for?* I decided right then and there thet he wasn't, an' I dried my eyes and went on out an' had me a good time."

"And you forgave her?"

"No-o. Not then. Not for many years, in fact. Ya see, I wasn't a Christian when I was a girl. So I was still foolish enough to carry thet grudge. It wasn't until I was grown-up and met yer grandpa's God and became a believer thet I had sense enough to see thet I didn't need to forgive Cherry. I needed Cherry to forgive me."

"What did she say?" asked Melissa.

"Say?" queried Marty. "Oh, ya mean when I asked her forgiveness? Well, that's the sad part. I never got to ask Cherry. I was way out here and Cherry had never left our home town. I wrote a letter. It came back to me. All it said on the envelope was one word—'Deceased' it said, jest like thet, 'Deceased.' "

"You mean—?"

"Cherry died. I found out later that she had died in childbirth. But I've always felt sad I wasn't able to tell her thet I was sorry—to ask her forgiveness. Ya see—I hadn't been very nice 'bout it all. It really wasn't Cherry's fault thet Clifton liked her better'n me."

Melissa began to weep again. Marty reached down and gathered the girl in her arms.

"Oh, Grandma," she sobbed, "I like him so much."

"I know," said Marty, stroking her hair. "I know."

"I don't think Belinda even *likes* him," continued Melissa, sounding exasperated.

"She likes 'im," said Marty. "She jest doesn't like 'im in the same way thet you do. An' she feels bad thet he keeps doin' an' sayin' things thet hurt ya."

"Did she say that?" asked Melissa, turning swollen eyes to look at Marty.

"She said thet."

"I guess I should talk to her," Melissa whispered, and a fresh batch of tears started.

"Thet would be a good idea," said Marty.

"Do you—do you think she'll forgive me?" Melissa sobbed.

"Oh my yes," Marty assured her. "But I tell ya what. Before ya go off to have yer talk with Belinda, why don't ya an' me jest have us a little talk with God? Ya see, there's someone else involved here thet we haven't even talked 'bout."

Melissa's eyes studied the face of her grandmother.

"Jackson!" went on Marty. "Jackson is in this too. Now he is a fine young man an' apparently—well—sometimes we don't do a whole lot a choosin' in one we love—our heart jest does it fer us—an' it appears thet fer now, Jackson thinks thet his heart has chosen Belinda. Time will tell thet, of course. Ya are all very young, an' sometimes—well, sometimes the heart changes its mind agin. But, in the meantime—well, we don't want to hurt Jackson, do we?"

Melissa's eyes dropped to her hands, twisting her handkerchief round and round. She shook her head. She did not want to hurt Jackson.

"So we need to pray—fer all three of ya. Fer Belinda, fer you—an' fer Jackson. Thet each one of ya might be able to let God help ya with yer choosin'. Ya see, He knows! He knows how things should be for our very best. So iffen we leave it to Him, then He can work it all out."

Melissa nodded and they knelt down beside her bed together.

The days that followed were much happier for everyone, and Marty thanked the Lord daily. There were still times when

Jackson unintentionally hurt Melissa with his continued interest in Belinda, and Belinda cringed inwardly and subtly tried to divert his attention toward Melissa. But even though Melissa still cried alone in her bedroom once 'n a while, the tension between the two girls was gone. They could even talk about the situation together and at times they brought their problem to Marty. It always seemed to help when the three of them prayed together about it.

Chapter 20

Helping Luke

Belinda arrived home from school in a flurry. From her flushed cheeks and heavy breathing, Marty knew she must have run a good deal of the way. When Marty had first seen her slight figure flying up the lane, her heart had started to pound in her chest. Surely something was wrong! But the girl's first panted words put her mind at ease.

"Luke stopped by the school," she gasped out. "He's goin' out to change the bandages on the little Willis girl. He said fer me to join 'im there. He might need my help."

"Is thet the one with the bad burn?"

Belinda nodded, still puffing.

"Ya gonna take the sleigh?" asked Marty.

"No, I'll jest ride Copper. Thet'll be faster." And Belinda was off up the stairs on the run. Marty knew that as soon as she changed clothes for riding she would be back down.

Marty grabbed a warm sweater from the clothes hooks by the door and headed for the barn. At least she could saddle the horse and save Belinda that much time.

Copper, in the corral beside the barn, came when Marty shook the pail containing a small amount of oats. The other horses came, too. It was not a problem for Marty to catch Copper. It was a bit of a problem for her to get rid of the other horses.

She led Copper into the barn and was almost done saddling

him when Belinda appeared, still breathless. Marty wasn't sure if it was from running or from excitement.

They led Copper from the barn and Belinda mounted.

"Now, mind ya, don't run 'im too hard," Marty cautioned her. "Luke won't be that anxious fer ya to git there."

Belinda nodded, called a goodbye and was off down the lane. It was then that Marty remembered that Belinda hadn't even taken time for a snack, and the youngsters were always so hungry when they got home from school. Well, for Belinda, her daily bread seemed to be her nursing.

Belinda pushed Copper. She was mindful of her mother's admonition, but she did not want to keep Luke waiting. She had not been with Luke when he had first tended the child, but he had explained to her in detail about the burn the little girl had received. He was quite concerned. Besides causing the young child a great deal of pain, Luke was afraid it might become infected and cause permanent damage to the arm. So Luke planned on keeping a very close eye on the girl. This meant a frequent change of bandages—and that was a difficult, painful process. Because of the oozing of the open sores, the bandages stuck—sometimes badly, and they had to be carefully and slowly soaked off. It was important to be patient in the process, both to prevent pain and to cause as little damage as possible to the wound beneath.

Belinda wasn't sure what her role was to be. She had never been with Luke on a burn case before. Burns made her stomach flip. She had once burned herself when she was a little girl—not bad as burns go. In fact, they hadn't needed a doctor; her ma had treated it herself. But it had been terribly painful, and Belinda had not been able to use two of her fingers for days. At the time, she wondered if they would ever be useable again. Of course they were. In fact, now Belinda had a hard time remembering which fingers it had been.

But this burn—according to Luke—this burn would be different. The little girl had spilled hot grease all down one arm. Some had splashed on her chest too but those burns weren't too deep.

Even as Belinda felt herself drawing back from what lay

ahead, she pushed Copper as fast as she dared toward the farmhouse. Luke needed her. The little girl needed her. They must do all they could to save the use of her arm.

Luke's team was already there, tied to the hitching rail out front, when Belinda urged Copper down the lane at a gallop. She hastened to dismount and wrap the reins securely about the rail. If he was not tied carefully, Copper had a bad habit of leaving for home before his rider. Then Belinda hastened to the house.

The lady of the home greeted her. Belinda did not know the family well. They did not have school-age children as yet and did not attend their church. Belinda had seen them occasionally at community gatherings or on the street in town. She nodded to the woman now and her eyes searched the room for the patient.

Luke sat on a couch on one side of the room. A little girl— perhaps three years old—with a big bandage sat on his knee. He was letting her play with his stethescope. She put the instrument in her ears like she had seen the doctor do and grinned impishly at him.

She doesn't look too bad, thought Belinda. *Why, she can even smile!* Belinda had expected to encounter screams of pain.

"Well, here's my nurse," Luke announced to both the mother and the little girl. "Guess we'd better get to work, huh?"

The woman took Belinda's coat, and Luke sent Belinda to the washbasin in the kitchen to carefully wash her hands. She knew that when she had finished, he would also insist on pouring a strong-smelling disinfectant over her hands. She didn't mind the smell but the kids at school teased her about it—it stayed with her for days. But Luke always insisted on the thorough cleansing, and Belinda did not even think of fighting it.

"Now, Mandie," Luke said to the little girl, "let's take a look at that arm of yours."

The little girl pulled away. She did not want her arm touched. Instinctively she knew that it might be painful. She could bear the present pain—it still hurt, but it was bearable. But it had been worse. The memory of the pain she had endured made her draw away.

Luke gently lifted her and placed her on the table to take advantage of all the light he could. The child began to cry. Luke tried to soothe her but the tears and shrieks just increased.

Luke turned to the mother.

"You might want to go for a bit of a walk, ma'am," he said softly to the woman. Already her eyes were filling with tears. She slipped on a warm coat, lifted the baby from the floor and wrapped him securely in a blanket.

"I'll be at the barn iffen ya need me," she murmured.

The door closed gently and the woman and baby were gone.

"Now," said Luke above the cries of the child, "I'd hoped you could keep her attention elsewhere, but that's not going to work. You'll have to hold her while I get this bandage off. First, let's get organized."

Luke poured hot water from the kettle on the stove into the basin and added some of his strong-smelling disinfectant. He swished the water round and round, making sure the sides of the basin had been cleansed, then he walked to the door and down the path a few steps to dispose of the water. When he returned, he poured more warm water into the basin and again added disinfectant. With the basin on the table, he laid out sterile pads and all of his instruments. Then he nodded to Belinda who was holding the child, trying to comfort and assure her.

Belinda placed the little girl back on the table and the screaming began again. They would not even be able to converse during the procedure. Luke nodded to Belinda above the child's head and she took a firm hold of the little girl.

Belinda never would have dreamed that one so small could be so strong. It was all she could do to hold on to the child.

The first several rows of bandage came off quickly and easily, and then it began to get more difficult. Luke soaked and cut, soaked and cut, and the size of the bandage gradually decreased. And all the time they worked the little girl screamed and fought.

Belinda wished Luke could hurry. She was getting exhausted. She wondered how the little one had the strength to go on fighting against the procedure.

But Luke did not hurry. He took his time, and carefully, oh, so carefully removed each layer.

By the time he was down to the last of the bandages, Belinda was aching and covered with perspiration. The bandages, put on so clean and sterile, were now heavy with blood and liquid from the oozing sores. The smell was a strange mixture of the body fluids and the medication Luke had used on them before. Belinda wondered for a few minutes if she was going to be sick, but she fought desperately against it. This was not the time to be feeling queasy. She held fast to the little girl.

"Doesn't look too good," she heard her brother say over the cries of the child, and Belinda let her eyes drop to the burned arm.

Her stomach lurched and she shut her eyes and counted, trying to shut out the sight. The wound looked terrible.

"I'm gonna have to clean it up," Luke almost hollered at her in order to make himself heard. "Don't like to use chloroform on one so little, but might have to put her under for a bit."

Belinda watched as Luke poured a small amount of chloroform on a clean cloth. Then with a quick but gentle movement, he covered the child's nose and mouth. Almost immediately Belinda felt the small body relax in her arms. Luke carefully laid the little girl down on the clean sheet covering the kitchen table.

"We're going to have to work quickly," he said. "I didn't want to give her much. Now, you keep a close eye on her. Check her pulse often just as I showed you, and watch her breathing. I'll do this as fast as I can," and so saying Luke took his scissors and began to trim away the burned and lifeless flesh.

Belinda was glad she had something to do other than watch Luke. She checked the small girl's faint pulse, thankful that it remained even. Her breathing, too, did not alter. Belinda lifted the eyelid and studied the pupil's response to light. The child seemed to be doing fine.

"I don't think she'll stay under much longer," Belinda informed Luke, watching her eyelids flutter. "Do you want to give her a bit more?"

"I'm almost done. We'll try to make that do. I don't want to give any more if I can help it."

Luke was just finishing up the removal of the infected flesh when the girl began to stir. For a moment she looked about her uncertainly and then she began to scream again. Luke moved her to a sitting position and Belinda held her, talking to her soothingly.

The heavy medication on the bandages was nearly overpowering. Belinda felt her legs turning to rubber. She held the tiny arm as Luke pressed the sterile cloths carefully onto the burned area and began the process of rebandaging. Still the girl screamed. Belinda did not know if the cries now were from pain, fright or anger.

At last the job was done and Luke lifted the wee girl into his arms. Speaking softly in a hushed voice, he began to walk the floor with her, gently rocking her in his arms and murmuring soft words of comfort.

Gradually the child calmed. Luke continued to croon, telling her over and over what a brave, big girl she was and how she was going to be all better soon.

He turned to Belinda, collapsed into a nearby chair. "You might want to tell her ma that she can come in now," he suggested.

Belinda reached for her coat. *Fresh air!* she thought in relief. She left the house and headed for the barn.

The woman was lying face down on the hay. Beside her, bundled warmly against the weather, slept the baby.

"Ma'am," said Belinda, bending over the grieving form, "ma'am."

The woman stirred, turning a tear-streaked face to Belinda.

"We're all done. Ya can come in now."

"Thank God!" the woman muttered, and Belinda looked at her carefully.

How did she mean the words? They had not sounded like a small prayer of thanks, the way they did when her ma or pa spoke them. No, they had sounded quite different somehow. Belinda wished she knew what to say.

"Yes, ma'am," she faltered after a moment. "We do thank God. It's only Him thet can make the treatment work—make thet arm to heal."

The woman looked at Belinda with a very strange expression on her face, then lifted herself from the hay, gathered up her sleeping baby and hurried to the house.

By the time they reached the kitchen, Luke had completely calmed the child. He had bathed her teary face with a warm cloth and smoothed back the tangled hair.

Except for the swollen eyes, one would not have known she had just been through such an ordeal.

The child reached for her mother, and the woman hurried to lay down the baby so she might take the little one from Luke.

"I'll see you again in a couple of days," Luke was telling her.

"How—how many more times do we need to go through this?" the young mother asked him, her eyes filled with agony.

"I really can't say," Luke said honestly. "The burn doesn't look good at this point. It's going to be a fight to keep out infection. We'll have to keep a close watch on it. But I hope—I hope the healing process soon begins. Once it starts to heal properly, it might improve quite quickly. With a child, it often does," he assured her, patting the child's head.

Luke smiled at the woman. "We'll do the best we can," he promised her.

She nodded. She was too overwrought to even think of a thank you, but Luke understood.

He gathered all his belongings, threw the dirty bandages into the kitchen stove so the woman would not need to see the reminder, and reached for his coat.

Outside, Luke laid his hand on Belinda's shoulder. "Thanks," he said. "I never could have done it without you."

She smiled weakly.

"Do you mind coming back a few times to give me a hand?"

"No—I don't mind. I'll help."

"It's not very nice, is it?"

"No," admitted Belinda.

"It's always so much harder for me when it's a child," said Luke, shaking his head. "I just hope and pray I never need to treat one of my own. I don't know if I could bear it—or any of our family's children, for that matter. It would be so hard. The poor little things just can't understand the pain—and the treatment."

Luke shook his head. Belinda knew that he felt it deeply.

"You okay?" Luke sincerely asked her, searching her face.

"Fine," said Belinda.

"You looked a bit pale in there."

Belinda smiled again. "I felt pale for a few minutes, too."

Luke gave her a quick hug and turned to untie his team.

"I have to go on to the Williams'. They think they have a case of measles. Let's plan to meet here on Thursday right after school, okay?"

"Sure," said Belinda.

"Maybe next time it won't be quite so bad," said the doctor, "but—I can't make any promises."

Belinda nodded and mounted Copper. She was anxious to get home.

Chapter 21

An Accident?

Belinda let Copper choose his own speed going home. It was a good thing the horse knew his way. Belinda was not paying much attention to the animal—her mind was still full of what she had just seen.

The amputation of the Simpson boy's arm had been terrible. Belinda thought it might have been the worst thing she had ever seen in her life. But the little girl's burns would certainly rate a very close second. It was a terrible thing to see and, imagining the child's unbelievable pain, Belinda cringed each time she let the mental picture into her mind.

Maybe I'm not cut out to be nurse after all, she pondered. It was so painful to see the suffering. Maybe she should do like Melissa and become a schoolteacher. An artist, like Amy Jo, was out of the question—she didn't have an artistic bone in her body.

But then Belinda thought about Luke, about his dedication to this service, this ministry to people. She saw him again as he carried the child back and forth in the kitchen, soothing and comforting her. *Luke needs me,* she thought. There were too few nurses, he had said. Doctors could not handle all cases on their own. They needed assistants. Deep inside, Belinda knew this was her dream.

Of course she would not enjoy seeing the pain. Of course she would find some cases distasteful. But someone needed to be there, to fight against pain and suffering like Luke was doing. He would always be there, and with God's help she would be there, too.

As Copper ambled along toward home, Belinda's thoughts turned to Jackson. She *liked* Jackson, but she just couldn't seem to make him understand that she *loved* nursing. At this time she did not want to even think about boys. In the first place, she was way too young, though she did admit to mildly enjoying the girlish flirtation games on occasion. But, on further thought, Belinda could think of no good that would come of flirting. If the boy responded—well, that meant even more trouble, for Belinda knew that if she wished to be a nurse she would need to dedicate the next several years of her life to training. What would she do with a special beau then?

Besides, Melissa was the one who seemed to really care for Jackson. Melissa was young, too—too young to be thinking seriously about fellows. But Melissa seemed inclined to think about them anyway, and it certainly didn't help matters any that she had about made up her mind Jackson was the fellow for her. Now, it wouldn't have been so bad if Jackson had shared the feeling. But Jackson's attentions to Belinda were difficult to deal with. Fortunately Amy Jo's painting had captured her imagination so Belinda didn't have her niece to worry about too. She was glad Jackson would be going off to school someplace come fall. Perhaps that would solve the problem for all of them.

Without warning, a shrill crack suddenly split through Belinda's thoughts. Before she knew what had happened, Copper had spooked, tossing his head into the air and leaping wildly to the side. Belinda grabbed for the saddle horn and the reins but was unable to control the animal or her own body.

Frantically, she realized she was flying through the air. Time seemed to freeze before she struck the ground. When she did land with a sickening thud, all of the air was knocked out of her body, and she lay there on the ground in a daze. Copper tossed his head again in fright and headed for home at a gallop.

In the bush next to the road, the hunter heard the commotion. He had not seen or heard anyone around when he had fired at the rabbit and would never have shot if he had. But from the noise on the nearby road, he feared that the gunshot had meant trouble for someone. He ran to the road.

The first thing he saw was the fleeing horse, his head flung to the side to avoid stepping on the dragging reins. Then he looked the other direction and saw a motionless form lying on the roadway. The hunter cried out in alarm as he ran to the body.

It was a girl, a young girl, lying in a crumpled heap like a discarded sack. He knelt beside her, nervously looking for signs of broken bones or other injuries.

What should he do? Where should he go for help? He wished that a horse was available. He stared anxiously down the road, hoping the animal had stopped, but it was just disappearing over the crest of the hill.

The girl moaned softly. He turned back to her, inwardly praying fervently that she was not seriously injured. He dared to touch her face—to smooth back her hair. *What should I do?* he lamented.

The girl moaned again and began to stir. He watched her face carefully. *Who is she? Where does she live?* He should go for help. Get her parents. Something. But he couldn't leave her here alone. He cradled her head carefully. *What if her neck is injured?* his frantic thoughts tumbled over themselves.

She moved again and he saw her eyelids flutter. Was she coming around? Would she be okay? *Oh, please God, please God,* he pleaded with a God he did not know nor understand.

Belinda fought against the unreal world she so precipitously had entered. *What happened? Where am I?* She struggled to fill her aching lungs with air. She hurt. Her whole chest hurt.

Gradually she began to breathe again. The pain was subsiding and her thinking began to clear. She forced her eyes to open. Someone was bending over her, gently stroking her face as though coaxing the life back into her body. She strained to make her eyes focus on the world swimming around her.

And then she saw the dark eyes and the black hair. She knew him immediately. It was the boy, the boy with one arm. She fought to get control of her breathing, straining to sit up.

What happened anyway? she tried to ask.

"Easy," he was saying softly. "Easy. Don't try to move yet."

"What—? What—?" tried Belinda again but her lips would not work properly. She let her head drop against his supporting arm, closed her eyes and willed the world to stop spinning.

What had happened? Where was she? Why was she here? Slowly, oh so slowly things began to fall into sequence. She had been helping Luke. They were done—had finished the bandaging of the little girl's burned arm. She was on her way home. She was riding—

"Copper," said Belinda, straining to lift her head again. "Where's Copper?"

"Sh-h," the boy hushed her. "Take it easy. Yer gonna be all right." He prayed that he was right about that. "Jest rest a few minutes."

"Copper," repeated Belinda.

"Copper?" asked the boy, wondering what Belinda was muttering about, and then it dawned. "Is Copper a horse?"

Belinda looked at him, her head still foggy. *Of course Copper is a horse. My horse.* And he should be here—somewhere.

"I'm afraid thet Copper went on home," the boy said.

Belinda's head was clear enough now for her to understand the implications.

"Oh, no," she groaned, moving her head to the side. The boy was relieved to see that she could move it properly.

"Oh, no," said Belinda again. "Ma'll be frantic!"

"What?" questioned the boy.

"Ma—she'll be worried sick when thet horse comes in without me. I gotta git home—fast as I can."

Belinda struggled to get to her feet, but the boy held her. Belinda was surprised at the strength in his one arm.

"Don't," he said. "Not yet. You might be hurt bad—have a broken bone or somethin'. It's not safe to move jest yet."

"I'm fine," Belinda protested. "Really!"

"You don't seem so fine to me," he insisted. Then he looked at the pretty girl that he held securely on his one arm and flushed deeply. "Thet is, you might be hurt some. We don't know yet."

Belinda wondered why the boy was so flustered, but she did not try to figure it out. All she could think about was her mother. She knew Marty would fear the worst when Copper arrived home riderless. She had to get home—and quickly—but first she would just rest a minute and be sure that she was really okay. The boy was right about that.

She closed her eyes and relaxed. The trees had stopped swirling around, her breath was coming much more easily and her chest no longer pained. Here and there she felt bruised but nothing seemed to hurt unbearably. She was bound to ache some, and would doubtless be quite sore for a few days, but she did not think she had broken any bones. Bit by bit she mentally went over her body. No, she was sure she was all right.

She looked up at the boy again. His eyes were anxiously studying her, his face pale. She did not try to fight against the arm that held her. Instead she spoke to him, evenly and coherently.

"I think I'm ready to get up now. I'm sure I have no broken bones. I jest had the wind knocked outta me, thet's all."

"Yer sure?" He still did not release her.

"I'm sure," she assured him. "Iffen ya'll jest help me to my feet—"

"Take it real easy," he cautioned, "and let me know if anythin' gives you pain."

He stood to his feet then, gently lifting her along with him. Belinda felt things beginning to spin again, but she held tightly to his arm and closed her eyes until the whirling stopped.

"How is it?" he asked solicitously.

"Fine. Be jest fine in a minute. No—no bad pain—jest a few bruises."

Belinda tried a smile. It was a bit weak but the boy responded, his dark eyes lighting up.

"Yer a good sport," he said admiringly.

At that Belinda chuckled softly. "A good sport? Well, I didn't exactly choose this way to—"

"I know," said the boy. "It was my fault. I'm sorry." His eyes darkened with remorse.

"Yer fault?" asked Belinda. "How—yer fault?"

"I didn't notice you comin'. I shot at a rabbit, an' it frightened yer horse. I didn't even know you were around 'til I heard the commotion. I—I—but it was already too late. Yer horse was runnin' off an' you were a-layin'—"

Belinda stopped him. "Did ya git the rabbit?" she asked softly.

He looked at her. Was she teasing him? Then she smiled and the next thing he knew they were laughing together.

"I dunno," he said truthfully. "I think I did."

"You'd best go see," Belinda prompted him. "Don't wanna waste it."

"Yer serious?"

"It was nearby, wasn't it?"

"Right over there, behind those bushes."

"Then go check. I'll brush a bit of the dirt offa me and then I'd best be gittin' home."

He soon was back with the rabbit, grinning as he held it up for her inspection. Belinda could see that it had been a clean shot. *Must be good with a gun,* she thought.

"Good meat, rabbit," he informed her. "I should know. Thet's about all we've been eatin' this winter."

Belinda nodded, still busy trying to remove the dirty snow and road clutter from her clothes. He reached out a hand and brushed her hair gently. "You got it in your hair, too," he said softly.

Belinda tried a step. Her legs seemed to be working fairly well, but he quickly reached out and took her arm.

"Why don't I git rid of this first?" he said, indicating the gun and the rabbit that lay at his feet.

Belinda waited until he had crossed to a nearby tree and deposited the gun and the game in the branches. "I'll pick it up on my way back home," he informed her. "Now, let's get you on home before yer mama comes lookin' for you."

They walked very slowly at first, his hand carefully assisting her. She was not in any real pain but she did notice there were many parts of her body that seemed to be crying out for attention. She would be stiff and sore tomorrow, that was for sure. At least they did not have far to go.

"Is it okay?" he asked her repeatedly, and each time she stoutly insisted that she was fine.

They had not gone far when they heard a horse rapidly approaching and Clark came over the nearest hill riding Copper at a brisk gallop. As soon as he reached them he slid to a stop and dismounted in one fluid motion.

"Ya all right?" he asked Belinda anxiously.

"I'm fine," she answered, "jest a little bruised, thet's all."

"What happened?"

"Ol' Copper here spooked an' threw me."

"It was my fault," explained the boy. "I shot at a rabbit."

"An he got it too," put in Belinda admiringly while the boy colored and looked embarrassed.

Clark's eyes traveled from one to the other of them. The boy still supported Belinda protectively.

"Well, I'm glad yer okay," Clark said quietly. "An yer mama will be greatly relieved too. Didn't know what to think when thet horse came in like he did. I tried to tell yer mama that he jest might have slipped rein again and left ya stranded at wherever ya were. But we had ta check to be sure."

"I tied him carefully like ya said," Belinda informed him.

"Well, let's git ya up on this horse," said Clark.

"You ride, Pa," Belinda argued, thinking of Clark's wooden leg.

But he would not hear of it, and soon Belinda was boosted up into the saddle and they were on their way home again at a brisk walk. No one thought to question the boy's continuing on with them. He could have gone back for his gun and his rabbit and gone home. But for some reason he did not think of that, and Clark and Belinda both accepted his presence. It seemed right somehow for him to continue on home with them.

Marty hurried out to meet them when they entered the lane.

"What happened?" she asked, her eyes large with concern.

"She's jest fine," Clark was quick to assure. "Jest took a bit of a spill. Ya know ol' Copper. He spooks awful easy."

Clark lifted Belinda down and went on to the barn with the horse. The boy took her arm again, and with Marty fluttering anxiously before them, they went into the house.

It wasn't until they were safely seated at the kitchen table that Marty turned to the boy.

"So you two finally met?" she commented. "Seems thet it's accidents thet bring ya together."

The boy looked puzzled.

"Guess Belinda will have plenty of tales to tell in the comin' years 'bout her nursin' experiences," Marty went on. "Thet's where she was tonight, too—when this happened—helpin' Luke. But I guess ya knew all 'bout thet. This one was a burn case."

The boy turned to Belinda, his dark eyes wide—questioning. This—*this* was the girl he had been told was there when they took his arm?

Chapter 22

Introductions

Belinda noticed shadows darkening the boy's eyes. She saw the questioning look on his face. His lips parted as though he was going to say something, and then they closed tightly and he turned away.

He did not bolt, though she feared for a moment that he might. The knuckles on the hand that gripped the edge of the table were white. His face was even more pale then it had been when he had bent over her in the road. She wanted to say something—anything, but didn't know what it would be.

Marty had not noticed the exchange. She had supposed they knew each other. Belinda, having recognized him immediately, had taken it for granted as well. But of course the boy would not have known who she was. He had been unconscious the whole time that she was with him after his accident.

Clark's appearance helped to break the tension. With no idea of the undercurrent in the room, he hung up his coat and hat on the proper pegs and walked toward the table.

"Sure can tell thet summer is 'most here," he said in a good neighborly fashion. "The days are gittin' to where they're worth somethin' agin, an' the air is actually warm. Be mighty glad to see warmer weather, too. I've had 'nough winter fer a while."

There was no comment from the two at the table. Marty brought thick sandwiches and milk for each of them. Belinda looked shyly across at the boy. Would he refuse it? She was afraid he might. But no, he mumbled a polite thank you and began to eat the sandwich.

"How's yer pa doin' on his loggin'?" Clark asked the boy.

His eyes lifted from his plate and met Clark's. "Fine," he replied, but offered no more than that.

"It's nice havin' yer ma comin' to sew every day," put in Marty. "I enjoy her company."

The boy nodded.

Clark pulled up a chair and joined them at the table. Belinda had said nothing. Inside she felt a deep ache. She couldn't explain it—she just knew that she hurt deeply. She felt this emotional pain more keenly than she felt her aches and bruises from the fall.

Something was wrong. She had hoped that the boy had adjusted to his arm being gone, had learned how to go on without it, had understood those who had been forced to take it to spare his life. But from the dark shadows in his eyes and the frown on his countenance, she knew that it wasn't so.

Does he still hold the surgery against Luke, too? Belinda wondered. *Perhaps he does*—but Marty was talking. From the looks her way, Belinda knew the question must have been directed to her.

"Beggin' pardon," she responded and shook her head slightly.

"Yer not hurt, are ya?" asked Marty, coming forward to touch the girl's forehead.

"No, no, I'm fine—really," Belinda quickly answered.

For just a moment Belinda saw concern in the boy's eyes again, and then it was gone and the darkness returned.

"I'm fine," Belinda insisted again, "I jest wasn't listenin'. Was thinkin'—thet's all."

"I asked about the little girl. How is she?"

"Mandie?"

"Is thet her name?"

"Mandie. Mandie—" Suddenly Belinda could not remember the family's last name. Near panic seized her. Was there something wrong? Had she hit her head? And then it came to her.

"It's Willis," she said with confidence and relief. "Mandie Willis."

Marty looked at her quizzically and Belinda hurried on. "She's—she's—" She wanted to say that the little girl was jest fine, but in honesty said instead, "She's burned real bad. Luke is worried 'bout infection. We have to go back on Thursday."

Marty frowned in concern. "Terrible thing, those burns," she said. " 'Specially fer a little child."

Belinda nodded.

"Ya've hardly eaten a thing," Marty scolded. "Ya missed yer supper an' now—"

"I'm jest not hungry," said Belinda and pushed the plate away from her.

"But ya need—" began Marty and was interrupted by Clark.

"Might be better fer her stomach if she don't put nothin' in it fer the present."

Marty removed the plate.

"So what did ya do?" she asked Belinda.

Belinda looked at her quizzically, not understanding.

"How did ya help yer brother?"

"Oh! I—I held Mandie—while Luke took off the old bandage an'—then I—I watched her after she was put to sleep, to see thet—thet—she was okay an'—an' everythin'."

All the time they had been talking Belinda could feel the eyes of the boy on her face. She couldn't read the expression in his eyes, but she really did not want to know. Did he hate her for her part in the tragic surgery? She wished she could go to her room. That he would go home.

"I think thet's enough medicine talk," Clark said, and Belinda sighed in agreement.

Clark's hand slowly moved down to rub his injured leg. He was not aware of his action, but the boy noticed it. *How much does his leg still hurt him?* the boy wondered. Did it still shoot fire up the limb, making it seem like it was still there and badly damaged? Did the pain never quit? "Phantom pains," they called it. Well, phantom or not, the pains were very real. The boy winced just thinking about it.

"Don't believe I've been told yer name," Clark was saying

to the boy. "We never were introduced like. I'm Clark Davis, this is my wife Marty and my youngest girl, Belinda. But then, ya already know her."

He didn't. He hadn't. Not really.

The boy mumbled his acknowledgment to the introductions. When Belinda was presented his eyes met hers for a moment, but the coldness was still there.

"An' yer name," Clark prompted.

"Drew. Drew Simpson. Andrew really, but everyone calls me Drew."

Belinda repeated the name mentally. Drew. It suited him somehow.

"Well, Drew, we're right glad to make yer acquaintance. An' we are thankful to ya fer carin' fer our Belinda."

"It was my fault—"

"Nobody's fault," Clark stopped him. "Thet fool horse always was bad fer spookin'. Don't know how to go about gittin' 'im over bein' gun shy. He's always been thet way. Well, we'll jest watch 'im a little more closely, thet's all."

Drew had finished his milk and sandwich. Marty offered him some crumb cake but he politely turned it down.

"I've gotta get home before my folks get ta worryin' 'bout me," he said and reached for his cap. "Didn't realize how late it's gettin'."

Both Clark and Marty thanked him again. They invited him to return any time in the future. Drew did not say whether he would accept their invitation. For just a moment his clouded eyes met Belinda's and then he turned away. She wanted to say something. To thank him for his kindness, but she choked on all of her intended words.

And then he was gone, the door closing firmly behind him. Marty was speaking as she cleared away his dirty dishes, "He seems like an awful nice young boy. I do hope thet he ain't harborin' any bitterness over his arm."

Belinda excused herself. She wanted the privacy of her own room.

Spring was quickly followed by summer, and after school

was over, Belinda busied herself with accompanying Luke. Mandie's burned arm gave them a real scare. Luke even thought at one point that she, too, might lose it. But he fought— my, how he did fight—and the arm finally began to heal. It would always bear ugly scars, but she still had the use of it.

Belinda did not see Drew again, though she frequently wondered about the boy. Was he still nursing his grief? She did not know. They did see his mother—almost every day, in fact. She still came to sew. Over the days and weeks Marty had seen the woman's eyes go from despair, to acceptance, to hope, to renewed faith in life. True, the family was still in difficult circumstances, but they were on their way to independence. Well, they had always been independent enough, but now it looked like they might one day be able to take what they considered to be their proper place in the community.

The woman now wore a new dress, one she had made for herself. She even walked straighter with more confidence now that she was no longer wearing the many-times-mended garment. There were even moments of brief conversation between her and Marty as they took little breaks for tea and discussed weather, gardens or neighborhood events.

Marty learned that Mrs. Simpson's two sons had never been to school—not for a single day of their lives. And yet both of the parents put great stock in education and had taught the boys everything they could, bringing home extra books to help them keep up with other youngsters their age. Mr. Simpson himself had been a college graduate, Marty discovered to her great surprise. And Mrs. Simpson had at one time tutored special English classes to immigrant families. Marty understood a bit more about the pride that kept them from "accepting charity."

But though Belinda saw Mrs. Simpson often, she did not ask about Drew. Not that she did not care. It was just that she feared to ask the question because the answer might not be the one she wanted to hear.

Jackson still hung about—a hard one to avoid, Belinda decided ruefully. Even though school was out for the summer, Belinda saw him each Sunday at church and he always lingered about, looking for some opportunity to serve her or suggesting some outing they might enjoy together. Belinda tried to be kind and firm, but Jackson was not too good at taking hints.

Melissa still sighed and longed for Jackson to take notice of her. There were other boys who would have gladly showered Melissa with their attention, but she ignored them completely.

How foolish we be, thought Marty as she watched silently from the sidelines. *Each wantin' exactly what one can't have.*

When fall came, Jackson packed his bags and went off to school in the city. He'd been counting on an intimate chat with Belinda to ask her if she would wait for him, but he could never get an opportunity. Belinda was always busy. He never saw a girl so taken with her work. So Jackson went off to college with a heart slightly heavier than his steamer trunk. A year was a long time to be away, and Belinda was growing up awfully fast. His only hope was that her nursing would keep her so busy she wouldn't notice the other boys who hovered around.

The school year began with Marty dreading the thought that this would be the last one at the local school for both Belinda and Melissa. But as she watched them go off together, she was pleased that they were chattering and enjoying each other's company. *It should be an easier year for all of 'em,* Marty thought with relief, *havin' Jackson a good two hundred miles away!* Marty sighed. *Poor Jackson!* She did feel sorry for him. He was a fine young man.

Well, the girls were still young. There would be lots of time for beaus. She could just imagine Missie praying that Melissa would meet no fellow of special interest while she was back east going to school. Missie would not be any more anxious to lose her Melissa to the East than Marty had been to lose her Missie to the West.

Marty sighed again and turned from the window. She was afraid that the year ahead was going to pass all too quickly.

Chapter 23

Birthday Party

The team moved at a brisk trot, faster than usual, Marty felt as she cast a quick glance Clark's way. But she did not question him. He urged the horses on a bit, not holding them back as he normally did when they were homeward bound on a beautiful June day. Marty turned to try and enjoy the wild roses that lined the roadside. Their fragrance reached out to her as the light wagon hurried on by. They truly were pretty, but Marty's thoughts were on other things.

Strange, mused Marty to herself. But she did not make any comment aloud. Still, the whole thing did seem unusual.

Marty was very aware that today was her birthday—and though Clark had made no remarks to indicate that he remembered, she was sure he had not forgotten. Clark had never forgotten her birthday in all the years of their marriage. Yet, birthday or not, he had seemed awfully anxious to hustle her away from the house, and his excuse of "Ma Graham needin' some cheerin' up" now seemed a flimsy one at best.

Marty had agreed to accompany Clark to the Grahams', expecting to find a lonely and sombre Ma, but she had been her usual cheerful self, serving Marty tea and fresh strawberry shortcake and chattering away about all the new achievements of her many grandchildren.

Clark had left Marty to visit there and had gone on to town. Marty was very cooperative with the plan, but she found herself watching the clock and chafing a bit as the afternoon slowly moved along. Clark seemed to take longer than usual, and Marty was most anxious to get home.

Her birthday always meant a family dinner. The offspring took turns year by year to host the celebration. Marty did not try to keep track of where the birthday dinner was to be. The girls always knew, they informed Clark, and without discussion of where they were to celebrate, Clark always got Marty to the right home at the appointed time.

Most years Marty enjoyed the little game. She purposely tried not to think of whose turn it should be so that she could savour the "surprise," but as Clark clucked again to the team, Marty found herself going back over the last few years of birthday dinners.

It had been at Arnie's and Anne's last year, and the year before, at Nandry's and Josh's. Before that? Marty had to really concentrate. Oh, yes. It was at Clare's and Kate's. But, no, surely this year it was to be at Kate's or they would be late for dinner.

It was a weekday so the dinner would be the evening meal. They always had an early dinner together on a weekday and even then it tended to be rushed. Marty cast an anxious eye at the sky. It was getting late. Before too long the cows would need milking. Marty stirred restlessly on the seat. She did hate being rushed. Time with family always seemed so short.

It must be at Clare's and Kate's, she argued with herself. There just wouldn't be time to drive to one of the other homes. *I'm mistaken about three years back. That year must have been at Luke's and—. But no.* She interrupted herself. *I can distinctly remember Kate's chicken and dumplings.* For some reason, Luke and Abbie were unable to have the family this year and so Kate was taking their turn, she decided.

Marty's thoughts turned to worries. *Was Abbie not feeling well? No one had told her—*

"Did ya have a good chat with Ma?" Clark unexpectedly broke into her thoughts.

Marty shifted her attention back to her husband. His face was relaxed, his hands firmly holding the reins as he expertly guided the team down the country road.

Marty blinked, surprise showing on her face. Why was he asking about Ma in the middle of thoughts of birthday? And then Marty realized that just because her mind was totally absorbed with her birthday dinner, that was no reason Clark's thoughts should be taken with it as well. Perhaps this time he *had* forgotten. *Perhaps—*. Marty had a little stab of disappointment. But *once*, in all of the years of their marriage? Surely she could forgive him this once.

"Oh, yes—yes," Marty stammered. "We had us a good chat. Ma's as perky as can be. Full of plans and tales of grandkids an'—," she hesitated. "Where'd ya get ya the idea that she was feelin' down?" she asked, turning on the seat so that she could look full at Clark's face.

"Feelin' down?" Clark echoed. "I don't recall ever sayin' Ma was down."

"But ya said—ya said she needed a bit of a visit—some cheerin' up, ya said."

Clark just smiled his teasing smile. "I know yer visits always cheer Ma up. Jest by yer bein' there I know."

But Marty was not in the mood to listen. Something seemed to be wrong here. A little hurt stirred within her. Had her whole family forgotten her birthday?

Straining forward as the team was slowed to make the turn down the lane that led to their farm, her eyes scanned the hitching rails expecting to see the teams of Arnie, Luke and Josh, but no teams stood placidly swatting at annoying flies. No wagons sat empty in the farmyard.

They have, sighed Marty. *Ever' last one of 'em. They've all forgotten.*

Marty felt an unaccustomed heaviness as Clark helped her down from the wagon. Was age catching up with her? She hadn't noticed it before. Oh, true, she was slowing down some. She was aware of it as she hoed her garden or hung out the wash, but she had done nothing all day long and yet she felt weary—nothing, that is, except needlessly "cheer up" Ma Graham.

Marty turned to go up the walk. She was almost to the door

before she realized that Clark, who usually went right on down to the barn with the horses, was at her side. Ignoring her questioning look, he opened the door for her, and she led the way into the big back porch.

Her mind was already in the kitchen. The hour was late. What would she prepare for their supper? She hadn't planned on having to get the meal this night. It should have been her special birthday dinner. She wasn't to have had to think of leftovers or—

Just as Marty opened the door and stepped into her large kitchen, a sound of "Surprise!" "Happy Birthday!" exploded all around her. She heard her own voice catch in a sharp gasp and felt Clark's hand of support on her arm.

"Oh, my!" said Marty, taking a step back, away from the noise and confusion. "Oh, my!"

They were all there. Everyone of them. The horses and wagons had been carefully hidden from sight. The trip to Ma's had been a ruse—one that Ma herself had shared and supported. Clark had gone to town and whiled away the hours until the time the family had told him to have Marty back home.

But this time it was the girl's surprise. Belinda, Melissa and Amy Jo. They had insisted to the family members that it was "our turn" to have Marty's birthday dinner. They had even gotten an excused absence from their schoolteacher in order to have the afternoon free to get the meal. They had prepared it all from start to finish. Marty could only exclaim over and over as she swallowed the tears that insisted on crowding against the back of her throat.

A small bouquet of fresh spring wildflowers graced the table that was carefully set with Marty's good china. Everything was in readiness, and Clark quickly urged the family to take their places at the table "before the food gets cold," the girls insisted.

After Clark's prayer, the mothers fixed plates for the younger ones and the older children waited on themselves. With a flurry of noise and commotion they headed for their favorite spot on the back veranda. When things quieted, the adults began their meal, Belinda, Melissa and Amy Jo hovering nearby to pour the coffee and wait on the table.

The gravy was just a bit lumpy, the biscuits a bit too brown and the fried chicken a teeny bit dry, but to Marty, the meal was delicious and she kept telling the girls so, over and over.

"Did we surprise you? Did you guess?" Amy Jo kept asking.

"I had me no idea," Marty assured her, but she didn't add that she'd been a mite worried that her family had forgotten her. "Ya did it all? Yerselves?"

The girls laughed merrily, pleased that their plan had worked so well, and pleased, too, that Marty seemed so surprised at their achievement.

"We all shared in the cooking," Melissa explained. "Even Amy Jo. She did the potatoes and the cole slaw."

"An' Melissa did the chicken an' the biscuits, an' Belinda the vegetables," quickly put in Amy Jo to give proper credit where credit was due. "And Belinda made the cake, too," she added as an afterthought.

"It's yer favorite. Spice," Belinda told her.

After the meal was over, the children were called in from the porch and the whole family joined together in the singing of Happy Birthday, the little ones anxious for the fun of handing out the gifts. Marty exclaimed over and over as the lovingly chosen and handmade gifts were presented to her.

The three girls saved their gifts until the other members of the family had all presented theirs.

"I wanted you to have this, Grandma," said Melissa, passing Marty a carefully wrapped gift in light-blue paper.

Marty unwrapped it to find a beautifully bound edition of *The Pilgrim's Progress*. Marty knew it was taken from Melissa's private library, making it all the more meaningful to her.

Amy Jo came next. Her gift was not as carefully wrapped, but the colorful paper was festive. Marty began to unwrap the present, noticing that her hands trembled from excitement.

She lifted away the paper and found herself looking straight into the eyes of Melissa—from Amy Jo's first attempt at a portrait. There really was a likeness, and though Amy Jo's art would need years of polishing and perfecting, Marty was amazed that the girl had done so well. "Oh, my, Amy Jo! You did good—real good on this picture," Marty exclaimed, and other family members began to crowd around to see Amy Jo's art. There were many congratulations and enthusiastic comments, and Amy Jo beamed in response.

When the excitement died down, Belinda pressed forward. She handed Marty a small package. "Remember the lace collar ya saw and liked?" she murmured. "Well, I couldn't afford to buy it, but I found a pattern almost like it, an' I crocheted ya one myself. It's not as nice but—."

Marty slipped the lace collar out of the paper. Belinda had done a beautiful job. Marty traced the delicate floral pattern with a tip of her finger.

"Why, it's even prettier," she said softly, her eyes thanking Belinda even more than her voice did. "Thank ya, Belinda. Thank ya everyone. I do believe this is the nicest birthday thet I ever had."

Clare began to laugh. "Ma," he said, "seems to me ya say thet every year."

"An' every year I mean it too," insisted Marty.

Then all eyes turned to Clark. The family knew well the tradition of Clark presenting the final birthday gift.

"My turn, is it?" said Clark, rising to his feet.

Clark's hands were empty.

"Well, this year," he said slowly, "I have nothin' to give." He hesitated. All eyes were on his face. No one spoke. Clark cleared his throat. None of his children believed for a minute that he had nothing to present to Marty.

"Leastways," he continued, "nothing here at hand. My gift is outside. In the garden. Anyone who be wantin' to see it has to follow me out there."

No one remained behind. Clark led the way, taking Marty by the hand and leading her to the end of the garden. All the other family members trailed along behind, several of them making guesses as to what the gift might be. Marty heard the laughing and the teasing voices all around her, but her mind was busy trying to guess, too, what Clark had for her.

"There it be," Clark said, halting before a small, waist-high tree. It was not magnificent in appearance, but Marty knew it must be "special." She reached out a hand and turned the tag that hung from a small branch, fluttering in the soft evening breezes.

" 'Jonathan Apple,' " she red aloud and then, with a little cry she threw her arms around Clark's neck. "Oh, Clark where did ya find it? Where did ya get it from? I been a wantin' one but no one 'round here—."

"I sent away fer it," said Clark as he held her. "Sneaked it in here an' planted it yesterday. Was scared half to death thet you'd catch me at it."

Marty looked around at her family. She reached out to try to pull all three of the young girls into her arms at one time. Each one of her gifts was so personal, so special. Her family knew her well. Her family showered her with love. She felt blessed beyond expression. Her eyes brimmed over with tears.

"Go ahead," she challenged them with a smile, "laugh iffen ya want to, but this truly—*truly* has been my best birthday ever!"

Chapter 24

A Caller

All through the spring and summer Drew struggled with his bitterness. Why had he lost his arm? If there was a God who cared about him, why had it been allowed to happen? Why hadn't the doctor just let him die? He would rather be dead. At least he *thought* he'd rather be dead. Yet, at times, even Drew breathed deeply of the fresh spring air or exulted over the brightness of the summer sky, or tilted his head to catch the song of a bird.

Almost daily he thought of Belinda. And always his thoughts were troubled. He did not know how to sort out his feelings toward the young girl. Why was she so interested in nursing? How could she stand to see her brother cut people up? Didn't she have any kind of feeling? At the same time he questioned her interest in nursing, he admired her in a strange sort of way. He was quite sure he wouldn't have been able to face some of the situations that Belinda did.

How does she do it? WHY does she do it? The whole thing puzzled him. He couldn't understand her. He couldn't understand this whole strange family. And Drew certainly could not understand his inner conflict.

In some way, Drew took pleasure in his self-pity. And yet there was something else that kept fighting to be free of the bitterness. He seemed to be at war with himself. He wondered why he didn't just give in to his bitter feelings.

But how was Drew to know that he was the subject of daily prayers? How was he to understand that the strange longing, the reaching for something beyond himself, was the result of God's working in answer to the prayers of people who really cared.

But just as he felt ready to let his anger go, his stump of an arm would catch his attention and a new wave of pain would sear, seemingly from fingertip to shoulder. Sobs of pain and anguish would cause Drew to bury his head in his pillow or flee the house in renewed bitterness.

And so Drew struggled with himself. One minute he was content to wrap himself securely in his shell of bitterness and pain, and the next minute almost responding to the urge within himself to let go of his bitterness—to try to find some other way to live with what "fate" had handed him.

Another thing puzzled Drew. He felt there was something different about his mother, subtle changes he couldn't put into words. Was it just his imagination or was it really there?

For the past several years, Drew's mother had been shut away in silence and self-pity. She had not wanted to go West, had resisted with all her being. Oh, not in so many words. That was not her way. But they all knew how she felt. It showed in the tightness of her lips, in the stiffness of her stance, in the darkening of her eyes. Though she had never been one to laugh and chat easily, she became a woman living in a shell. It was as if the real person did not even share the dampness of the crowded soddy with the rest of the family. She became cold and withdrawn, even from her children.

There had been one thing that had seemed to bring life and fire to Drew's mother, and that was lesson time. How her dark eyes flashed if the boys were reluctant to study. Her chin thrust forward stubbornly when she declared that she did not intend to rear unlearned children—West or no West. Their father, too, made sure time was found each day for books and learning.

At the beginning of the new school term, Drew had watched his younger brother Sidney being ushered off to school. Now that Sid was dressed in proper garments, their mother had insisted he should be in a real classroom where he belonged. Drew

watched her holding her breath that first morning. *How would
he fare among the other students?* Drew knew was her worry.
Would he have years of catching up to do? But the first report
of Mrs. Brown was filled with incredulous praise. The boy was
unbelievably ahead of his age group, she stated, and she com-
mended the Simpsons heartily for their excellent job in super-
vising the boy's education.

Drew knew his mother had been tempted to send him, too,
off to the local school. She undoubtedly would have insisted had
it not been for his age and his missing arm. She did not say so,
but Drew knew that her mother heart, though shriveled and
broken by her hard life, ached for him. She knew it would be
difficult for him to face the world.

Drew's father did not seem to feel comfortable in Drew's
presence. He did not discuss the accident or Drew's handicap.
In fact, he seldom talked to Drew at all. But he did make it
quite clear that he did not wish Drew back in the woods felling
trees.

Even Sidney let his eyes skim quickly over the empty sleeve
and then directed his gaze elsewhere. Drew began to feel he
would go through all of life with people conveniently overlook-
ing him.

So Drew was left to his gun and his wandering. He probably
would not have been able to make it through those first difficult
months had he not known that the family needed meat, and
that he, even though missing a limb, was still able to supply it.

But in recent weeks Drew had been sensing a newness of
life and hope in his mother. Oh, true, she still had very little to
say, and she still never laughed, but her eyes looked different
somehow. She seemed—she seemed warmer, less chilled and
cut off from the rest of the family. Could it be that something
was changing on the inside? *And if so, why?* Drew wondered.
Was it simply because she was winning the struggle for sur-
vival? Oh, they were still in need—that was for sure—but they
were not in debt to any man. They had lost nearly everything
they'd owned, so there was really nothing more for anyone else
to claim. But they were dressing better now—were eating more
than rabbit stew. His mother even had her own garden, and

come fall she would not be beholden to the neighbors.

But was that the whole reason for the hope in her eyes? Or did it have something to do with that Davis family? She shared the house with Mrs. Davis three times and even up to five times a week. Was some of that other woman's optimistic spirit rubbing off on her?

Drew watched his mother closely, hoping with all his heart that the change might continue and that she would begin talking to him, chatting as mother to son, perhaps even allowing him a chance to talk about his missing arm. He studied his mother carefully each day when she returned from the Davis farm.

Drew did not understand the Davis family. But he could sense that they were different in some way. He had never seen a woman who seemed to be as sensitive—as caring—as Mrs. Davis. Drew longed to see that look of love and caring in the eyes of his own mother. *If only—if only*—his heart kept crying. *If only we could talk. If only Mother felt free to speak what she feels. If only she would ask me how I felt.*

And what about the Davis father? The guy with just one leg? How had it happened and how come he could accept it— even *joke* about it? Why did he seem to have such a warm and generous spirit? His little schemes of the year before had not been missed by Drew. He knew Clark had "invented" ways to help the family through their first winter. He had seen the Davises' woodpile. He had seen the farm. Drew knew Clark wasn't the type of man to need outside help to keep things in order. *What makes the fellow tick, anyway?* he asked himself.

The whole thing was beyond Drew. He couldn't figure any of it out. He stayed as far away from the Davises as he could get.

And then one fall day when the wind was rattling the red and gold leaves and the geese were crying overhead, Drew had found himself walking toward the Davis farm. The gun was tucked in the crook of his missing arm. He always carried it that way. It made him feel that his arm such as it was—was still good for something. But today the gun was forgotten. He would not have thought to shoot even if a rabbit or a grouse had crossed his path. Drew, deep in thought, decided he had to find some answers. With sudden resolve he quickened his step toward the only person who might be able to help.

Drew was relieved to find Clark clearing fallen leaves out of the spring. Drew did not wish to go near the house. He did not want to risk a chance meeting with Belinda.

"Drew!" Clark greeted him warmly. "Out huntin' agin I see. No luck?"

Drew laid the gun aside, his cheeks flushing a bit. He hadn't really been looking for game.

"Not yet," was all he answered.

"I'll jest be a minute here," Clark told him, "and then we'll go on up to the house an' see what Marty might have to munch on."

Drew leaned over the gurgling water and swept more leaves out into the current with his right hand.

"Were ya left- or right-handed?" Clark surprised him by asking.

"Right," answered Drew.

"Thet's one thing about losin' a leg," Clark stated matter-of-factly, "don't make much difference." When Clark chuckled, Drew smiled to join him.

"How's yer pa doin' with his loggin'," Clark asked further.

"Good," said Drew. "He found himself a mule somewhere. He's real pleased with himself."

"Thet'll help him a lot," said Clark. "Don't know how he managed last winter without one."

"Oh, he and ma jest hooked on ropes and hauled 'em out."

One sure could not accuse the Simpsons of being lazy.

"I'm after Pa to let me get back to helpin' him," Drew went on.

Clark looked directly at the boy. He felt he knew what Drew was trying to say.

Prompting him a bit, Clark commented, "He don't want ya in the woods?"

Drew shook his head. "Won't let me go near—ever since the accident. Thinks it's his fault, I guess. Thet's just silly. Wasn't anybody's fault—jest one of those things."

Clark was silent for a few moments as he scooped out soggy leaves and tossed them aside. "Guess I can understand his feelin's," he said.

Drew nodded. He guessed he could understand his pa's feelings, too, but it did seem foolish when his pa needed all the help he could get.

"Well," said Clark, straightening up, "guess thet'll be good enough fer now. I'll need to clean it once or twice yet 'fore winter freezes it in."

A flock of Canada geese passed overhead, calling out their forlorn cries. Clark and Drew both looked skyward.

"Always did think thet the cry of a goose be one of the saddest sounds I know," Clark observed. "Does it hit ya thet way?"

Drew nodded solemnly. It did. He wasn't sure why, but he had felt the same way.

"I don't know what there be about it," Clark went on, "but it most makes me shiver." And shiver he did.

"Let's go git somethin' to warm us up," he suggested. "Marty'll have somethin' hot fer sure."

Drew sucked in his breath. If he went now he might never find the courage to talk to Mr. Davis again.

"I was kinda wonderin' if I might talk to you some?"

Clark's face softened. The boy's eyes told him that he needed someone—needed someone badly. He lowered himself to a soft bed of leaves and nodded to the boy to go on.

"I—I hate to take your time like this but—but—"

"I've got me more time than anythin' else," Clark assured him.

"Well, I—I—noticed—truth is, I've been wonderin'. You see, I figured if anyone should know what a body goes through in losin' a limb, then it should be you."

Clark broke a small twig and cast it into the spring water. The current swirled it around a few times and then carried it off downstream.

"I only lost a leg, boy," Clark said softly. "Ya lost an arm. Now I ain't even pretendin' thet there ain't a big difference there."

The boy swallowed hard. Clark was making light of his own loss.

He looked at Clark evenly. "I happen to know myself well enough to know that I wouldn't a taken kindly to losin' a leg either," Drew said.

Clark nodded. The boy was at least honest.

"How long ago?" Drew asked.

"Long time now," said Clark lying back against a tree trunk. "Long, long time. Before Belinda was even born."

"How'd it happen?"

A shadow passed briefly over Clark's face, telling Drew even more than his words did.

"Couple a kids were messin' around in an old mine shaft," Clark began. "It caved in on 'em. I went in to get 'em out. They were 'most buried in it. Afore I got the second one out, it caved in agin. The heavy timbers got me."

"How'd you get out?" asked Drew.

"Men—friends from our son's ranch—dug fer me."

"Did you—did you give yer permission to the doc? To take yer leg, I mean?"

"Nope!" said Clark. "Didn't know a thing 'bout it. Actually, I didn't lose my leg right away. An' there weren't a doc within miles, far as anyone knew. It was Marty thet tried to clean it up an' disinfect it. It was crushed, too. An awful mess, they tell me. Then gangrene set in. I shoulda died I guess, but God had other plans. Sent along a doctor—right from among the neighbors—and he took care of the leg while I was wild with fever."

Drew's face had become white as Clark told the story simply, without drama.

They sat silently for many minutes, both busy with his own thoughts.

"What did you think when you—when—"

"When I came to my senses and knew what'd happened?"

The boy swallowed hard. He could not speak.

"Well, at first—at first I thought my whole world had fallen apart. I wondered how I would ever be a man agin—how I'd care fer my family—what I'd think about myself. Fer a while—fer a little while—I wished thet I had died—at least thet's what

I *thought* I wished. But not fer long. God soon reminded me thet I had a lot to live fer. That my family loved me and would keep right on lovin' me—one leg or two—an' thet God hadn't forgotten me. Thet He was still with me, still in charge of my life. It took a while, but God helped me to accept it. Don't miss it too much anymore at all."

"It still hurts you though, doesn't it?"

Clark's head came up. He looked at the boy. "What makes ya say thet?" he asked.

"I've seen you. I've seen you reach down an' rub it. I know— I know how bad it can ache. Even though it's gone, it can still—"

"Phantom pain," Clark finished for him.

The boy nodded.

"Yers bother ya much?"

"Sometimes. Sometimes it's not bad."

Clark nodded knowingly.

"How long you had thet—thet—?" the boy began.

"Wooden one? 'Bout five years now, I guess. Works real good too. Don't know how I ever got along without it. Luke, my doctor son, talked me into it."

"They don't have—they don't have—things for arms, do they?"

" 'Course they do. Not jest like this. Sorta hooks an' things, but Luke could tell ya all 'bout 'em."

Clark stopped. The boy who had been discussing the loss of a limb so calmly just a moment before had suddenly put his head down on his one good arm and was sobbing convulsively. Clark moved quickly to put an arm around him and draw him close.

"Cry," he said, tears brimming in his own eyes, "go ahead an' have a good cry. I did. Let me tell ya, I did. Scream, iffen ya want to. Git it all out. Ya got somethin' worth cryin' over. Go ahead an' cry."

The boy shook with his sobbing. "I hate it!" he screamed out. "I hate it! I don't have an arm. I don't have a God. I don't have *nothin'*."

Clark held him until he quieted. Then he passed him a large checkered handkerchief and let him blow. With an arm still around him he spoke quietly. "Son," he said. "I can't do nothin' 'bout gittin' ya an arm but—but I do know where ya can find yerself a God."

The boy looked up, his eyes still wet with tears.

"Ya don't even need to go a-lookin' fer 'im," Clark said, "fer, truth is, He's been lookin' fer you. He loves ya, son. He loves Ya. An' He wants to come into yer life, ease yer hurt and give ya a real reason fer livin'."

The boy shook his head. "I—I—I've done lots of wrong things. I don't think thet God would want—"

"That's the beauty of it," Clark continued. "He doesn't need to wait until we're without wrong. He'd wait forever iffen He did. We've all done wrong. The Bible tells us thet—an' there's no way we can change from our sinfulness on our own. And there's a serious penalty for sin—death." He paused to look into the tear-stained face before him.

"But the Bible also tells us thet while we were yet wrong-doers, Jesus Christ loved us enough to die fer us," his voice continued, strong and confident. "Now, thet means thet the death penalty fer those wrongs—those sins of ours—Christ paid. So we come to Him and jest thank 'im for what He's done and accept the new life He offers. Thet's all there is to our part. An' then He does His part. He forgives us our wrongdoin'—an' He gives us the peace an' fergiveness we been lookin' fer. It's as simple as thet."

The boy still looked doubtful.

"How—how do you do it?" he asked.

"Jest pray—jest talk to yer heavenly Father 'bout it. Ya ever prayed, boy?"

"Only once," the boy admitted. "At least I guess I prayed. It was when Belinda got hurt. I was so scared, I—"

"An' God answered yer prayers, didn't He?"

"Did He? I never thought about it. I—"

Then the boy turned pleading eyes to Clark's. "Will you show me how?" he asked.

Clark's arm tightened around his shoulders. "I'd be most glad to," he assured him.

Chapter 25

Sorting It Out

There was much joy in the Davis household that evening when Clark told his good news to the rest of the family. Marty let her tears fall freely and Clark led the family group in special prayer for young Drew. Though Belinda's face shone too over the announcement, she said very little. And then when she was finally free to slip away unnoticed, she went to her room and fell down beside her bed.

She wept there. She wasn't sure just why. There were so many emotions swirling around within her. She was thankful that God had answered her prayers. She hoped that Drew would now be at peace with himself. She prayed that his bitterness would be gone. She knew that there would still be many bad days in store for him, but with God's help and the prayers and support of friends he could make it, she knew he could.

Would he be able to forgive her also? She prayed that he would understand that she and Luke had only done what needed to be done. That they had taken no pleasure in the doing.

It was a long time until Belinda felt relieved enough of her burden to be able to prepare for bed. Even as she crawled between the soft flannel sheets, she wondered if she would see Drew again. Yes, she would, she reminded herself. Her pa had said that Drew had promised to come with them to church on Sunday. For some strange reason Belinda's heart gave a little skip. What would it be like? What would they say to one another? Would he smile? Belinda went to sleep with a strange feeling of anticipation. She hoped the days until Sunday would pass quickly.

The next day, a Thursday, Luke stopped by at school to ask if Belinda would be interested in helping with a delivery. Lou Graham's wife was expecting again, and she had told Luke she would not object to Belinda being present.

Belinda squealed with enthusiasm and rushed home to change her clothes. She would meet Luke at the Grahams'.

"Don't dawdle," he warned her. "You never know how much time you might have when waiting on a baby."

Belinda laughed and promised she would hurry.

Belinda barely made it to the Grahams' in time. The delivery was the most exciting event she had ever witnessed. Over and over again she thought of the story her mother told of how her sister Ellie had been the only one to assist at Belinda's delivery. She wondered if Ellie had been as excited as she was now.

Once it was well on the way, the birthing was all over so quickly. Belinda was given the privilege, under Luke's watchful eyes, of taking care of the new little girl. After bathing her and wrapping her in her warm flannels, Belinda placed her gently on Mary's arm. The woman beamed down at her new offspring.

"Meet Amanda Jane," Mary said. "Amanda, this is Belinda, yer nurse. Didn't she do a fine job now?"

Ma Graham moved forward to claim her new granddaughter, and then before Belinda could turn around, all the family members were pouring into the room, squealing and shoving and coaxing to hold the new sister.

Belinda was in an especially lighthearted mood as she mounted Copper and set out for home. She could hardly wait to share the experience with her family. *Why, even squeamish Melissa will enjoy this story,* she thought.

Belinda, her thoughts on other things, was brought swiftly back to the present when Copper flicked his ears forward and looked off to the side. Belinda tightened her hand on the rein. Perhaps a small animal was in the bush. But it was Drew who stepped from the undergrowth, his rifle tucked firmly under his arm and whistling softly to himself.

Drew was as surprised to see Belinda as she was to see him. They just looked at each other, neither one speaking. There was so much that could have been said, but no words came. It was Drew who finally broke the silence.

"Don't worry," he said, "I won't shoot."

Belinda began to laugh softly. "Good," she replied.

Drew laid down the rifle, lest even the sight of it should make Copper bolt, then moved toward Belinda.

"I was hopin' to see you before Sunday," he said simply.

Belinda's eyes met his. They were still deep and dark but there was no shadow in them. She waited for Drew to speak again.

"Have you been helpin' yer brother again?" Drew asked.

Belinda nodded, unable to keep the shine from her eyes.

"Where this time?"

"The Grahams'. Lou Grahams'. They jest had 'em a new baby girl. It was my first time fer a delivery."

It was obvious to Drew that Belinda had enjoyed the experience.

He smiled easily. "Guess thet beats takin' off arms, huh?"

Belinda's eyes dropped and Drew wished he hadn't said that.

"Are you in a hurry?" he surprised her by asking.

"Not—not really."

"Would you mind if we talked a bit?"

Belinda shook her head.

Drew looked up at her and laughed, "Would you mind comin' down off yer horse before I get a crink in my neck?"

It was Belinda's turn to laugh. She passed him the reins to dismount. Drew could not hold the horse and assist Belinda as well. He wanted to help her. He wondered if the horse would bolt if he just dropped the reins, but he didn't dare take the chance. Copper didn't have a very good record. Belinda did fine on her own.

"I'll tie 'im," he said.

"Tie 'im tight," called Belinda. "He loves to break free an' go home."

"Seems this horse of yers has 'im lots of bad habits," said Drew, and Belinda laughed again.

Belinda stood stiffly until Drew joined her.

"Would you like to sit?" Drew asked and he led Belinda to the side of the road to a fallen tree. Before Belinda could protest, he removed his coat and spread it on the log.

Belinda wasn't sure how to begin the conversation so she let Drew do the leading.

"S'pose yer pa told you about the other day," Drew began.

Belinda nodded. The boy would think she was tongue-tied if she didn't soon come up with some words.

"I don't know how it works—but it does. I really—feel different. Somehow, I—jest—I jest know there really is a God—an' thet He really does change you when you ask Him to."

"I know," smiled Belinda. "He changed me, too."

"You know—I didn't know much about God," Drew went on. "I'd heard people talk about Him. Mostly cussing. But—when you got thrown that day an' I was scared to death, somethin' deep inside me told me thet there really is a God who I could pray to. I prayed. I didn't even know how—or what to say or anythin', but I prayed for you."

Belinda's eyes looked about to fill with tears. "I've been prayin' fer you, too," she admitted.

Drew swung around to face her. "You have?" he asked incredulously.

She nodded her head again. "Ever since—ever since that day—I even prayed for ya when ya were still layin' there. Right after we had—had taken yer arm. Luke took out the—crushed pieces—an' I watched ya an'—an' prayed."

"What did you ask?" asked Drew.

"That you'd get better. Thet you'd—you'd git over it. Wouldn't be bitter."

Drew became very quiet. He studied the clenched fist on his one remaining hand. He watched it slowly relax.

"Bet you thought God hadn't heard your prayer, huh?"

"Sometimes it takes a while," answered Belinda simply. "We need to learn patience when prayin'. Pa is always sayin' thet."

"I like yer pa," said Drew.

"Me, too," said Belinda, and her eyes shone again.

"Well, it might have taken a while longer than it should have. If—if I just hadn't been so bullheaded, but I want you to know thet God did answer yer prayer. All of it."

"I'm so glad," Belinda said, and her eyes threatened to spill over again.

They sat silently, each wrapped in thought.

"You really like yer nursin' times, don't you?"

Belinda nodded.

"Why?" asked Drew. "I mean yer so young—an'—an'—" He wanted to say pretty but he wasn't sure how Belinda would take it.

"I—I've always hated to see things suffer," Belinda responded. "Even when I was little. I would find birds or little animals an'—I'd try to make 'em well agin. Sometimes I would even take 'em to Luke. He'd help me. We'd do all we could to make 'em better agin. Luke, he—he hates to see sufferin' too. An' he will do anything—anything—to help people."

"Funny," said Drew. "I thought much differently about the two of you for a long while."

"I know," acknowledged Belinda. "I'm sorry." Her voice was no more than a whisper.

"I'm the one who's sorry. I—I was stupid, thet's all. Full of self-pity an'—an' anger. I shoulda been thankin' you for what you did, an' instead I was actin' like a—a baby."

"Oh, no," protested Belinda. "I knew how you felt. I mean—well, Pa, he's been through that, too, an' we knew—"

Drew laid his hand on her arm, his hand warm against her skin. She felt protected somehow but she didn't understand the feeling. They sat in silence for several minutes and when Drew spoke again, the subject had changed.

"This your last year of school?" he asked her.

She nodded.

"Then what?" he asked again.

"Luke's gonna let me work in the office in town. He'll train me and I'll help him there an' with his house calls. After thet—I don't know."

Drew was silent.

"What 'bout you?" asked Belinda.

"I wanta get some trainin', too," he told her. He had never shared his dream with anyone before, but it seemed so natural, so right, to share it with Belinda.

"It woulda been tough, I know that—but I wanted to be a lawyer."

Belinda's eyes widened.

"A lawyer?"

"Guess I wanna help people, too. Only in a little different way."

"Like?" asked Belinda.

"My pa wouldn't have lost everythin' he had if he woulda had a lawyer. The other fella had no legal claim on it, but he had more money and more power than my pa. He ate up one little rancher after another."

Belinda nodded her understanding.

"Why—why do ya say 'wanted to be'?" she asked him.

He looked down at the dangling sleeve, Belinda's eyes following his.

"It woulda been tough enough when I—when I had—both arms, but now—well—I'd—I'd never be able to . . ."

Belinda let her eyes rest on his arm for only a moment. Then she looked back into his face. "Thet makes no difference," she boldly stated. "Ya don't need two hands to think—an' lawyers mostly think—an' talk. Ya can still do thet."

He looked doubtful.

" 'Course ya can," continued Belinda. "Ya got a good head—jest like yer brother. So—you haven't been to school? In the classroom? But ya been taught. Taught real good, too. Teacher's always talkin' 'bout how much Sidney knows. An' I'll bet thet ya know even more, and you can keep right on learnin', too. Ya can still study. No reason ya can't still be a lawyer iffen ya want to."

"You—you really think I could?" he stammered.

" 'Course!"

His hand tightened on her arm. What if she was right? Maybe she was right. Belinda wouldn't say it if she didn't think it was possible. It would be tough—really tough—but it might work.

He wanted to hug her—to tell her just how much it meant to him that she not only shared with him her dream, but she gave him back his. He could feel the tears stinging his eyes. He didn't want to cry. He had cried enough over the last months to last him for a lifetime. He lifted the dangling sleeve to his face and quickly dabbed his eyes, hoping that Belinda would not notice.

They sat silently, Belinda swinging one free leg back and forth gently. She was deep in thought, wondering just how she could help Drew realize his dream.

He interrupted her thoughts.

"Do you have a beau?"

Belinda blinked.

"Do you?" he pressed further.

She shook her head dumbly.

"I—I'd—" he began, but Belinda cut in quickly.

"I don't think thet I should have one now. I mean—it'll take a long time to learn about nursin'. It wouldn't be fair to—to ask a boy to wait."

Drew sucked in his breath. He hadn't thought of that.

"Yeah," he said at last. "Yeah, it will take me a long time to become a lawyer, too."

Belinda nodded. A little thrill went through her at his words. *He is believing in himself agin,* she exulted silently.

"So I guess we both have to wait, huh?" said Drew.

"I guess," replied Belinda.

Silence again. This time it was Belinda who broke it. She stood up, looking over toward Copper.

"I'm glad we had this talk," she said honestly, smiling shyly. "I was worried some about Sunday. I—mean—"

"I know what you mean," answered Drew. "I was worried some, too."

"I better git home," continued Belinda. "They'll be lookin' fer me."

"I'll get yer horse," said Drew.

Drew led Copper to the road and Belinda followed. He

handed her the reins as she went to mount. He wanted to have his hand free.

Belinda was about to put her foot in the stirrup when Drew stepped close to her.

"Thanks, Belinda," he whispered and she turned to look at him.

She hadn't realized he was standing so close. She hadn't realized just how magnetic his dark eyes were. They held hers as he stepped even closer. His hand went out to rest on her waist and he drew her slightly nearer. Then he bent his head and kissed her firmly, yet gently.

It took Belinda's breath away. She had never dreamed it would be like that. So sweet, so tender. Her first kiss.